BONDAGE Ł

GOLDEN ANGEL

GOLDEN ANGEL LLC

Cover designed by Eris Adderly

Edited by Personal Touch Editing

Copyright © 2021 by Golden Angel

All rights reserved.

No part of this book may be reproduced in any form or by any electronic or mechanical means, including information storage and retrieval systems, without written permission from the author, except for the use of brief quotations in a book review.

❀ Created with Vellum

PROLOGUE

MITCH

"Bondage buddies?" Domi raised her eyebrows, leaning back with her arms crossed over her chest, the position pushing up her breasts even more than the corset she was wearing. She looked skeptical but intrigued.

Barely standing five feet tall, petite in every way, with a riot of dark brown curls that danced around her head, she was a whole bunch of sass and bravado, despite her small stature. Whenever she was at the club, she dressed like she meant business, with full-on goth aesthetic that warred against her fae-like appearance. She looked like a goth-metal fairy most of the time.

Anyone thinking she was a pushover just because she was short or because she was a submissive should be warned by her outfits, but there was always someone who underestimated her. Domi sometimes pushed back just to show she *could*. It meant a few of the Doms at Stronghold and Marquis, the BDSM clubs they both belonged to, weren't interested in playing with her.

Right now, they were at Marquis, the club where they'd met. He'd been one of the instructors for new submissive members, and she'd been one of the students. Marquis was the fancier of the two clubs and the only one that provided dinner. A regular restaurant down-stairs, but its second floor served as an exclusive kink retreat for dinner and a show and a back hall with fetish-themed hotel rooms. Stronghold was Marquis' sister club, but they were as different as night and day. It was the original club and far more utilitarian, though it had more room to scene. The atmosphere was completely different, so Mitch had chosen to ask Domi to Marquis instead.

Tonight was as close to a date as Mitch had been on in years. First dinner—and his proposition to Domi—which would hopefully be followed by some seriously hot play and/or sex while they watched tonight's show. Giving her his best wicked grin, Mitch leaned across the table where they were sitting at.

"It's like fuck buddies, but with kink."

She pressed her full lips together, and he was pretty sure she was trying not to smile. The expression on her face was blank, but he could see in her dark eyes, she was thinking about it. His grin widened.

He liked Domi.

Mitch enjoyed her fire and sass. He especially liked it when he managed to push past it and reach the woman underneath. Feel her melt. Then make her fly.

She was a sweet masochist whose need for pain-filled pleasure matched his sadist's need to deliver it, which was even more of a bonus. Mitch didn't have to do a hardcore scene every time to be satisfied, but after a while, the *need* would build until he couldn't ignore it anymore. Hearing a woman beg and scream, then beg and scream for an entirely different reason, flat out did it for him. He needed her to enjoy it, though, which meant he needed someone like Domi, who loved every second of the wicked things he did to her.

"You had fun with me during your subbie classes," he pointed out, winking at her. All the submissives had been fun in their own way, but Domi was the one whose tastes most aligned with his.

Their last class together, when he played doctor, had been his favorite, especially since initially, she had scoffed at the idea of medical play. The little subbie had thought he wouldn't be able to hurt her the way she wanted. Mitch had thoroughly enjoyed proving her wrong. They'd had a discussion then about playing in the club, no commitment, but so far, she'd proven elusive and hadn't given him a straight answer.

Which was why he'd finally told her to meet him for dinner and a show at Marquis. He hadn't been sure if she actually would, but figured she'd be intrigued enough to come find out what he wanted.

"I did..." She tilted her head at him, chewing her lower lip, the uncertainty on her face making her look more vulnerable than usual. Her halo of curls bounced slightly when she shook her head, and his cock sank a little in expectation of rejection, then she surprised him. "No dating, just sex, right? Here in the club?"

"Here or at Stronghold," he confirmed. Coming to Marquis was more of a special event since membership was incredibly expensive, but as a member of Stronghold, they could visit Marquis one night a month without having to pay extra. He didn't want to rule out Stronghold since they'd be able to meet there far more often.

Domi rolled her eyes at him as if to say *duh*. "That's what I meant."

Sliding his feet over to her side of the table, he trapped her legs between his. It wasn't painful, and she could have easily pulled her legs up if she wanted to, but it was a reminder—he was the Dom, she was the sub. Domi sucked in a quick breath, her gaze flitting up to his, then dropping down to the beer glass in front of her.

That was Domi. Sassy brat right up until she was challenged, then her submissiveness took over. Sometimes, it was a bit more of a fight than others, but deep down, she *wanted* to submit. It just had to be earned. The challenge never failed to turn him on.

"If we're going to play together, you'll need to be more respectful... at least in the clubs," he said firmly. Outside of the club, she could roll her eyes all she wanted. He didn't care what she did when she wasn't in his space. He just wanted to play with her when she was.

"Sorry, Sir." Her contriteness only lasted another few moments before she looked back up at him. Still considering, her fingers tapped nervously against her beer glass. "Would there be a club contract? Would we still be able to play with other people?"

"I'm fine with or without a contract. As for playing with other people, I just want first dibs." Mitch grinned at Domi's slightly confused reaction. "If we're both at the club, and neither of us has scened yet, we get first dibs on each other. If I'm not around, you can play with whoever you want and vice versa. My work schedule can be a little unpredictable, so I'd rather keep it casual. If you prefer setting times to scene, I can do that, but it will need to be on a week-by-week basis."

"No, dibs works," she said, a slow smile curving her lips and bringing out the cute little dimple he liked to see. Mitch enjoyed making people smile and liked making them laugh even more. Domi could be a bit of a challenge, as she was in most things. Any time he got that dimple to peek out, he mentally high-fived himself. She snorted. "Dibs. I like that. That's so you. Do you have this arrangement with anyone else?"

"Nope, just you." Her expression didn't change, but he could sense she wasn't sure how she felt about that. "It would be hard to have first dibs on more than one person. What if you were both there at the same time?"

"That's true," she said, then shrugged, picking up her beer to take a sip. "So, why me?"

"I like the way you scream." He winked as heat flushed her face, turning her cheeks a dark red, and her eyes widened slightly. God, he loved kink. Only in a BDSM club could that sentence be considered foreplay.

Domi's tongue flicked out over her lower lip, swiping up a tiny droplet of beer, and Mitch's cock twitched with interest. She had beautiful lips and a talented tongue, and he would very much like to explore her mouth with his cock again. Soon.

"Is that it?" she asked, her voice huskier. The rise and fall of her breasts in her corset as she took a deep breath was easy to see. His cock was ready to go, but they still had a few details to hash out before he could get his hands on her. BDSM was big on communication—something that had been drilled into him when he'd taken the Dom class required for Marquis and Stronghold's membership.

"It's a big part of it." His voice became more serious. "We have complementary kinks. I like torturing you. And neither of us is looking for anything serious." In fact, Domi often flat out refused to scene with the same guy twice, which was why Mitch wanted to put his offer on the table, so they both knew exactly where they stood. "There are nights when I'd just like to be able to come to the club scene and not have to worry about my submissive getting ideas beyond that."

Mitch was always very clear about where he was in life and that he had no interest in a relationship. He didn't want to hurt anyone, so there were some submissives he wouldn't scene with because he knew he wasn't what they were looking for.

"How's that going to work out for you if I'm already scening with someone?" Domi asked, resting her cheek against her hand, leaning onto her elbow.

"I'll live." He shrugged. "You usually don't jump right into scening with anyone, so I figure I have a pretty good shot at being there when you decide you want to."

Domi

The offer was almost too good to be true, which was why Domi was so cautious.

She'd come out tonight because she'd been so surprised Mitch Elliott—*Master Mitch*, the Playboy Dom—asked her out on what amounted to a date, she had to know why. Her best friend, Rae, would have demanded it, even if Domi's natural curiosity hadn't driven her to it. They both needed to know what he wanted.

His offer wasn't entirely unexpected. It was similar to what he'd told her he wanted when she was still in training, but she hadn't realized he was quite so serious about it. This was even more tempting than before, and not just because he was hot as hell. Tall, blond, piercing blue eyes, with broad shoulders and muscles in all the right places, he always managed to make her feel both small and safe with

5

him. He was kind of the club clown, always looking for a laugh, but when it came time to take charge, he did so with an intensity that always left her breathless.

His offer appealed to her on a level she hadn't expected.

Domi preferred stability. She didn't want a relationship, but jumping from Dom to Dom every time she was at Stronghold didn't hold a lot of appeal. She'd already found most Doms didn't want to go to Marquis for a single hookup. Marquis' setup was unique, both where the shows were held and the private rooms. In a lot of ways, she was more comfortable at Marquis than Stronghold since she was more of a voyeur than an exhibitionist. This was where she'd done all her training, but she hadn't been able to find any Doms willing to accompany her.

Maybe that was another reason she'd said yes to Mitch's invitation. She'd been dying to come back to Marquis with someone other than her bestie. Watching the shows with Rae was fun, but it left them both horny and unsatisfied afterward.

"Okay." She couldn't think of a single downside. While she was sure there must be one, it wasn't leaping out at her, so she might as well enjoy herself until she found it. Especially because she wanted to enjoy *tonight*. She was back in Marquis with a hot Dom who wanted to fuck her into oblivion, and the show was going to be starting soon.

Domi wanted her orgasm.

A wicked grin lit up Mitch's face, his blue eyes flashing bright with anticipation. He hadn't been sure of her answer until she gave it, which was nice. She'd hate to be predictable.

"Let's kiss on it," he suggested, reaching out to grab her wrist and pull her around the leather seat of the curved booth. Domi went willingly, although she pretended to be less eager than she actually felt. Her body was already buzzing from when he'd trapped her legs between his—she still didn't know why that was so hot.

When she was close enough, leaning toward him, he lowered his lips to hers.

He was a damn good kisser, and Domi loved kissing. It started gentle but demanding, his lips opening and his tongue sliding between hers. His hand glided down her back, then pulled her toward him, dragging her across the seat. Her short skirt rode up to her hips as he moved her.

One hand dipped down between her thighs, cupping her pussy... He jerked his head back when he realized she wasn't wearing panties. Blue eyes blazed with desire and satisfaction.

"No underwear? Good girl." He practically breathed the words, then his lips crashed down on hers again, rougher and with more intent. Domi whimpered as his fingers slid between her wet lips, exploring her swollen folds and rubbing her needy clit. "Do you consent to sex tonight, sweetheart?"

Domi moaned. "Yes, Sir." *Please, Sir.* She wasn't going to beg unless he made her. However, if he didn't fuck her, she was probably going to stage a revolt.

He chuckled. "Thank God." His fingers swirled around her clit as a reward, although she knew he probably would have done so either way. "Condom?"

"If you want." Domi knew firsthand, condoms weren't always trustworthy, but she never objected to a man taking responsibility for birth control, even though she had her own. She would have insisted on them if they were just doing a one-night hookup, regardless of his club membership, but since they were going to have dibs on each other, she'd make an exception for him. Truthfully, she liked the feeling of skin on skin better, anyway.

"That's a no, then," he said, pushing his fingers slightly inside her. Domi shivered, her eyes half closing as her body stretched for him, her wet sheath welcoming him in.

Not knowing where to put her hands, she left them where they were, one still on the table, the other beside her on the booth where he'd dropped it so he could touch her.

Even with her eyes closed, she knew when the lights dimmed. The show was about to start. The design of the booths made them very private, although not entirely soundproof, and she could hear the murmur of anticipation from everyone else in the room. Marquis' stage room was set up like a theater in the round, with private booths all around the edge of the room and a large stage in the center where all manner of kinky demonstrations and shows happened. Domi's arousal surged even more. She loved a good show.

Breaking off the kiss, Mitch swirled his fingers against her clit, his other hand moving up to the top of her corset. Her figure was too slight to really have cleavage, but the corset gave her the closest thing to it.

"This is going to have to come off," he murmured.

"Quick release," Domi purred with a flirtatious smile. It was why she liked the steampunk-style corsets. A few quick flicks to undo the front closures, and she was free. Mitch's eyes lit up with appreciation as the sides of the corset fell away, leaving her upper body naked.

MITCH

Even in the dimmed lights, it was impossible not to appreciate Domi's naked beauty. Her nipples stood out from the small mounds of her breasts, just begging to be pinched, bitten, and tormented. Her lips were parted, eyes alight, and cheeks flushed with eagerness. Mitch rubbed her clit a little harder, and she moaned, the slick heat of her pussy growing wetter with every stroke of his fingers.

Music, slow and languorous, with throbbing bass, filled the room. The regular lights dimmed even further, and a couple walked onto the slightly raised stage in the middle of the room where all the brightest lights were now focused. The way the lights were aimed kept them out of the darkened booths, though there were also privacy curtains available at each one, including black sheers for those who wanted to see out but didn't want to be seen. Thick red velvet drapes could enclose the booth completely, turning it into a little oasis of privacy, which would mean not being able to watch the show. Mitch didn't bother with either—he and Domi didn't care about being seen.

Master Michael, one of the owners of Marquis, and his girlfriend and submissive, Ellie, stepped onto the stage. Like Mitch and Domi,

Michael was a sadist, and Ellie was a masochist, a show guaranteed to appeal directly to them.

Michael was tall, muscular in a lanky way, with brown hair that brushed the tops of his cheeks and constantly getting in his eyes. In contrast, Ellie was short, generously curved, with creamy pale skin and nearly black hair. Her short silky robe accented her curves, thanks to the belt tied around her middle, and the skirt fluttered around her thighs. They were an attractive couple with a connection that was palpable.

Walking to the center of the stage, Michael turned to face his sub, leaning down to give her a soft, tender kiss on the lips. Barefoot, Ellie stretched up to meet him, the expression on her face adoring.

Mitch pulled away from Domi's pussy, ignoring her whimper of disappointment. He pressed his wet fingers to her lips and bit back his own groan when she accepted them, cleaning off her juices with her tongue. The mimicry of what he wanted her mouth to do to his cock was hot as fuck. Curving his other arm around her, Mitch brought her flush against him, so he could more easily play with her breasts. He pulled his fingers from her lips, taking a breast in each hand. They fit into his palms, allowing his fingers to close around the full mounds and reach her peaked nipples.

Rather than teasing her, he gave each one a hard pinch, making her gasp in surprise and pain. His cock jerked at the soft sound, which she'd tried to muffle. Tightening his grip, he tugged on them, making her arch her back and lean forward, squirming with arousal.

On the stage, Michael had already stripped Ellie out of the robe she was wearing, revealing the weights attached to her nipple rings, pulling them down, and a flash of jewelry between her thighs, likely something to torture her sweet pussy.

Mitch rolled Domi's nipples painfully, eliciting a high-pitched whine from the back of her throat. Leaning closer to her, he kissed the muscle where her throat met her shoulder and then nipped at it, dragging his teeth over her sensitive skin. His cock was rock hard and pressing against his leathers, begging to be let out.

"I think your nipples could use some jewelry, don't you?" he whispered, twisting and tugging on the small buds. "I wouldn't want you to get jealous of Ellie."

"Yes, please, Sir," Domi said, her voice soft and needy. Her back arched, thrusting her breasts forward as though her body was repeating the plea.

He nearly groaned at her eagerness. Only a sweet little masochist would take the pinches and twists to her nipples he was doling out and ask for more.

"Keep watching Master Michael and Ellie," he murmured into her ear. "Don't take your eyes off of them." Releasing the little buds, he grinned when she let out a long breath, her body relaxing from the tension. That bit of relief wasn't going to last very long, and he knew neither of them wanted it to.

On stage, Michael had secured Ellie's wrists to a rope hanging down in the center of the stage and her ankles to a spreader bar that forced her legs wide apart. He was wrapping rope around Ellie's body, focusing on figure eights around her large breasts that made them jut out even more, her pale skin turning pink as they were bound. She was panting, her eyes almost glazed over. With her legs spread, Mitch could see the clamp on her clit.

Reaching into his pocket, Mitch pulled out the clover clamps he'd brought. Their initial pinch wasn't bad, but tugging on them made them tighten, increasing their bite. Perfect for Domi.

Domi

Normally, watching Master Michael and Ellie wouldn't be a hardship, especially because being a voyeur to this intense scene was a pleasure unto itself, but not being able to look over and see what Master Mitch had for her was its own form of torture—which she was sure the jerk knew. Her nipples were already throbbing from his abuse, and her pussy was pulsing in time, clenching with need.

She was so aroused, it took willpower not to reach between her legs and touch herself for relief, but she knew better than to do that next to a Dom. That was a surefire way to an evening without a single orgasm. The best way to get what she wanted was to be a good girl and do what she'd been told.

So, she watched as Master Michael tied off the end of the rope, leaving Ellie in a rope shirt that covered nothing and added to the torture of her breasts. Domi couldn't help but wonder if such bondage would be as effective on her since her own boobs were so much smaller than Ellie's. She would love to try.

Mitch's hand moved back around her back and cupped the breast farther away from him. She'd expected a pinch, but instead, his fingers gently stroked her abused nipple, teasing and making it feel even more sensitive.

It wasn't until Master Michael picked up the flogger hanging from his belt loop and sent it slashing through the air, the pinch came. Domi cried out just after Ellie, her nipple throbbing from the sharp, stinging pain that jabbed through it. A moment later, Master Michael brought the flogger down on Ellie's other breast, and Master Mitch quickly clamped Domi's other nipple.

Gripping the table in front of her, her eyes unfocused as the flogger rose and fell, panting for breath as her body adjusted to the exquisite agony. It hurt so much and felt so good as her pulse pounded in time with Ellie's cries.

The room echoed with whimpers, moans, and groans from other booths, adding to the show on stage.

"Up, sweetheart," Mitch ordered. She cried out when he used the clamps to move her, dragging her forward by her nipples, so she was bent over the table.

Tears gathered in her eyes from the sharp pain, then the dull throbbing that replaced it when he let the clamps go. On stage, Master Michael aimed the flogger at the tender undersides of Ellie's breasts, making her shriek at the impact, then again as the weights on her nipples bounced along with her breasts. Domi's nipples throbbed in erotic sympathy.

Smack!

Master Mitch's hand slapped her ass, making her cry out in

surprise. Her cheek stung where the blow had landed. Like when he'd pinched her nipples, he wasn't giving her any warm-up time... and her body loved and hated him for it.

Smack!

She moaned, lifting her hips up for more.

Smack! Smack!

Thwap!

She shrieked, her pussy pulsing with pain from the particularly hard smack. Oops, she'd dropped her head, taking her eyes off the show. Jerking her head back up again, she shuddered with the erotic pain as Master Mitch started spanking her again, covering her entire ass with hard swats. Propped up on her elbows, she could feel her breasts swaying beneath her, the clamps tugging on her from the movement.

On stage, Master Michael dropped the flogger and moved to Ellie, quickly undoing the rope and making her cry out as blood rushed back into her tortured breasts. Tears dripped onto the abused mounds, and she screamed, jerking slightly when he removed the weights from her nipples and gave each of them a sharp pinch. The insides of her thighs were glistening with the evidence of her arousal, even as she shuddered and sobbed.

Moving behind her, Master Michael undid the front of his leathers, taking his cock in hand. Retrieving a small tube from his pocket, he squirted shiny liquid onto his cock, and Domi moaned when she realized his intention. Fuck, this was going to be hot.

Ellie's sobbing breaths turned into another shriek as Master Michael lined his cock up with Ellie's ass and thrust in at the same time, Master Mitch thrust into Domi's pussy. She cried out with relief at finally being filled, her muscles clamping around him. One of Mitch's hands pulled at the back of her hair, keeping her head up, so she was staring right at Master Michael and Ellie. Moving his hands around to Ellie's front, closing around her tormented breasts and squeezing, he began fucking her ass with a hard, pounding rhythm.

Master Mitch kept one hand in Domi's curls, the other wrapped around her hip as he fucked her pussy as hard as Master Michael was riding Ellie's ass. Domi shuddered, bracing herself against his hard thrusts, her breasts bouncing, nipples protesting the abuse whenever the clamps brushed against the table, digging into her flesh. Every slap of Master Mitch's body against her spanked cheeks reignited the sting from his hand. Her pussy convulsed around him, her passion climbing higher.

Watching the show with a Dom was everything Domi had imagined and more.

Another scream from Ellie echoed around the room. Master Michael had removed the clit clamp, and the fingers of one of his hands were buried in her pussy, rubbing roughly against the sensitive nub, increasing both her pain and her pleasure. Echoing his movement, Master Mitch released one of Domi's nipples and thrust his hand between her thighs.

Ecstasy exploded inside her, twisting around the stinging pain into its own unique creation that flooded her body. Domi's cries joined the others filling the room, her orgasm pulsing inside her, along with Master Mitch's cock. She could feel him throbbing, flooding her pussy with his cum.

MITCH

Fuck.

With a strangled cry, Mitch emptied himself into Domi, the silky walls of her pussy gripping and squeezing the life out of his cock with each pulse of her orgasm. The incredible eroticism of fucking the hell out of her while they watched another couple playing and fucking... He was definitely going to be bringing her back to Marquis in the future.

Normally, he wouldn't consider that because it might give a subbie ideas, but this was *Domi*. If anything, he'd probably have to reassure her *he* wasn't getting the wrong idea. Marquis was date-like.

But he had dibs.

He had to admit, it was one of his better ideas.

Whimpering, Domi went limp in front of him, still panting, her pussy quivering around his shrinking cock. On stage, Michael had already removed the restraints from Ellie's wrists and was bundling her up in his arms to carry her offstage. From the expression on her face, she was still flying high.

The lights around the room went up to the dim setting that had indicated the show was about to start. It would stay that way until everyone left, giving them just enough light to make their exit but keeping the booths completely shadowed. In a few minutes, servers would make the rounds, dropping off water and anything the table had ordered for aftercare and taking orders for those who hadn't done so beforehand. Knowing Domi's love for lemon, Mitch had taken the liberty of ordering her a slice of lemon meringue pie.

Sitting down, Mitch pulled Domi toward him, turning her around to face him. She had a similar expression to Ellie's, and he allowed himself a few moments of smug satisfaction over making her look like that. He got another bolt of enjoyment when he removed the clamp from her right nipple, and she wailed, back arching, hands automatically coming up to fend him off as the blood rushed back into the crushed nubbin. If she hadn't been totally undone by the scene, she never would have reacted that way.

Easily grasping her wrists in his hand, he leaned forward and took her nipple in his mouth, suckling her through the pain. Little sobs of breath heaved her chest, and she shuddered, slowly coming down from the high. When he removed the one on the left, she was clear-eyed enough not to fight him and moaning in enjoyment as he soothed the sting with his lips and tongue. Mitch's cock twitched again at the sultry sound, but he knew it wasn't actually going anywhere.

One slice of pie and two glasses of water later, Domi was completely recovered and happy to agree to schedule future visits to Marquis—no 'dibs' needed. Which was good since Marquis required a reservation. Mitch walked her to her car, gave her a hard kiss, and said he hoped to see her soon. With a wink, of course.

Strolling back to his own car, he whistled a merry tune.

CHAPTER ONE

Six months later

<u>Domi</u>

"I love you."

"And I love *you.*"

"I love you *more.*"

"Uh-uh, I love *you* more."

"Uh-uh, I love you *most!*" Ana giggled, the way only a five-year-old who had just bested her mother could. Ever since she'd learned that "most" was, well, the *most*, she'd been thrilled to use it, and Domi was happy to let her. Especially in little contests like this.

Seeing Marcus' car coming up the driveway of the house she and Rae rented together, and where Ana lived with them half the time, Domi hugged her daughter tightly. She and Ana had been watching for him from the couch, which was tucked under the big bay window next to the front door. She could see Julia, Marcus' wife, in the passenger seat, and Domi sighed inwardly even as she waved.

"Daddy! Daddy! And Ju-ju!" Ana bounced on the couch in excitement, waving her hand at her dad and stepmom.

It wasn't that Domi didn't like Julia. The woman was almost everything she could ask for in a stepmother for Ana. She loved Ana, treated her like she was her own, and was good at knowing when to indulge her and when to be firm. Unfortunately, *Julia* didn't like Domi... at all.

Domi couldn't really blame her.

To say Ana had been unplanned was a vast understatement. Domi had been rebounding hard from a college relationship that hadn't worked out, thanks to her ex's super bigoted parents, and Marcus had been having a good time while he and Julia were on a break. No, no, a real break, not a Ross and Rachel from *Friends* kind of break.

Julia had gone to Europe for a year for work. She and Marcus had been together since high school and decided to take that year to 'discover themselves.' They'd planned to reconnect when she got back and see how they both felt, but they didn't have any contact and considered themselves single.

A few weeks before Julia was scheduled to return home, Domi and Marcus had been at the same party. She'd been angry and heartbroken after being dumped. He'd been missing Julia while simultaneously terrified everything between them would have changed, and Domi had been a good distraction. Both of them had been a little drunk, but they'd been what each other needed that night.

They hadn't even exchanged phone numbers. Still, ironically, while Marcus had been worried everything between him and Julia would be different after a year apart, it hadn't been. Not right away.

Julia came home, had her planned meetup with Marcus, and the two of them had been headed straight for happily-ever-after. Then Domi had to hunt him down three months later to let him know she was pregnant, and it was his. Poor Marcus had been torn between the love of his life and "doing the right thing." Domi had made it clear she didn't want the latter—*at all*—but Julia had to live with the knowledge Marcus had considered leaving her for Domi and Ana. It became even worse when they started trying for a child of their own, and it quickly became clear getting pregnant was going to be a struggle for Julia.

She never, not once, took that out on Ana.

But sometimes, she took it out on Domi. Domi tried to be understanding but was only willing to tolerate to a point. She also couldn't help but roll her eyes every time Marcus came by to pick Ana up and Julia was with him. It was literally a five-minute drive, and Julia had only missed it twice in five years—once when she was on an unavoidable trip for work and once when she was with her mom at the hospital. It was as though she thought if she wasn't there, Domi would throw herself at Marcus and change his mind about becoming a family.

Watching Marcus get out of the car, Domi could admit he was a good-looking guy. Tall, dark, and handsome with a great smile and broad shoulders, he was a total catch, but he was so vanilla, she'd rocked his world by suggesting doggy style during their night together. Great guy, great dad, but she had absolutely no romantic or sexual desire for him. Maybe one day, Julia would actually believe that.

The woman in question got out of her side of the car, waving at Ana with a smile, but pointedly didn't look at Domi. Almost as tall as Marcus, curvy—aka, totally stacked—with pale skin and red hair, she looked like a young Christina Hendricks.

Domi was mostly comfortable being short and skinny at this point in her life, but she still struggled to understand how someone who looked like Julia could be insecure over someone who looked like her.

"I'm gonna miss you, Mommy," Ana said, throwing her arms around Domi's neck and smacking a kiss against her cheek. Every other week, she said the same thing, and Domi knew it was true, but Ana was also excited to spend time with her Dad and Julia.

"I'll miss you more," Domi countered, squeezing her tightly.

Thankfully, Marcus and Julia lived close, so it was easy to split up time between them. Ana went back and forth each week, which meant Domi was only a single mom about half the time. She both dreaded and looked forward to Ana's weeks away.

The alone time was blissful, the chance to catch up with her friends was wonderful, but she missed her baby girl the whole time she was gone. She was growing up so *fast*.

"I'll miss you *most!*" Ana said, giggling wildly, giving Domi another kiss before jumping off the couch to run and let her father and step-mother in. She was far too big now for Domi to pick up and carry to the door. The thought made Domi's chest ache a little with nostalgia. Unlike Domi, Marcus was still able to pick up Ana, even if he couldn't carry her for the distances he used to. She threw her little body at him, squealing with happiness.

"Daddy, Daddy, Daddy, I missed you!"

"I missed you too, baby girl," he said, giving her a kiss on the fore-head as he tucked his arms underneath her.

"I missed you too, Ju-ju!" Ana said, reaching out her hand toward Julia, who laughed and caught the little hand in hers, giving it a kiss.

"And I missed you, Ana-bug." Julia grinned. "Are you ready to go to the zoo today?"

Ana cheered, wriggling enough Marcus had to put her down so she could jump around in excitement. "I want to see Monkey Island!"

All of them laughed, and Marcus curved his hand over Ana's brown curls, which were so much like Domi's. "I think we can make that happen." He looked up at Domi, still smiling. "Do you want to come with us?"

For the sake of their daughter, the three of them did a *lot* of things together, including holidays, but the innocent question still made Julia's lips tighten into a flat line. Her expression softened with relief when Domi shook her head.

"No, thank you. I have things I need to get done today."

Specifically, things to get herself ready for a night at Marquis. Every weekend Ana spent with Marcus and Julia, Domi spent either at Stronghold or Marquis. Tonight she wasn't going with Master Mitch, though. She and Rae were having a ladies' night to see the fire play scene that had been scheduled. Neither of them had ever seen fire play and were both fascinated by the idea.

Ana pouted but ran over to hug her around the waist. "Bye, Mommy."

"Bye, baby girl. I'll see you on Wednesday for dinner." Domi reaching to hug her back. For just a brief moment, she wished her daughter could stay with her all the time... but that wouldn't be fair to Marcus. She would enjoy some time for herself. At least for the first few days. That was why they had family dinner every Wednesday, then Ana would be back with her next Saturday morning.

"Can you take Ana out to the car, hon?" Marcus asked Julia, surprising the hell out of Domi—surprising her even more when Julia just nodded in agreement. Domi and Marcus watched them walking to the car, Ana already chattering about what she wanted to see at the zoo before Marcus turned back to Domi. There was something in his expression that made her realize that whatever he wanted to say to her, it was big. He kept his voice low, even though it was unlikely Ana would be able to hear them, even if she wasn't talking.

"Julia is pregnant."

Domi slapped her hands over her mouth to stifle her squeal of joy and excitement. She didn't want to draw Ana's attention when Marcus and Julia were clearly not ready to tell her yet, but it was so hard. Even with the strain between herself and Julia, she felt nothing but joy for the couple. Marcus' eyes dance with happiness.

"Oh, my goodness!" she whispered before jumping forward to hug him. Even if it made Julia mad, she couldn't help it. "I am so happy for you two! The IVF?"

Chuckling, Marcus hugged her back, seemingly not at all worried about his wife's reaction. It wasn't as if they hugged for more than a moment before stepping away. Marcus shoved his hands in his pockets, rocking back on his heels and grinning widely.

"Yeah, this round worked. She's three months along, officially, as of tomorrow. We want to tell Ana this week, but we couldn't decide if it was better to do it with just us, or if you prefer, we'll wait until Wednesday."

This was why her co-parenting relationship with Marcus and Julia *worked*. As much as Julia might want to cut Domi out of their lives entirely, she knew she couldn't and, when it came to the big stuff, she didn't try to. If it might be better for Domi to be there when they told Ana, then Julia wanted Domi there.

Domi blew out a breath, thinking quickly. Ana knew her Dad and

Julia wanted a baby and was excited about the idea of a sibling, but enough time had passed from when the idea was first introduced, she might have settled into the idea it wasn't actually going to happen. Also, it was one thing to think about having a baby brother or sister and another to face the reality after five years of being the main focus of all three of her parents.

"I think... you should do what feels right," she said slowly. "If a good moment to tell her comes up, I think you should take it. If a good moment doesn't come up before Wednesday, you can tell her at dinner."

Nodding, Marcus' smile seemed a little dimmer... more nervous. "How do you think she'll take it?"

"I think she'll be excited, but she's also going to have a lot of questions," Domi said frankly. "After the idea sinks in, she might start to get worried or anxious, but I think she's going to be a great big sister."

"She definitely is." Marcus shot a fond look to the car where Julia was buckling Ana in and laughing at something she said. "Julia bought her a book about being a big sister. I have no idea if it'll help, but she does love books."

"Yes, she does." Domi laughed. That was an understatement. Ana had loved books even as a baby, especially when the book came with a stuffed animal of the main character she could hold while the book was read to her. "I bet it'll help. That sounds like a great idea." One that had Julia's mark all over it—in a good way.

Domi still had to sigh internally when Julia straightened up and looked back at them, the frown on her face the expression most often directed at Domi.

"Marcus? Are you ready to go, or do you need another minute?"

There was barely held impatience in her tone and just a tinge of accusation as if she thought Domi was purposefully holding him there to talk to her. Maybe Domi was projecting a little, but that's what it felt like. Pushing a smile on her face, she grabbed Ana's bag and passed it over to Marcus.

"Here you go. I'll see you Wednesday. And congratulations." It was all she could do not to reach out and hug him again. With Julia's gaze already boring holes through her, she decided not to, but only because Julia was pregnant and likely to be more emotional. That didn't stop her from turning and waving at the other woman. "Bye, Julia!"

Pressing her lips together so tightly, it looked like she had to poop, Julia managed to curve her lips in the semblance of a smile and wave back with a grudging little twist of her fingers.

Domi stood in the doorway as they pulled out of the driveway, giving one last wave to Ana as her daughter waved to her from the backseat. Stepping back inside, she closed the door behind her and sighed. She wished she and Julia could have a better relationship, but it could be worse.

She glanced at the clock. Rae wouldn't be home from the gym for close to another hour. The house was going to be wonderfully, gloriously empty until then, which meant she could just sit and do absolutely nothing... at least for the next hour.

MITCH

Muscles straining, Mitch put on a final burst of speed... to no avail. His fingers reached out and flailed through the air, touching nothing. The lack of contact threw him off balance, and he tumbled forward, rolling onto the grass. Rather than trying to jump back up, he laid there panting, staring up at the blue sky, streaked with wispy white clouds.

Zach was just too damned fast. There was no catching him.

The whooping when Zach crossed into the end zone was echoed by the rest of his teammates—Zach's teammates, not Mitch's.

A face popped into view, blocking off the pretty sky. Brown hair, amused hazel eyes, and a slightly off-center nose—probably broken sometime in his youth—Brian smiled sympathetically at him, offering a hand to help Mitch up.

"You almost had him, man."

"I always *almost* have him," Mitch grumbled, accepting Brian's hand. He sighed, getting to his feet and brushing the grass and dirt off of his shorts and t-shirt. Looking over at the other team, high-fiving and bumping chests and fists in celebration, he sighed again. If they'd managed to keep the football out of Zach's hands, they'd have won the game.

Ah, well, couldn't win them all.

Half an hour later, he was at Murphy's Meals with his friends. Any time they managed to make it to the weekly game, Brian, Kincaid, Zach, and Mitch went out for lunch afterward. The four of them had been pretty tight since completing the Dominants 101 class together at Stronghold, even more so after serving as extra hands-on instructors for the Submissives 101 class.

Mitch was aware they were getting looks from some of the women in the restaurant, which happened every time they went out. They were all tall, good-looking guys, though in different ways. Mitch was the only blond, his hair trimmed short, and he liked to wear tank tops that showed off his muscles whenever it was warm enough. Today, they were all wearing t-shirts, though Mitch's still did a decent job of showing off his biceps.

Kincaid was even bulkier in muscles than Mitch, taller, dark-haired, with a permanent tan. While he couldn't match Kincaid for height or bulk, Zach had a dapper GQ thing going on that even being sweaty from football didn't diminish. Next to the rest of them, Brian joked he was the average one—brown hair, brown eyes, boring personality... but he was fooling himself. The submissives jumped at a chance to scene with him. He was an attractive guy with a good build, not nearly as intimidating as Kincaid, and far more serious than Mitch.

Having kinky friends, he could hang out with outside of the club had turned out to be pretty great. He'd lost touch with his high school friends when he'd gone to college, then with his college friends after graduation as they spread out in the quest to find jobs. While he had some work friends, their schedules were always so crazy, finding time to hang out outside of work wasn't easy.

"Are you going to Marquis tonight?" Kincaid asked. Mitch immediately knew he was asking because of the fire play scene scheduled.

Mitch had never seen anyone do fire play and would love to. Unfortunately...

"Can't," he said with a sigh. "Working." Otherwise, he would have made a reservation for him and Domi. Taking her to watch a fire play scene? *Hot.* Pun fully intended.

"That sucks," Kincaid said sympathetically before turning his attention to Brian. "We got a booth if you want to join us. We're interested in watching the technique." By 'we,' Mitch and Brian both immediately understood Kincaid was talking about himself and Zach.

They must be interested in *just* the technique if they were inviting Mitch and Brian along. It was a pretty open secret that Kincaid and Zach were... *involved.* Exactly what that involvement looked like seemed to change day to day. Although Kincaid was openly bi, they'd all thought Zach was straight until he and Kincaid started doing whatever it was they were doing. It was kind of like Fight Club—none of them talked about what Kincaid and Zach were doing.

The thing was, Zach still scened on his own with women at Stronghold and occasionally Marquis. Kincaid didn't scene with anyone unless he and Zach were scening together with one woman, and they both topped her and didn't actually interact. But every once in a while, they would go to Marquis, together, without a woman.

Brian and Mitch had talked about it, both of them curious as fuck, but they'd always come to the same conclusion—*not my business.* If Kincaid or Zach wanted to talk about it, they'd bring it up.

"Are you sure?" Brian asked. "I'm a little interested but hadn't planned to go since I didn't have anyone to go with."

"Well, now you do," Zach joked, grinning. "I think I'm more interested in it than Kincaid is, honestly."

"I'm not *un*interested," Kincaid said, but his shrug indicated Zach's statement was basically correct. If Mitch had to put a label on them, Kincaid was a Dom who liked a bit of sadism, and Zach was a sadist who liked to top. Actually, depending on what Kincaid and Zach were doing, Zach might be a sadist and a switch.

A buzzing sensation against Mitch's thigh had him pulling out his cell phone. He grinned when he saw the message and quickly typed back. *Yes*, he was absolutely willing to trade his shift tonight for one tomorrow. He hadn't made plans tomorrow, and he was just as curious as Zach about the fire play scene. Hell, it might be better to go with his fellow Doms than with Domi. He'd actually be able to focus on watching and maybe learn something.

"Is it work?" Kincaid asked. He was a police detective, so he knew he could be called in at any time, putting him in the same boat as Mitch, even though they had very different jobs.

"Yup, but good news for once," Mitch said, shoving his phone back in his pocket. "I'm in for tonight!"

CHAPTER TWO

MITCH

Arriving at Marquis before the evening had really started was always interesting. He and Domi had never been late to a show, but since the night they'd made their agreement, they only had appetizers or dessert before the show started. Tonight, he and the guys had decided to have dinner beforehand, but on the second floor rather than in the restaurant, which was an option offered to anyone who had reserved a table for the show. There was more privacy upstairs, and they wouldn't have to worry about anyone overhearing what they were talking about. Everyone else would be there for the same thing.

The restaurant downstairs had become so popular, it would be packed on a Saturday night, with lots of vanillas who had no idea what was located right above their heads. Mitch found the whole thing both genius and hilarious.

At the top of the stairs, Freddy was waiting. He'd once worked the front desk at Stronghold and was now managing that part of Marquis, but he still scheduled himself for at least one shift a month to check people in. Mitch hadn't known until about a month ago, Freddy was also a lawyer at a pretty prestigious firm downtown. Kincaid had seen him in action, helping out some other members of the club, and said he was a total shark.

No one looking at him right now would guess it. He had spiked his blonde hair with some kind of gel that made it glittery with pink highlights, the white button-down shirt he had on had ruffles around the collar and wrists, and with a hoop hanging down from one ear, he looked like a very pretty pirate. Well, if pirates ever had glittery hair and actually wore eye makeup like Johnny Depp.

"Master Mitch, hello," Freddy said, glancing down at the computer in front of him, a slightly curious expression on his face. Mitch grinned and sauntered up to the front desk, leaning his elbow on it.

"Hey, Freddy. Think you can sneak me in tonight?" he asked with a wink.

Freddy froze for just a moment, then he frowned at Mitch almost fiercely and wagged his finger. "You are bad, Master Mitch. Whose guest are you?"

Chuckling, Mitch straightened. One of these days, he'd be able to pull one over on Freddy, but today was not that day. "Just keeping you on your toes. I'm with Kincaid and Zach."

"You're the first to arrive. Would you like to be seated, Sir?"

"Yes, please."

The black leather pants Freddy was wearing added to his piratical air, and Mitch grinned in appreciation as he followed him into the main room. The stage was already set up with a padded leather table, a bucket of water, and a tray waiting to be filled with whatever Mistress Lisa would use for the scene.

He wasn't the very first to arrive, although there were only a few other people already sitting down. Scanning the room, Mitch was surprised when his eyes fell on Morgan sitting alone in a booth.

She'd been one of the submissives in the same class Domi had taken, and well, the things he'd learned about her during that time had made him feel extra protective over her. Truthfully, he was that way over all the submissives from that class, even if Domi was the only one he'd been interested in calling dibs on afterward. Domi and Rae didn't really *need* anyone watching out for them, though. They watched out for each other.

Morgan and Samantha, the other two subs in the class, didn't have that. They'd both come to the class alone and hadn't really bonded, thanks to having very different personalities. Actually, Morgan seemed to have trouble making friends in general. Mitch wasn't sure if it was because of her past or her personality, but he suspected a combination of both. She was also incredibly easy to take advantage of, which was why his concern rose when he saw her there on her own.

"Thanks, Freddy, I'll be right back," Mitch said, tapping his fingers against the table Freddy led him to. Seeing where Mitch was looking, Freddy nodded his head in approval and left the menus on the table.

"Enjoy your evening, Master Mitch."

Sauntering over to Morgan's table, Mitch smiled broadly when she looked up at him. She perked up, eyes sparkling with happy surprise and a smile lighting up her face. Morgan was, in a word, stunning— long red curls tumbled over her shoulders and down to the curve of her very large breasts, wide green eyes with thick lashes, and pale skin that marked up beautifully under the lash. She knew exactly what makeup to wear to emphasize her assets, and he knew she took a lot of pride in doing so, now that she could.

"Hello, Morgan, is it okay if I sit down?" he asked, gesturing to the booth. With anyone else, he probably would have just slid into a seat, but Morgan needed practice saying both yes and no.

"Yes, please, Master Mitch." She beamed at him like an eager puppy who knew they'd just passed a test. Mitch grinned back at her in approval.

"Are you here on a date tonight?" Even though he knew Freddy would be watching over her, that didn't mean he couldn't do the same. He knew Kincaid, Zach, and Brian would all feel the same way when they arrived.

To his surprise, Morgan shook her head, almost gleeful. "I'm meeting friends here! Submissive friends!"

Well, damn. Warmth expanded in his chest, and it took him a

27

moment to realize what he was feeling was pride. All of them had worked with Morgan on fitting into the club scene, but her background had been working against her. Though she'd asked that information not be shared with anyone unnecessarily, all the Doms who worked with her had to know so they didn't accidentally add to her trauma. She was still in recovery from being abused by a bad Master —on every level. It was too bad since it might have helped her if the other submissives understood what was actually going on with her. She'd had trouble adjusting to the idea other submissives weren't competition and might even *want* to be friends with her.

"That's wonderful," he said, reaching out across the table for her hand, which she immediately took so he could give it a squeeze. Morgan responded to both verbal and physical cues of approval from anyone she considered dominant to her, but she craved touch more than anyone he'd ever met, though she never asked for it. "Anyone I know?"

Domi

Swaying on her high heels—six inches were a torture device on their own, but she didn't plan to be on her feet for very long—Domi sashayed into the back of Marquis with her bestie by her side. For once, she was taller than Rae, who had chosen to wear cute kitten heels rather than stilettos. That was Rae, though, dressing like a baby girl even though she swore up and down she had no interest in a Daddy Dom.

Domi had been to Marquis once a month with Mitch for the past six months for the shows, so she knew if she actually wanted to watch and pay attention to a scene, she was better off coming with Rae.

The rear entrance to Marquis had been instituted once the owners realized the restaurant portion of the building was too crowded to provide complete coverage for people who were just coming for the kink on the second floor. Domi liked it because when she was all decked out in leather and lace, she didn't exactly blend with the restaurant patrons.

Rae—with her multitude of long braids pulled into pigtails with purple bows, a purple corset pushing her boobs up like a platter, and black and purple tutu—would have stuck out even more. At least Domi was dressed in all black, whereas the virulent purple of Rae's corset and ribbons looked radioactive. It was also stunningly gorgeous against her dark skin and black hair.

Sometimes, Domi wished she could wear something other than black, but she had a hard enough time getting people to take her seriously. She knew what she looked like. 'Fairy-like' was the term used most. More than one Daddy Dom had approached her, hoping her hard exterior was really just a brat covering up a vulnerable Little. While she didn't mind a bit of roleplay, that particular role didn't do much for her unless it was combined with the stuff she liked. It wasn't one she could sustain outside of a scene, no matter how she looked.

Rae, on the other hand, was totally a babygirl, she just couldn't bring herself to admit it. Just coming to the submissive classes had been a struggle for her. A strong feminist who believed women should be able to do whatever they wanted—including submitting to a man— she'd had trouble with the idea of *her* submitting. After the class where Rae had tried out age play with Daddy Dom Brian, Domi had thought her bestie might quit, all together.

But Rae had insisted on joining Domi if this was what she really wanted to do because she wasn't going to let her face "all that kinky shit" alone. Loyalty had outweighed her struggle with her own desires. That or she was using Domi's interest to give her an excuse to keep exploring kink as well. Probably a bit of both.

"Stupid stairs," Domi muttered under her breath as her heels sank into the plush carpet. They *could* have used the elevator, but she would have felt lazy doing so for only one floor when there were people who actually needed the elevator.

"Should have worn shorter heels," Rae said, snickering at Domi over her shoulder. In her much shorter heels, she was having no trouble climbing and got to the top in half the time it took Domi.

"Shut it," was Domi's super creative comeback. By the time she made it to the top of the stairs, her thighs and calves were burning, and she was panting slightly. That last part, she was going to blame on her corset.

Rae was already chatting with Freddy and Tracey, who were manning the front desk. Show-off. Pretending she didn't feel the burn in her legs, Domi sashayed her way over to the front desk, tugging her pleather skirt back into place. Greeting Freddy and Tracey, she chatted with them a bit before Freddy led her and Rae into the showroom.

The booths were already filling up, most of them with groups rather than couples, interestingly enough. Domi glanced around the room, looking to see who was there. They were mostly familiar faces, a few people with the curtain drawn across their booth for more privacy before the show started, and... Master Mitch.

Not just Mitch. Brian was sitting next to Morgan in a booth, Mitch across from her, while Kincaid and Zach were standing on either side, leaning in for the conversation. As usual, Morgan was the center of male attention, just like she had been during class.

Domi didn't get what the Doms saw in her. She was superficial, shallow, and constantly hanging off of the guys to get their attention... Hmm. Okay, maybe she did get what the Doms saw in her, but she really expected better from them—especially from Mitch.

Wasn't he supposed to be at work? That's what he'd told her. Domi hadn't thought twice about it, knowing he worked some crazy hours.

A thread of jealousy wove its way through her, making her stomach churn. Was he here with Morgan? Domi thought she was the only one who came to Marquis with him. That's what he'd said, but he was sitting across from her... although when he brought Domi here, they always sat in the back of the booth, right next to each other.

Except the first night—when they'd been negotiating their dibs.

"What, are they her harem now?" Rae asked, her footsteps slowing alongside Domi's. There was a note of possessive jealousy in her voice. No matter how she insisted she wasn't a baby girl, and she didn't want a Daddy Dom, she could never hide she had a thing for Master Brian—aka Daddy Brian.

He was the only Dom whom Domi hadn't had sex with during the classes because she'd known how that would make Rae feel. The others had been fair game, but not him. Even if Rae wouldn't admit her feelings, Domi respected that boundary.

Too bad Morgan didn't respect anyone's feelings. Something else that had been made clear during the classes.

"It must be the boobs," Domi said. "When you pay for them, you can make sure there's enough for four men to handle."

Rae snickered. "Hair color from the bottle, boobs from the surgeon... do you think any part of her is real?"

"I'm sure her feelings are." The low, sharp voice interrupting their observations made both of them jump guiltily. Domi hadn't realized they were talking loudly enough for anyone else to hear, but Freddy must have come back to fetch them when they'd slowed down to ogle Morgan's table. Domi had never seen that particular expression on his face—unfriendly, cold, and censuring. Shameful heat rose, turning her cheeks red. Freddy crossed his arms over his chest. "Is there a problem between the three of you I'm unaware of? Something that she's done to you?"

"No," Rae and Domi both whispered at the same time. Domi's gaze dropped to study her shoes, and out of the corner of her eye, she could see Rae doing the same. Freddy was one of the nicest people in the world unless he saw someone stepping out of line, and the fact he'd caught her and Rae was mortifying. Especially because she really had no defense. Everything Domi could think of to say to try to excuse herself sounded hypocritical and judgmental, even in her own head.

She's always trying to get attention from the Doms.

So what? Most of the single submissives were. On any given night, Domi might be, too. Just because lately, she'd been focusing her attention on one particular Dom didn't mean she hadn't been part of that in the past. Rae still was.

She really does have fake boobs.

Yeah, Domi didn't think that was going to fly with Freddy. He didn't seem like he cared. Domi didn't really either; it had just... come out—something that made her feel slightly sick now that she was thinking about it. She really didn't know anything about Morgan... If she'd had breast cancer or something, Domi was going to feel like a total asshole.

She's not friendly. Or at least, she's only friendly with the Doms.

Morgan wasn't the only submissive who could be described that way, either. Some of them were kind of aloof. Recently, Domi had overheard someone talking about her and Rae that way—they tended to stick together at the club and hadn't really branched out. They'd been like that in their daily lives as well. As long as they had each other, they hadn't really needed anyone else.

Yeah, Morgan had annoyed her a little during classes, but back then, Domi had just rolled her eyes and ignored her. She definitely hadn't felt the need to trash talk her.

So why was she being such a catty bitch tonight?

I'm jealous.

The realization hit her like a freight train.

After months of being Mitch's first dibs, months where she'd scened with other people, months where she'd been totally fine knowing he was scening with other people, she simply wasn't anymore. When was the last time she'd even scened with someone else? A month and a half ago, or about that, with a new Dom to the club, Master Law. Lawrence was his real name, but one of the subs had called him Master Law when she found out he was a lawyer, and it had stuck. Since Domi hadn't scened with him before, they'd agreed to no sex. She'd been relieved he hadn't expected or wanted that from her.

She hadn't wanted to have sex with anyone but Mitch. She just hadn't known it at the time or hadn't been willing to admit to it—even to herself.

Fuck.

Years of not wanting a relationship, of not finding a single guy she was interested in having a relationship with, and *now* she had to go and develop feelings? And for Master Mitch, the playboy Dom, of all the Doms she could have gotten a crush on.

"What's going on over here?" The sound of Master Mitch's deep voice made her want to bang her head against the wall.

Not right now! She was still dealing with the whole "I think I've developed feelings" thing. It was like her thoughts had summoned him before she was ready to actually face him. *Crap, crap, crapola on toast!*

"Is everything okay?"

Oh, good, not just Master Mitch. They'd also attracted Master Brian's attention. Rae must be dying.

Neither she nor Rae apparently felt up to answering, so there was a long beat of silence before Freddy finally spoke up.

"The ladies have an issue with... another member and were expressing their opinion about that member." Freddy's voice was clipped, although not disapproving as it had been when he'd first rounded on them. In his own way, despite what he'd overheard, he was still trying to follow the unspoken subbie rule of Stronghold and Marquis—*look out for each other*—a rule Rae and Domi had just broken.

That made her feel even worse.

She peeked up to see Mitch and Brian exchange looks. Yeah, they weren't fooled. In fact, Domi wouldn't be surprised if everyone was looking at them now—hopefully not knowing exactly what was going on.

Voices coming in made her glance over her shoulder. Tracey was leading three other women into the room. Domi was relieved to see no one in the booths on that side of the room was looking over at her and Rae, so maybe they hadn't drawn as much attention as she'd thought. She felt even worse when Tracey led the three women over to Morgan's table, and Morgan greeted them with complete delight.

She hadn't been here with Mitch at all. Or Brian. Or any of the Doms. She was here to meet friends. Domi recognized two of them— Caroline, who had a reputation for being mean but who didn't come to Stronghold very often, and Amy, who was a total sweetheart. Which meant she and Rae had been completely off base.

Although she didn't think Freddy would have excused their words, even if they hadn't been—and he shouldn't—but Domi felt even worse if that was possible.

"Why don't we go have a chat?" Master Mitch suggested, his voice deceptively mild, the kind of voice he used in a scene right before he got all bossy.

Shit.

"How bout we don't?" Rae muttered under her breath, and Domi stifled a groan. She knew better than to sass Mitch when he used that voice, but Rae obviously had missed the threat in his tone.

"No one asked you, little girl." Brian stepped up next to Rae, his voice harder than usual, as Mitch's fingers wrapped around Domi's arm. "Freddy, are any of the rooms open?"

"Everyone's here for the show, so you have your pick for the next two hours," Freddy said.

Fuck.

CHAPTER THREE

Domi

"What? No, why can't we talk together?" Rae's voice was half angry, half horrified, and Domi started to turn to look behind her, but Mitch's grip on her arm kept her from being able to spin all the way around.

Master Brian had the door to the Little Girls' room—the youngest age-playroom in Marquis—open, and Rae was obviously balking.

"You and Domi feed off of each other. I think Master Mitch and I will have better luck getting to the bottom of this if you're separated." Master Brian's voice was firm. "You can safe word, or you can come in."

"But... Domi..." Rae's head swung toward her, and Domi could see the conflict in her expression. She hated and loved that room. She wanted Master Brian, but she didn't want to want him.

"That's not your safe word," Master Brian said as he crouched slightly, flipping Rae over his shoulder. Shrieking her outrage, she slapped his back, but she still didn't say *Red*.

"I don't like this room!"

"That's why it's a good punishment, little girl."

As the door shut behind them, the hallway filled with silence.

Domi bit her lower lip and turned her head to look at Master Mitch. So far, tonight was not going anything like she'd thought it would, and she still didn't know how to deal with her newly realized feelings for him. She couldn't remember the last time she'd liked a guy enough to even *consider* having a relationship.

"In here," Mitch said, opening the door to the Dungeon. It was Domi's favorite room at Marquis, and they both knew it. Her brow furrowed, trying to figure out what he was thinking but went in obediently. Moving to the center of the room, she turned to face him but couldn't quite meet his eyes. "Do you want to tell me what you and Rae said that had Freddy so riled up?"

Heat filled her cheeks again, and she *really* couldn't look at him. "Do I have to, Sir? I realize what I said was shitty, and I regret it."

"Why don't you want to tell me?" He walked forward, circling around her, fingers trailed over the back of her bare shoulder, making her jump. Her stomach rolled. Shit. Realizing she *like* liked him was messing with more than just her head.

"I don't want you to think less of me, Sir," she admitted, going for a hard truth. Doms liked hard truths, so if she confessed this one, hopefully, she could avoid worse.

The fingers moving over her skin paused. "All right."

"Really?" Relief suffused her. That was so much easier than she'd thought it would be. It didn't make the guilty shame curdling in her stomach go away, but at least she didn't have to describe to Master Mitch how catty she'd been. "So, um, is that it?"

Smack!

His hand slapped against her ass, hard enough to sting, even through the fabric of her skirt, and Domi jumped in surprise.

"Is that it, *Sir*," he corrected. "And no. You don't have to tell me what you said, but I do feel, as your sometime-Dom, it's my duty to correct your behavior when you step out of line."

"That's really not necessary, *Sir*," she said, rushing the words as respectfully as she could. "I promise, I already learned my lesson... and I'd hate to make you miss tonight's show. I know I don't want to miss it."

She also didn't know if she could handle a scene with him—not without feeling things she shouldn't.

Unfortunately, the reminder about the fire play demonstration didn't move him. Master Mitch chuckled, moving around her again until he was in front of her, his eyes roving over the bare skin of her chest as if he was mentally undressing her.

"Then not getting to see the show sounds like a good punishment, doesn't it?"

One last scene...

That's what this could be. One last scene to enjoy, then she'd have to cut herself off cold turkey from him. Continuing to have sex with him when she had feelings and he didn't was a recipe for disaster. Domi's tongue flicked out, wetting her suddenly dry lips.

"But isn't that a punishment for you, too, Sir?" After all, he'd come here tonight for the same thing she had.

The smile that spread across his lips matched the wickedly cruel glint in his blue eyes.

"I'm sure I can find a way for you to make it up to me."

MITCH

He didn't know what Domi and Rae had done to agitate Freddy but knew it couldn't be good. When he'd looked up and seen her standing there, he'd had the excited thought maybe he could watch with her, then he'd realized she and Rae were having a face-off with Freddy. That had thrown him completely, and he'd immediately gone to see what the problem was.

As much trouble as he had imagining Domi and Rae doing something really wrong, he knew nothing else would get Freddy's hackles up. If he'd read between the lines correctly, they'd been gossiping—or worse—about another club member.

There were always members who didn't get along and were encouraged to avoid each other. Marquis made that easier than Stronghold since everyone was separated by booths, so there was really no reason to interact. Sometimes, people still said things they shouldn't, but it was frowned upon. Freddy, in particular, was protective of the members, and if it was a member he'd taken under his wing... well, double that.

That Domi was still flushed with guilt and didn't want to admit what she'd said confirmed how bad it must have been.

Mitch was disappointed to miss out on the fire play scene tonight, so he wasn't kidding about Domi making it up to him. Since he hadn't thought he'd get to see her this weekend, in some ways, this was a treat. She looked gorgeous in a black corset and a tight black skirt that left very little to the imagination, eyes dark with both eyeliner and mascara, and lips painted a vivid red. He was looking forward to messing up all that carefully applied makeup.

"So..." She squirmed slightly, peeking up at him, looking like a little girl trying to figure out how much trouble she was in—she'd likely kill him if he voiced the comparison. There was a tiny glint of anticipation in her eyes. "Is missing the show my only punishment?"

Aww... Sweet little subbie. Delusional little masochist. Delightful little newbie. She thought a punishment scene would automatically mean a hard paddling, maybe even the whip, more intense than usual, more painful than usual. While Mitch's sadistic side would thoroughly enjoy that, he didn't need to cause her physical pain to feed that part of himself. He could get off on fucking with her... period.

"Oh, no, sweetheart," he said, smiling wickedly. "We're just getting started." Her dark eyes lit up with anticipation, and Mitch nearly laughed aloud. She was going to be a lot unhappier when she realized what he had planned. "This way, little subbie."

Moving her to the deceptively simple wooden table, Mitch helped her with her corset. Once the laces were loosened, he easily pulled it over her head before running his hands over the red marks it left on her skin, purposefully avoiding her breasts. Domi let out an appreciative hum as he caressed the marks, relaxing under his touch.

Dropping his hands down to the zipper on her skirt, he peeled the fabric away, shimmying it down and raising his eyebrows when he saw her thong. The pause in undressing her made Domi open her eyes and look at him to see what had happened. Seeing his focus, she shrugged.

"I didn't know you were going to be here tonight, Sir."

"Fair enough," he conceded, enjoying the disappointment that flashed across her face. Even though she would have protested, part of her had been hoping he'd punish her for wearing underwear. Which, of course, was why he didn't.

This was a punishment scene—a real one. Any enjoyment Domi received from it would be after Mitch was thoroughly assured of her remorse.

Hooking his fingers around her thong, he dragged it down with her skirt, leaving her totally naked, a sight he never got tired of. With his face right next to her mound, the sweet, musky scent of her arousal filled his nose, tempting him to lean forward and take a lick between her folds... Mitch controlled the impulse.

Starting with something she'd enjoy would send the wrong message.

"Hands behind your head." He moved back to a standing position so he could loom over her in an appropriately Domly manner. It didn't require greater height, necessarily, although that helped. Mostly, he stood too close to her, crowding her space and claiming it as his own.

Eyes focused on the center of his chest, Domi's breath hitched as she lifted her arms. The position pushed her breasts forward, her brownish-pink nipples begging for punishment.

Mitch was going to enjoy this.

Domi

A little confused why she hadn't immediately been put on the torture table—Mitch's name for it, not hers, from previous times they'd been in this room—Domi found her anticipation rising. One of the things she liked so much about scening with Mitch was he was rarely predictable. Keeping her guessing heightened both her anxiety and excitement about a scene.

She was also relieved to find scening with him didn't feel any different, just because she'd realized she had a crush on him. Part of her even wondered if maybe she was wrong about those feelings, but then she imagined him doing this with someone else—*anyone* else—and the sick, jealous twist in her stomach made it clear her feelings for him had *definitely* changed. In the first few months, they'd scened together, she hadn't cared at all when he'd scened with someone else. In fact, she'd been kind of relieved to know he was, absolving her of the need to commit.

His hands cupped her breasts, fingers plucking and teasing her nipples as she watched, bringing her back to the present. Domi pushed her emotions, her thoughts about the future, aside. If this was their last scene together, she was damn well going to enjoy it.

Well, as much as she could enjoy an actual punishment. She was still a little nervous to discover what that might entail. Being a masochist, she could take—and find pleasure in—a decent amount of pain, but she didn't know how far Mitch would be willing to push her.

Right now, he wasn't pushing her at all. His touch was gentle, more of a tease than anything else. The eager pulse between her legs was growing needier, her nipples tingling for more than little tugs and pinches. Doing her best to suppress the impulse to squirm, Domi thrust her breasts out a little more, hoping Mitch would take the invitation.

Instead, he stepped back, dropping his hands. Domi whimpered, rocking back onto her heels. She hadn't even realized she'd been leaning forward.

"Stay right there, sweetheart," Mitch said, turning away and moving to the toy cupboard on the far wall.

Yay! Toys! Her pussy clenched in excitement. Toys meant they were about to really get started. Anticipation sliding through her, she pressed her thighs together right as Mitch turned back around, so of course, he saw the movement.

"Legs apart," he barked, turning from regular bossy Mitch to stern

Master Mitch in a heartbeat and spiking Domi's arousal even more. The almost icy look in his blue eyes made her mouth dry. "A little wider than your shoulders, and don't move from that position unless you want me to get the spreader bar."

A shiver went up her spine. Did she want him to get the spreader bar? Domi loved the feeling of vulnerability, but she also hated knowing she'd disappointed him by failing to follow an order. She spread her legs, feeling the cool air on her heated flesh, which did absolutely nothing to soothe her growing desire.

Moving behind her, she could hear him putting things down on a table outside of her view. She was tempted to sneak a peek, but if she got caught, it probably wouldn't be worth it. Besides, she was going to find out what everything was soon, right?

He came back around in front of her, gaze dark, intent, and focused on her breasts. Neediness surged as he cupped one mound, lifting it with a motion she was very familiar with, and automatically held her breath, waiting for the bite of the clamp he was holding.

The pinch gripped... and disappointed. Domi's breath puffed out in surprise. Staring down at the rubber-tipped adjustable clamp, she immediately realized, while it was on its tightest setting, the tension was nothing near what she was used to. Her nipple throbbed slightly in the confines of the prongs but didn't really hurt.

It didn't burn.

It didn't do anything to ease the itchy, aching *need* inside of her.

She stared in near disbelief as Master Mitch pinched her other nipple with a matching clamp, the silver chain hanging down between them swinging, the cool metal brushing against her stomach. Saying the clamps 'pinched' her nipples was too generous. It was more like a slightly overenthusiastic hug.

What the hell?

MITCH

The baffled, almost insulted expression on Domi's face was almost too much for Mitch to bear. She was staring at the clamps on her nipples as if they were a puzzle she was trying to solve. Mitch actually had to bite the inside of his lip to keep from grinning.

He'd purposefully chosen the weakest clamps he'd ever used on her, ones that would tease rather than satisfy. For a newbie sub or one unused to pain play, these clamps on their tightest setting would be a punishment. For an experienced masochist like Domi, they were more like jewelry.

It also meant he'd be able to leave them on her for longer than some of the harsher clamps he could have used.

"Bend over at the waist, sweetheart," he ordered. Domi's gaze snapped up to his, searching for answers, but he kept his expression carefully blank. Her brow furrowed in the center, but she bent forward. "Keep your hands where they are."

"Yes, Sir," she muttered, her tone perilously close to being disrespectful.

Smack!

The hard swat to the back of her thigh made her jump and moan, low and needy. With her hands behind her head, she was bent at an almost ninety-degree angle, giving him complete access to her ass and pussy. With her legs spread, he could see the glistening folds of her pussy, soaked with arousal, and the crinkled hole of her anus above.

Scooping up the lube and plug he'd picked out, he opened the packages, making her wait, letting her squirm. Her buttocks jiggled as she shifted her weight side to side. Pulling on a rubber glove, Mitch flipped open the lid of the lube.

"Are you feeling remorseful yet, Domi-Darling?" he asked as he smeared the ginger lube over the plug. As plugs went, this one wasn't very big, maybe a little over an inch in diameter and about four inches long. Definitely not the biggest thing she'd ever had up her ass.

Like the clamps, that was the point.

"I already regretted my words before we even stepped in here, Sir," she retorted. Her curls shook as she tried to look over her shoulder. The movement nearly made her lose her balance, but she quickly settled back into place.

"Ah, but regret and remorse are different, sweetheart." He placed the tip of the plug against her anus, placing his ungloved hand on her lower back to help her balance and stay in place. "Deep breath."

When she breathed out, Mitch pushed the plug into place in one swift motion. Domi squeaked, rocking forward. She would have lost her balance if it hadn't been for his hand pressing down, holding her in place.

The base of the pretty pink plug looked so cute nestled between her cheeks, just above her swollen folds. Mitch took a moment to admire the view as he stripped off the rubber glove he'd used to protect his hand from the lubricant, but not because it would hurt his hand. He didn't want to get the lube anywhere but exactly where he meant it to go.

Domi was acquainted with ginger lube, although he hadn't used it in a while.

After a few moments, she gasped, her buttocks clenching, and he heard her mutter something under her breath, too soft for him to actually hear it. Mitch grinned. This was so much fun, and he was just warming up.

CHAPTER FOUR

<u>DOMI</u>

Fucking ginger lube.

She didn't need to ask Master Mitch why the slight burn from the plug's insertion was increasing instead of decreasing.

Intensifying.

Tingling.

Driving her wild while doing nothing to satisfy her.

The actual size of the plug had barely even stung, nestling inside easily, making her feel *filled* but not *full*. She wanted to be full so bad, even if it was her ass, not her pussy.

Her empty, needy, clenching pussy.

A low chuckle behind her reminded her Master Mitch was watching the show. Watching her squirm, well aware of how unsatisfactory the nipple clamps and plug were for her. The growing burn from the lube was making her pant—with desire, not with pain.

Fucking sadist.

He was getting off on this, even if she wasn't. Domi hadn't even considered he might torment her with *less*, not *more*. It was devilish and frustrating as hell. Especially since he was still just standing there doing nothing.

"Is this it, *Sir?*" she asked, taunting. "I thought you could dish out more than this."

Master Mitch laughed aloud. Some Doms were all business inside a scene, but not him. He wasn't afraid to laugh, and it never took away from his confidence or authority. In fact, his wicked sense of humor often made scening with him more fun. Sort of. Fun after the fact.

In the middle of it, sometimes it felt more like torture.

Like right now.

"All right then, Domi-Darling," he drawled, and she heard him pat the wood of the table beside them. "Up on the table."

Rat fink bastard. He helped her onto the table since she was petite enough to need the assistance. He also thoroughly enjoyed watching her 'hop' up and land on her butt, pushing the plug farther in and making her muscles squeeze around it in reaction. Domi's breasts heaved, her nipples tingling from the clamps, but nothing more.

The polished wood was smooth under her back as he laid her down. There was a myriad of ways the straps attached to the table could be attached. Domi was quickly spread out in an X shape, straps over her arms, legs, and middle, so the only parts of her body she could move more than a couple of centimeters were her head, fingers, and toes.

She wriggled, testing the boundaries, but the leather straps were secure. Master Mitch's fingers trailed over her breasts, teasing them with his light touch. Domi couldn't even arch her back, thanks to the strap over her rib cage, holding her in place. When his fingers brushed over the sensitive tips of her nipples, she groaned in frustration, squirming even more.

"So, is this when the real punishment starts, Sir?"

The sassy question made him grin again. Instead of pinching her nipples, tugging the chain, or doing *anything* that would make her feel more, he moved his hand away. Her nipples throbbing with the need for more stimulation, she bit her lower lip to keep from begging for it. One blond eyebrow arched, his gaze boring into her, and Domi knew she wasn't fooling him one bit.

"Ah, poor little masochist... is this not enough for you?"

Domi pressed her lips together to keep from answering. She was pretty sure that was a trick question.

MITCH

Untrusting little subbie. Mitch couldn't blame her. Even sexually frustrated and tied down, she knew when a question had no good answer. Not that staying silent was going to save her.

The table she was lying on wasn't actually one solid block of wood, although he wasn't sure she realized that yet. They'd been in this room more than once, but there were so many things to play with, this was the first time he'd put her on the table. It had been personally designed and built by a Dom who specialized in BDSM furniture and implements for Marquis. With plenty of joints and moving parts, it could be moved into multiple configurations, all designed to torment and fuck any submissive lying atop it.

Reaching underneath the lip, Mitch flipped open a latch so he could spread Domi's legs even farther open and also give him a space to stand between them. Her eyes widened with surprise when she felt her legs moving, and she wriggled some more, but the straps crossing her body held her tightly, regardless of the table's changing structure.

"Such a pretty, wet pussy." Mitch stepped between her legs and stroked his finger along the thin strip of hair she didn't shave. Everything else was beautifully bare, leaving her sensitive folds completely unguarded. Crouching, he heard her suck in her breath in anticipation, her body tensing for whatever he was about to do.

Gently resting his hands on either side of her pussy, using his thumbs to spread her labia apart, he leaned in and licked right up the center of her folds from the base of her pussy to her swollen clit. She cried out, jerking against the restraints as his tongue swirled around the nub, then away again.

His cock, already hard from the fun of clamping, plugging, and restraining her, jerked at the sound of her pleasured moans. The crouched position wasn't the most comfortable, so knowing his muscles would start to burn soon, he focused on pushing her quickly toward orgasm. The sweet taste of her coated his tongue, her hips moving as much as they could against the leather straps holding her down, her panting breaths coming faster and faster. Just before he was sure she was going to come, Mitch pulled away.

"No!" She jerked, shuddering. Standing, he watched as her eyes flew open, head lifting slightly, so she could glare at him.

Leaning forward, he was careful not to touch her while he picked up the final item he'd procured from the toy cabinet—a small, rubber flogger, with many tiny strands, not more than half a foot long, sprouting from the handle. It was meant for flogging particularly small, sensitive parts. Their eyes met again, and he let some of his enjoyment subside, remembering why they were actually there.

"Next time you want to say something nasty about someone, I hope you'll remember this and think again," he said, completely serious. "I know you regretted your words, but it shouldn't have taken Freddy confronting you to feel that way. If it's something you don't want me or him to hear you say, it shouldn't be said at all."

Raising the whip, he brought it down sharply on her swollen, heated pussy.

***

Domi

Finally!

Domi wanted to scream with pure relief as the delicious pain shot through her. The sting from the whip felt incredible against her aroused flesh. Her ass clenched around the plug, heating her all over again from the inside, and if she could have lifted her hips to meet the next stroke, she would have. Each slap of the flogger against her pussy reignited the string, the tiny strands never hitting in the same spot twice. Master Mitch angled the strokes differently each time, making sure not a single area was neglected.

If only he could focus the blows on her clit, she was sure she could come just from this...

When he stopped again, she let out a frustrated scream, her fists bunching as the stimulation jolted to a halt. Lifting her head to see what had happened, she tried to squirm away as he lowered himself between her thighs again, his eyes focused on her swollen, reddened, aching pussy.

"Nooooo..." She moaned the denial, and this time, tried to get away from his questing tongue and mouth, but she couldn't.

After the flogging, her pussy felt even more sensitive, and his tongue was almost painful as it rasped over the swollen folds. Of course, she liked the pain, so that just made her even hornier. Her entire body felt as if it was throbbing, coiling, like a wire being drawn tighter and tighter. She was going to snap at any moment...

Except Master Mitch wouldn't let her.

"Please!" She practically screamed the word when he straightened again, leaving her hanging on the edge of an orgasm.

There wasn't enough pleasure *or* enough pain to bring her over the edge.

It was awful and not fun at all.

Slap! Slap! Slap!

The flogger fell against her pussy again, even gentler than before, denying her the sharp bite her body craved. She writhed against the restraints, to no avail.

Tears sprang in her eyes, her body thrumming, screaming out for more... she was so close...

The stinging slaps stopped again. Domi literally screamed in frustration. If her hands had been free, she might have actually tried to strangle Mitch, especially when she heard his low chuckle.

This is not how she pictured her last scene with him, not how she wanted their last scene together to go. And it was all her fault. Not because she'd fallen for him—she would have realized that eventually and known she had to end things—but because she'd turned into a catty, jealous bitch.

Morgan might not be her favorite person in the world, but that didn't justify what she or Rae had said about her, especially not where someone could have overheard them. It was bad enough Freddy had heard them. What if someone else had heard and told Morgan what they said? How would Domi feel if someone had been talking about *her* body, *her* makeup, and *her* fashion choices that way?

Master Mitch was right. Regret and remorse *weren't* quite the same, but she felt both now.

Gentle fingers stroked over her thighs, bringing her back to the man standing between them. He was looking down at her, his eyes scanning over her face, examining her.

"There we go," he murmured. "That's more of what I was looking for."

"I'm sorry," she said, her voice thick with emotion. She was so very sorry for so many things. Sorry for saying shitty things about Morgan. Sorry for being a bitch. Sorry for making him miss the fire play demo. Sorry, this was their last scene together, and he didn't even know it.

There was sympathy on his face.

"I know you are, good girl," he replied.

Domi didn't feel very much like a good girl right now. Her body was still all wound up, but she was miserable.

MITCH

Poor little subbie.

At heart, Domi was kind. She'd acted out of character, been punished for it, and was sincerely sorry for it. The tears in her eyes were as much from sexual frustration as they were from remorse. Calling her a good girl barely made her twitch.

He'd broken her down—now it was time to build her back up again.

Easing some of the sexual frustration he'd been torturing her with would help. They'd never done orgasm torture before or edging, but it was clearly a good punishment for her. Discipline time was over, though—time to clean the slate and let her start anew.

Leaning down, Mitch pressing his mouth to her pussy, this time going straight for her clit, instead of teasing her, and Domi's shriek echoed around the Dungeon. His balls tightened in response to that beautiful scream. Her body quivered, pulling at the restraints as he sent her careening into orgasm.

Releasing the hard suction on her clit, he licked her with long, sensuous strokes to help bring her down gently from the peak of pleasure. His dick was throbbing against his zipper, aching to be buried inside of her, but his good girl deserved more of a reward.

As her body relaxed, Mitch kissed up her stomach, his hands moving ahead of him, reaching her breasts. Fondling the soft mounds, he closed his fingers around the clamps, crushing the buds.

Domi keened, gasping, arching against the straps. He pressed his lower body against her pussy, feeling her wet folds rubbing against the bulge in his leathers.

"Oh, fuck... oh, please..." The ragged need in her voice was stronger than ever, even though he'd just given her an orgasm. She was his sweet, little pain slut, and now that her punishment was over, he was going to give her everything she needed.

Domi

The tight, painful, throbbing squeeze of her nipples was exactly what her body had been craving. It didn't matter that she'd just climaxed. Hot need pulsed through her, her pussy quivering against the thick bulge of Master Mitch's cock.

Pulling the clamps, he yanked them from her nipples, and she screamed as the exquisite agony shot through her. It was a move he never could have done with the harsher clamps he usually used on her, and she loved it as much as she'd hated how teasing the clamps had been before.

"That's my good girl," he crooned, lowering his mouth to her nipple. "You took your punishment, Domi-Darling. The slate is wiped clean."

The words were like a balm washing over her, relieving her of her lingering guilt and assuring her she was forgiven.

His teeth closed around her soft flesh, hot and wet, scraping over her sensitive bits. It felt like her entire body was a hot, throbbing mess of need and lust as she writhed under his touch. For a moment, his hands went away, then returned, exploring her body while his cock pressed against her slick entrance.

"Fuck!" Her ass clenched around the plug when he impaled her.

The burn from the ginger had almost completely dissipated, but the incredible feeling of fullness that came from being penetrated in both holes was its own deliciously painful treat. Domi's muscles clamped down, shuddering in pre-orgasmic bliss, already eager to take her over the edge of ecstasy again.

Teeth nipped.

His hips drew back, then thrust forward, stretching her muscles and filling her completely.

Domi laid in her bonds and wallowed in her complete lack of control and the sensations washing over her. She was flying higher and higher, the pain and pleasure winding through her body, mixing until she couldn't tell which was which.

Straightening, Master Mitch's fingers curved over her breasts, gripping and using them as leverage to fuck her harder, faster. She keened at the intense rush of sensations, the throbbing heat that flowed through her, filling her and leaving her breathless. With the plug in her ass, he felt even larger, filling her completely.

"Oh, fuck... Master Mitch... please..." She squirmed, shuddering as another orgasm began to crest, deeper and fuller than before. Her pussy spasmed around him.

"Come for me, Domi-Darling," he growled, squeezing her breasts tightly, her nipples pinched by his fingers.

Thrusting hard, he leaned forward, his hips rotating, rubbing his hard groin against her swollen lips and clit. The building crescendo of pleasure and pain had finally reached its peak. The immense pressure inside broke, and Domi screamed, ecstasy exploding inside of her. Her pussy tightened around Master Mitch's cock, and she heard his low groan as he joined her in rapturous bliss.

CHAPTER FIVE

MITCH

Thank you for being my bondage buddy, I've really enjoyed it, but last night needed to be the last time. I'm sure I'll see you around at the club. Take care!

Scowling, Mitch reread the 'Dear John' text he'd received from Domi that morning as if the bare-bones message would be able to offer up answers it hadn't revealed the first ten times he'd read it. Seriously, what the hell? For months, they'd had what Mitch considered the perfect relationship—a *non*-relationship—and he'd thought Domi was on board with that. Granted, he'd figured she'd eventually want to move on, women often did, but she hadn't shown any signs of it.

He'd been starting to think he'd found the perfect woman—one who wanted exactly the same thing he did, in perpetuity. He hadn't thought he'd have to find another play partner any time soon.

Hell, he didn't want to find another play partner.

What had gone wrong?

Everything had been fine last night. He didn't think the scene had overwhelmed her, even though it started out as a real punishment scene instead of their usual play. Punishment, fucking, a little of cuddling aftercare, and a quick kiss goodnight before they'd both gone home. Nothing stood out as different. Not until this morning when she'd texted him.

He'd smiled seeing her name on his phone and had been frowning ever since he'd read the actual message.

"Fuck it."

He pressed the call button. For some reason, he couldn't shrug off her dismissal of him the way he normally did. It felt wrong, though he couldn't pinpoint exactly why.

This wouldn't be the first time a woman had broken up with him, though he had to admit it normally happened within a month or two because she either got tired of only being fuck buddies or they fell apart naturally, but he'd always seen it coming. There was a certain *feel* to a connection when it started to diminish. Mitch was practically an expert on that feeling.

The connection between him and Domi hadn't diminished at all, and if he'd been asked, he would have said they were both happily still going strong as friends-with-benefits.

The relief he felt when Domi picked up the phone, rather than letting the call go to voicemail, was disturbingly intense.

"Hello?"

It was hard to tell what she felt about him calling her from one word, which had been imbued with very little inflection.

"Hey, Domi, it's Mitch." He paused. Dammit. He really should have thought through what he wanted to say. "I, uh, I was just calling to make sure you're okay."

"Yeah, I'm fine." Amusement tinged her voice. "Is this about my text message? I thought I was clear."

"You were... I just... I wondered why, I guess. I wanted to make sure I didn't cross any lines last night or anything."

"Oh, no!" The almost horrified way she rushed to reassure him he hadn't done anything wrong loosened the tightness in his chest. It felt as though a burden he hadn't been aware of had lifted, and now that it was gone, he could breathe a little easier. "No... I, I'm so sorry, I never meant to make you feel that way. I..." Her voice trailed off, becoming hesitant.

"You..." Mitch supposed it didn't matter much. If she was done with him, she was done, and he would have to deal with it. The thought of never playing with her again hurt him more than he'd expected, but he would respect her decision.

Domi blew out her breath, the way she often did before making herself say something she wasn't completely comfortable revealing. Mitch had heard her do it often enough, either before or after a scene when he'd wanted to push her limits. What she said next threw him for an unexpected loop.

"I'm starting to fall for you." She said it matter-of-factly, with very little emotion as if she was talking about nothing more shocking than the weather. "So, I decided we needed to break up."

Wait... that was his line. Normally, when he sensed a woman was getting involved emotionally, Mitch would break it off—the polite thing to do, the gentlemanly thing to do—but he'd never had a woman break up with him because she was falling for him. He hadn't realized Domi was starting to have feelings for him. Granted, they'd been scening together for far longer than any of his previous partners, and he'd gotten used to always scening with her... Hell, he hadn't been *interested* in scening with anyone else in ages.

"I realize that's not what we agreed to when we first started playing," she continued as though she wasn't messing with his entire worldview. "I don't want to get hurt, and I didn't want to put you in a bad position. I think it's better we end things before my emotions get more involved."

"You're breaking off our agreement because you like me too much?" he asked, just to make sure he understood correctly.

Domi snorted. "When you put it that way, it sounds ridiculous, but sort of. I am emotionally involved, and you're not, which seems like a disaster in the making."

That was hard to argue with, but it also seemed she was making some assumptions. Like, the fact he wasn't emotionally involved. Sure, he might not be a relationship guy, but he still cared about her. Liked

54

having her around. Liked being with her. Those emotions might be confined to the times when they saw each other, which were all at Stronghold or Marquis, but they existed.

"I think I'm just past the point of wanting a fuck buddy." A little note of yearning entered her tone. "I think I want a relationship. I know it won't be with you, but I feel like we've been having a relationship of sorts, and it's made me realize I might want more. At least, I think I want to try."

Lots of 'thinks' and a 'might.' She wasn't sure, then, but even so, Mitch didn't see how that benefited him. She didn't want him, not in the way they had been doing things.

"We could just scene together until you find someone," he said lamely. The moment he started speaking, he'd known it was lame but hadn't been able to stop himself. While knowing she wasn't ditching him because of last night had loosened his chest, now there was an unhappy little ball of emotions right in the center of his stomach.

"As generous as that offer is, I'll have to decline," she said dryly.

Damn, he was going to miss her dry, sarcastic, sassy sense of humor.

"Yeah, no, I don't blame you." He looked down at his feet, staring at the carpet. The bland beige color did nothing to make him feel any better. "I... Yeah. Okay. Take care, Domi."

"You too, Mitch," she said softly, almost wistfully.

Hanging up, he stared at the phone and rubbed the achy spot in the middle of his chest. Unhappiness welled, along with the odd urge to kick something. To yell. To unleash the chaos of emotions that were beginning to swirl around inside him as he realized he wasn't going to get to scene with Domi again.

Wasn't going to be the one to make her scream, and cry, and beg, and plead, then scream some more as she cried out his name. Wasn't going to have her dry wit to balance out his own goofiness. Not that he felt particularly goofy now. No more sassy, little sprite brightening up his weeks.

Shit.

Dropping onto his couch, he leaned his head back and stared up at the ceiling.

Now what?

DOMI

"I can't believe you broke up with him."

"We didn't break up. We weren't really together," Domi insisted. Although it felt like a breakup. Enough so, Rae decided they needed to have a girls' night out, saying Domi needed a distraction. They'd gone to Marquis, but not the kink-club part, the regular restaurant part. It had good food, and they got a small discount for being members. Plus, they both felt comfortable there.

Tucked in one of the bar's booths, they could huddle together and talk about whatever they wanted without worrying they'd be overheard. The booths were leather, incredibly comfortable, and kept their conversation as private as they could get in public.

"You were basically together." Rae gave her a look.

Domi made a face but didn't argue, changing the subject instead.

"What happened with you and Brian last night? How did that go?"

Now it was Rae's turn to make a face. She tugged on one of her long braids, a sure sign she was uncomfortable with the emotions Domi's question brought up. They'd both gotten dressed up for the night to make themselves feel good, and Rae had put her braids into two pigtails, tied with thin green ribbons that blended into the green braids threaded throughout the black, which all matched the lime green top she was wearing. Domi had gone for purple and black, preferring to offset her diminutive stature with kickass fashion, so no one mistook her for a pushover. Sometimes, it was hard being petite.

"It was fine. He said a few things that made me think."

Fine. *Ha.* Normally, Domi would have called her on that, but she was curious about what Brian had said. Rae looked more uncomfortable than ever. Domi wasn't exactly proud of herself or what she'd said about Morgan, but she didn't know what Brian could have said to make Rae look the way she did now.

"Like what?"

"Like how we're very insular." Rae tugged her braid again, harder. "I told him it's not like Morgan was friendly to any of us, and he asked me how friendly we were to her or Samantha... or if we shut them out the way, we do to everyone."

Domi's mouth opened, then closed. Well... yeah. She and Rae were best friends. New people they'd just met weren't going to have the same kind of bond they did.

On the other hand, she and Rae hadn't actually tried to get to know the other two women in their new submissives class. Morgan hadn't seemed super interested in getting to know them, she really hadn't, but Samantha... well, she'd ended up talking to Morgan or being on her own a lot. By default. Because Rae and Domi had always been sitting and talking to each other, ignoring the other two.

More of the guilt she'd felt last night trickled through Domi.

"I don't want to be friendlier with Morgan," Domi muttered. She sighed. "But maybe we did Samantha wrong. She seemed nice."

"She did." Rae looked a little morose. "Are we... do you think we're the mean girls of the new subs?"

Two days ago, if Domi had applied that title to anyone, it would have been Morgan. The woman was constantly preening, trying to attract the men's attention, and often made incredibly insulting comments without seeming to even realize what she was doing. Now though...

"Shit. We might be."

"We should try to make more friends... be friendlier."

"Agreed."

"And find you a new boyfriend."

Domi made a face. She did think she wanted a relationship. Probably. If she could start falling for Master Mitch, maybe that was what she really wanted, but first, she needed to let the bruises on her own heart mend. It had been a little lowering how easily he'd let her go once he knew why.

Yeah, she got it. That wasn't what he wanted, so she couldn't blame him for not trying to keep her around. Still, it hurt.

Stupid heart.

MITCH

Looking around Stronghold, he didn't know whether to feel relieved or disappointed when he didn't see the familiar riot of curly hair he automatically sought out. As usual, there were plenty of beautiful submissives in the Lounge area, all chatting with their friends while they waited for interested Doms to come by, but he didn't feel the slightest inclination to initiate a scene with any of them.

Just like he hadn't for weeks.

Instead, he headed toward the bar where he saw Kincaid sitting, looking at the Lounge area with a contemplative expression. He was wearing his usual leather pants and vest combination, his dark hair waving back from his face. Mitch knew a lot of the subs at Stronghold and Marquis had massive crushes on him.

"What's up?" Mitch asked, settling onto the stool next to him.

He glanced over and realized Kincaid was watching Zach talking to one of the subs in the Lounge. The pretty blonde was a pain slut and long-time member who Mitch had played with before and made a good play partner. She was engaged, but her fiancé was vanilla and let her come to the club to get her needs met. Perfect for not getting attached. If Mitch hadn't made his arrangement with Domi, he might have considered one with Amy, but... well, he also liked sex.

And he'd *really* liked sex with Domi.

"Not much," Kincaid said, bringing his scotch up to take a sip. He glanced at Mitch and frowned, refocusing all the attention he'd been giving to Zach and Amy from afar. "What's wrong?"

Shit, was it that easy to tell something was up? Mitch shrugged but felt his shoulders tighten at the question.

"Domi ended our arrangement today." He stared out over the club. The dance floor had a few participants, bumping and grinding, but they didn't provide much of a show. No wonder Kincaid had been watching Zach and Amy. Well, that and because Kincaid had a thing for Zach.

Mitch didn't know exactly how far that went, and it wasn't his business, but he knew it was true. He was pretty sure Zach had a thing for Kincaid, too, although he was harder to read.

"I'm sorry, man, I know you liked her." Kincaid spun around on his seat, holding up his hand to draw one of the bartenders' attention. A moment later, Master Andrew appeared in front of them; his dark black hair waved back away from a tanned face, dark eyes intense as always. Mitch always thought he looked kind of like a bulkier, more muscular Antonio Banderas.

"What can I get you?" Master Andrew asked, eyeing them speculatively. There was a small group of Doms who were friends with the owner of Stronghold, and they all had a certain air of authority about them, even compared to the other Doms within the club. Master Andrew was one of those. As a Master Sadist, he'd helped give both Mitch and Zach some extra training once they'd made it through Stronghold's class for new Doms.

"Mitch here needs a breakup drink," Kincaid said, his hand coming down on Mitch's shoulder in commiseration. Master Andrew's face changed to an expression of sympathy.

"Aw, I'm sorry to hear that, man. You and Domi were good together."

"We didn't break up," Mitch said, scowling at Kincaid and shrugging his hand off of his shoulder. "We weren't really together, so we can't have broken up."

Both Master Andrew and Kincaid gave Mitch a questioning look, their expressions so alike, it was a little unnerving.

"How long has it been since you scened with anyone other than Domi?" Kincaid asked. Mitch's lips tightened, and he scowled harder, crossing his arms over his chest.

"Didn't you go on dates to Marquis?" Master Andrew asked, a smile starting to grow. Part of the reason he and Mitch got along well was they had similar senses of humor, so Mitch wasn't surprised to be teased, but he didn't have to enjoy it. "Even before you stopped scening with anyone else, she was the only one you took there."

"Does it feel like you're broken up?" Kincaid poked his shoulder. "You don't look like you right now, man. You look all sad and shit. How do you think I knew something was wrong?"

"Yup." Master Andrew nodded. "In fact, I know exactly what to make you. You need a breakup drink." He turned away to grab ingredients off the shelves behind him.

Groaning, Mitch let his head fall to the smooth wooden surface of the bar and banged it a couple times.

"What's going on? Why is Mitch banging his head?" Brian asked from behind him. A hand patted him on the back. "You okay, buddy?"

"Domi ended their arrangement today," Kincaid said blandly, his tone neutral, mimicking Mitch's words.

"Aw, Domi broke up with you? I'm sorry, Mitch."

Mitch groaned and banged his head again. Today sucked. Hard.

"Here you go." Master Andrew slid something next to Mitch's head. He turned and looked at it.

The drink was pink on the bottom, yellow through most of it, and had an umbrella sticking out of it with a maraschino cherry stuck on a little toothpick. Brian and Kincaid were looking at it with something akin to horror—they didn't do mixed drinks. Heck, Brian barely drank liquor.

"What is that?" Kincaid asked.

Mitch smiled. Master Andrew knew him well. "Pineapple upside-down cake."

"Will your man card be revoked after drinking that?" Kincaid quipped, his lips twitching.

"Hell, no. Only the bravest men drink these." Mitch straightened and picked up the drink with a flourish, feeling a bit more like himself. "The ones completely secure in their manliness."

"And those without tastebuds," Brian muttered, his lips twitching. The drink *was* sickeningly sweet, but it was also exactly what Mitch needed right now—something sweet to soothe the beast.

CHAPTER SIX

Domi

"Do you think the green is unprofessional?" Rae asked, peering into the bathroom mirror. Even the bathrooms in Marquis were posh, with lots of gleaming black-and-ivory tiles with red accents, a couch, and a little sitting room with extra full-length mirrors just inside the main door before reaching the actual bathroom. Rae was standing in front of the gilt mirror above the sink, more drunk than sober, staring at the lime green braids threaded through her hair almost suspiciously.

"I'm the last person you should ask," Domi said with a snort. "I wake up and put on 'work pajamas.' Sometimes, I don't even do that." One of the many benefits of working from home.

Rae rolled her eyes.

"You still know what looks professional." She frowned into the mirror.

"Is someone at work giving you a hard time?"

"Not exactly, but Sheila from HR has made a few comments about keeping hair colors more to natural colors." Rae made a face. "As if her fire engine red is natural. That's only natural on the Little Mermaid." Domi giggled.

"I don't think the green is *un*professional," Domi said, tilting her head and looking at it. It wasn't as if the green was all over Rae's head, just a few braids scattered against the black. Though Domi had to admit, she didn't think she'd seen too many accountants with green hair.

"Ugh, I want to quit so bad."

"You know what you have to do then," Domi said in a sing-song voice, stepping to the side, so she could bump her hip against Rae's. Her bestie had been writing erotic romances for years, but the only person who had ever read them was Domi, who totally thought Rae could make it as an author. So far, Rae had refused to put them up anywhere anyone could see them.

To Domi's surprise, instead of her usual denial, Rae ducked her head. Was that... was she blushing? It was hard to tell with her dark skin tone, but Domi was pretty sure Rae was blushing.

"Rae? Did you publish something?"

"Not exactly," Rae said, still avoiding Domi's gaze. "I put up one story on a free site for people to read."

"And?" Domi was practically bouncing on her tiptoes, waiting for the verdict. "Has anyone read it? What did they think?"

"They seem to like it." Rae shrugged as if it was no big deal. Rolling her eyes, Domi dug into her purse to pull out her phone.

"Where is it? I want to see." It only took a little begging and pleading before Rae gave in and shared the web address. Domi pulled up Their Sexy Secret—her favorite one Rae had written—and squealed when she saw the rating and the comments. "Rae, this is amazing! They love it!"

"Not everyone," Rae muttered. Domi hip-checked her again, still not looking up from the screen.

"Oh, shut up, almost everyone does, and you can't please everyone. Look! This person thinks you need to publish it for real, and this person is saying they'd totally have bought it, and—"

"Okay, okay, okay," Rae interrupted her. Yup, definitely blushing now. Rae gave it away by rubbing her cheeks as though she was attempting to rub away the heat filling them.

The door opened, and another woman walked in. Both of them jumped, looking up almost guiltily. To Domi's surprise, they knew the new occupant. Domi recognized her from the times she and Rae had come to Marquis for their submissive class before it was officially open. A pretty white woman, she worked in the kitchen and looked like she'd just come off her shift, although she'd changed out of her chef's coat. Her hair was still pulled back in a utilitarian ponytail, and the tight tank top she was wearing didn't leave much to the imagination. Damn. Domi wished her boobs looked like that. Heck, she wished she had *half* the woman's rack.

"Hey, Avery," Rae chirped. Right, that was her name. Rae was actually good at remembering names, unlike Domi.

"Hi, Avery!" Domi repeated.

"Hi," Avery came to a halt, looking at them apologetically. "I'm sorry, I don't remember your names."

That made Domi feel a little better about initially forgetting hers.

"That's okay," Domi reassured her. "I forgot yours, too. Rae remembers everyone's name, though. I'm Domi, and this is Rae."

"Nice to see you again," Avery said with a smile. Something flickered in her expression. "Hey, um… this might be a little weird to ask, but you two were going to that, uh, *class* upstairs, right?"

She knew they had been, but the uncomfortable way she asked and the pink tingeing her skin said she was asking for a reason. Rae and Domi exchanged a glance. Was Avery submissive?

"Yup, we were. The *special* class." Domi winked at her. "Did you want to know more about it?"

"If you don't mind."

Looks like I'm the only one not blushing tonight.

"We're about to head back to our table, but you should come join us. It's to the left of the bar, one of the booths," Domi said enthusiastically. Maybe she and Rae had fallen down on the job when it came to making friends with Samantha or trying to give Morgan a chance—though she still doubted they'd have ended up friends—but they could make up for that now. Make a new friend *and* help out someone interested in being a submissive.

"Yes! Come join us, and we'll chat." Rae was clearly on the same page... or maybe she was drunk and feeling extra friendly... either way.

They'd show Mitch and Brian.

Even if Domi wasn't supposed to care what Mitch thought anymore. Yeah, clearly, she was going to need to work on that.

MITCH

He needed new friends.

"Seriously, Mitch, why don't you want a relationship with Domi?" Kincaid's cop training was showing, refusing to give up the interrogation.

"It's not *her*. I don't want a relationship with anyone." That had always been his motto. "Relationships aren't my thing."

"Aren't your thing?" Brian asked incredulously. "Then what do you think you and Domi have been doing these past months?"

Mitch took another swig of his beer to avoid answering and give himself time to think. What had they been doing? Having lots of hot sex. Exploring each other's boundaries. With just each other and no one else. That made them exclusive lovers but nothing more.

Sex was easy. Make her scream, make her feel good, get her off. No promises, no expectations, and no hurt feelings.

Do you really think Domi's not hurt? If she wasn't hurt, she wouldn't be pulling back.

No, she was afraid of being hurt. That was different. He hadn't hurt her yet.

You sure about that?

No. No, he wasn't. And he didn't like that, either. That was the opposite of what he wanted. He wanted to make Domi feel good, make her happy. Because he liked her. Was going to miss her.

Was falling for her the same way she was falling for him.

Aw, shit.

Could it really be that simple?

"I think I'm falling for Domi." He said the words slowly, trying them out to see how they tasted.

"Hallelujah. I was starting to think you're dumber than I realized." Master Andrew threw his hands up in the air in mock celebration. Mitch scowled at him, but the corner of his lip twitched. A class clown always appreciated another class clown.

"So, you do want a relationship with her?" Kincaid pressed, clearly still in questioning mode. Brian chuckled. Now, Mitch felt like throwing up his hands.

"I don't know. What does that feel like?" He shook his head. "The last time I had a 'relationship' with someone was high school."

That had ended when they'd both gone off to college. No broken hearts on either side—they'd just drifted apart, easy peasy. After his parents' divorce, he'd decided his way was better. No screaming, no crying, no hurt, no putting on a brave face, no pretending things were just fine when they were anything but.

"Yeah, I don't think that counts," Brian said dryly.

Master Andrew pointed a finger at him. "Hey, don't knock high school relationships."

"You and Kate were high school sweethearts?" Mitch was confused. Club gossip said Master Andrew had been a bigger man whore than Mitch before he'd gotten together with Kate. How was that possible?

"We broke up for a few years." Shrugging with a nonchalance that didn't seem quite real, the bartender leaned against the bar, his eyes unfocusing and a little smile growing on his face. "I moved to New York, she went to California. Lost touch. Then we both ended up back here around the same time, and that was that."

"Sure... that was that." Mistress Lisa stepped around Andrew to grab a bottle on the other side of him, shaking her head. "You're leaving out an awful lot of drama."

"The important thing is," Andrew continued, raising his voice to drown out Mistress Lisa's commentary, "you both have to be on the same page. If Domi wants a relationship and you only want sex, it's not going to work out. Or vice versa."

"But how do I know if I want a relationship?" Mitch persisted, looking around at his friends. Brian and Kincaid were both unattached, but neither of them was anti-relationships the way Mitch was. They were open to them. Obviously, Master Andrew had managed to make the jump from being the club's biggest manwhore to being monogamous and engaged. Sure, he and Kate might not make it in the long run, but they were making it work right now.

It wasn't that Mitch thought long-term commitment and marriage couldn't work out for people. He just hadn't seen it happen very often. Marriage, relationships... they were all a bad bet a surprising number of people decided to gamble on, anyway.

Domi made him want to try.

"Do you want to see her outside of the club? Do you care about how she's feeling when you're not having sex? Do you miss her when she's gone?"

Well... yes.

They'd been texting between seeing each other at Stronghold and Marquis. It had started out as a way to set up their scenes but had evolved to chatting. Never about anything important, but any time his phone lit up, and he saw Domi's name, it made him smile. He looked forward to her texts. Looked forward to seeing her. Enjoyed having dinner with her at Marquis as much as he did scening with her after.

Shit.

Domi hadn't been the only one falling all this time. He had as well and hadn't even noticed.

"That was fascinating to watch," Master Andrew drawled. "Come to some kind of revelation?"

"I think I want Domi." He sat up straighter.

"You *think*?" Kincaid smacked him on the back of the head. "Seriously? You *think*?"

"Yeah, I think," Mitch repeated stubbornly. "Even that's pretty new to me, okay?"

"Argh. Hopeless." Kincaid gave him a hard look. Yup, between the two of them, Mitch knew who was in charge. "Do not go to Domi with you 'think.' Wait until you're sure."

"How long do you think that will take?" Brian asked with amusement, talking over Mitch's head as if he wasn't even there. "A couple of days before he realizes he's pining after her?"

Mitch glared at him.

"He might be really dumb and have to wait till he sees her scening with another Dom," Master Andrew offered, not bothering to hide his grin when Mitch scowled even harder.

Shit. He didn't like that idea at all. How fast was Domi likely to move on? Would she jump right into a scene with someone else?

"Oooh, somebody doesn't like that idea," Brian teased.

"Somebody needs new friends," Mitch grumbled, but he didn't mean it. Mostly. They sure as hell had given him a lot to think about, though.

DOMI

By the time Avery joined them at the table, she and Rae had already ordered another round of drinks and agreed they were going to make a new friend. Or, as Rae put it, "Add some vanilla to our caramel mocha latte." Which had made both of them giggle madly.

Sliding into the booth next to Domi, Avery let out a little groan.

"Oh, it feels so good to be off my feet."

"Long night?" Domi asked sympathetically. Avery shrugged, but the truth was in her drawn expression. She had a beautiful girl-next-door thing going on and looked great without a lick of makeup but couldn't hide her exhaustion.

"The longest." Avery leaned back and sighed, smiling as one of the cocktail servers came by to get her order before rushing off—much faster than he'd moved for Domi or Rae. "Nick, our executive chef, is a fantastic chef, but he's also an ass."

"He's the brother of one of the owners, right?" Rae asked. The silent owner, actually, but Rae and Domi had learned a lot about Marquis while they'd been attending classes there before it opened.

"Yeah, but trust me, he didn't get the job through nepotism. He's really good. He just also didn't get it through charm." Despite her venting, a smile curved Avery's lips, and Domi raised her eyebrows. Hmmm... maybe Chef Nick was a little more charming than Avery was letting on. "Anyway, I would love to talk about anything other than work if that's okay."

"Absolutely," Domi said immediately. "You wanted to know about the... special club upstairs?"

"Yeah." Avery paused as the server returned, giving her a beer before hurrying off again. She took a small sip before continuing. "Do you like it there? It's safe? Do you have to take the class to join the club?" The words came out in a rush, as though she had to get them out before she thought too hard about it.

Domi and Rae both blinked with surprise. It sounded as if she already knew she was interested in what the club had to offer.

"I don't think you have to take it to join," Domi said. "We did because we had no experience. If you know what you're doing and you're single, they'll pair you up with a Dom—or sub—and observe you before they let you play with anyone else."

"I went with Domi, so she wouldn't have to go alone," Rae said and shrugged, pretending to be more nonchalant than Domi knew she actually felt. Even more than Domi, Rae struggled with her needs. "I liked it more than I thought, so even though I thought she was perfectly safe, I stuck around."

Avery smiled and relaxed.

"You're interested in joining?" Domi asked, even though the answer was obvious. She wanted to get Avery talking. She was genuinely interested, and if this helped her keep her mind off Mitch for the rest of the night, even better.

"I belonged to a club before I moved here," Avery admitted, a wistful expression growing. It was clear she had good memories of the place. "It wasn't anything like Marquis, but I enjoyed it. Working down here, knowing what's going on upstairs... I thought maybe I should get back into the scene."

"That's great!" Rae beamed at her. "What else do you want to know?"

Avery turned out to be a lot of fun—they all bonded over their love of terrible chick flicks and bad shark movies, along with their interest in kink. Unlike Domi and Rae, Avery was neither a masochist nor a baby girl in denial. She called herself a 'service sub.' Domi found the idea kind of fascinating but not particularly appealing for herself.

So, the day wasn't a total loss. She'd lost a bondage buddy but gained a friend.

CHAPTER SEVEN

MITCH

Another day, another flurry of emergencies.

It could be worse. So far, nothing life-threatening had come in—sprains, a couple broken bones, two guys high as kites, and one dude who had lost a glass dildo up his ass. Mitch had had a quiet talk with him about stuffing his butt responsibly. Things that didn't have a base to keep a part of them *outside* the body did not belong in the butt. If only he could make that into a sign and put it up somewhere, people would actually read it. But by the time they got to the ER, it was too late.

All throughout the day, Domi hovered in the back of his mind, just as she had the past few days. He still didn't know what he wanted to do. The indecisiveness wasn't like him, but he'd wanted to take a few days to see if his life really was all that different now, without her in it.

One difference was he never got the little jump of excitement when his phone went off anymore because he already knew it wasn't her.

Another difference was he had trouble keeping his head in the game. He was constantly wondering what she was doing. What it would be like to try a relationship with her. Whether she'd even want to try with him. All the ways it could go wrong. On the other hand, they were already not together now. What's the worst that could happen? That they'd not be together *again*? Same boat he was in now.

Right now, she still liked him... he was pretty sure. If they got together and things crashed and burned, she might not like him at all anymore.

But what if it doesn't crash and burn?

Then... they'd be together. Stay together. Marriage?

For the first time, the thought didn't give him an itchy feeling that made him want to rub calamine lotion all over himself—which was disturbing all on its own. Shouldn't he still feel itchy and uncomfortable? What was so different about Domi?

"It's kinda slow in here today, don't you think?" Jane asked, coming up next to where he was standing at the computer, entering butt-stuff guy's details. Mitch winced. Jane was their new intern, fresh out of medical school, and she'd only been there a week.

"Shh, don't say that!" Dr. Brady, who was running the room that morning, glared at her. Despite only being five feet tall and one of the warmest, friendliest people Mitch had ever met, she could also be fierce as hell. Especially if someone jinxed them like Jane had just done.

"Sorry!" Jane clapped her hands over her mouth. When Dr. Brady turned away, Jane leaned in toward Mitch. "She's really superstitious, huh?"

"For good reason," Mitch said, shaking his head. "You'll learn, newbie."

Less than five minutes later, they were all running their feet off as victims of a multi-vehicle car crash were wheeled in. Jane looked sick to her stomach, but she followed along quickly enough when Mitch hurried toward the stretchers, along with the other nurses. Yeah, she'd learn.

DOMI

Watching Ana prancing around in her Elsa dress, Domi had to grin at the enthusiastic hand waving going on. It didn't matter the weather was warm or her name actually matched Elsa's sister—as far as Ana was concerned, she was the snow queen. She had a great imagination.

"Queen Elsa, I request permission to return to the house," Domi said finally, getting her daughter's attention. She was still sitting on the chair Ana had directed her to before doing her snow queen thing. "I have work to finish."

Ana's face fell, but she nodded. Domi's chest tightened. She hated disappointing her daughter, but she couldn't play all afternoon, as much as she might want to. Part of her was a little exasperated. It wasn't like Ana had included her anyway, but she knew Ana still liked having her there, even if Domi was only watching from her chair.

Then Ana brightened again.

"When the new baby gets here, she can be Anna!"

Domi had to laugh. Thankfully, Ana was very excited about becoming a big sister, just like Elsa. She hadn't even been bothered when Julia's morning sickness had become so bad, Marcus had asked if Ana could come back to Domi's early. Poor Julia had started throwing up almost constantly on Monday, and even though she was now on anti-nausea medication, Marcus wanted her to get a few days' total rest while she recovered from what had been a truly awful few days.

"It'll be a bit before the baby is able to play like that, but eventually, yes."

"I can't wait!" Ana spun around, throwing her arms out wide. Her happy grin was infectious, and Domi found herself grinning, too, her guilt fading in the face of her daughter's joy.

"Rae will be home soon," she reminded Ana. "Maybe she can play with you when she gets here."

It wasn't really throwing Rae under the bus. After sitting in front of a computer screen, working with numbers all day, she loved playing with Ana, and Ana brightened even more at the reminder.

"I'm going to pretend my new sister is here playing with me until

Aunt Rae gets home." Ana nodded her head decisively, and Domi laughed.

"Okay, have fun, sweetie."

Smiling, Domi turned and headed back into the house just as her neighbors, Karen and Jordan, were coming outside. They didn't have a fence between their yards, just flowerbeds, but thankfully they all got along really well. Jordan waved, and Karen nodded her greeting since she was carrying a tray full of drinks and snacks. They often sat in the backyard on nice days, enjoying the weather, so Domi wasn't too surprised to see them out today.

"Afternoon!" Jordan called out, smiling widely and brushing some of their grey hair out of their face. Jordan was the first non-binary person Ana and Domi had met, but both of them had learned how to use their pronouns quickly. "Isn't it a gorgeous day?"

"Gorgeous," Domi agreed, smiling.

"Hey, Elsa, looking good," Karen said, putting down the tray she was carrying and giving Ana a thumbs up. Ana smiled back and twirled, prompting a smattering of applause from their neighbors.

Feeling a little better now that Ana wouldn't be totally on her own for playtime, Domi headed into the house and sat down to get to work. Being an inpatient medical coder wasn't the most glamorous job in the world, but it was important. One missed code or forgotten rule could end up costing a hospital tens of thousands of dollars, which should have been covered by either insurance or the government. Domi liked knowing she was helping people who needed it by making sure every 't' was crossed and every 'i' dotted, which meant she needed complete focus on what she was doing.

Which was why it took her a moment to realize the sudden, loud sound she was hearing was screaming.

"Domi! Domi!" Jordan's voice was only slightly muffled as they banged on the back door.

Scrambling out of her chair, Domi accidentally knocked it over, her heart already pounding as she ran for the back of the house.

Ana. Something happened to my baby.

The high-pitched wail of pain had to be her daughter. Her airway constricted, making it hard to breathe, and the only thing that kept her from panicking was the knowledge Ana needed her.

"I'm coming!" Domi yelled down the hall. Jordan had already abandoned the back door the moment they saw Domi at the end of the hall and headed their way.

She burst through the back door, running straight for the line of trees at the back of the yard, and immediately knew what had happened—Ana *knew* she wasn't supposed to climb the trees without Rae or Domi there with her, but she loved to climb. Domi had suspected she sometimes did when they weren't around.

Karen was kneeling next to where Ana was lying on the ground. Jordan skidded to a stop beside them, only a few seconds before Domi did. It felt as if she'd leapt across the entire lawn in a single bound, she'd moved so quickly. Thankfully, Ana was no longer screaming, but she was still crying, great heaving sobs that only came with real pain.

"Oh, baby, baby, what happened?" Domi knelt down, reaching out tenderly, but her hands hovered, unsure where to touch.

Ana's little face was so pale, her eyes huge in a drawn face, tears rolling down her cheeks, and she was clutching her left arm to her stomach, but she reached for Domi.

"Shh, shh, baby, just lie there," Jordan said, getting down on their knees and pressing their hand against Ana's head. A retired paramedic, Domi trusted Jordan's judgment even though it killed her not to be able to gather Ana up into her arms. Jordan glanced at Domi, eyes serious and worried. "We don't know if she hurt her neck or back, so it'll be safer to keep her like this until the ambulance gets here with a neck brace and a backboard."

Domi pressed her hand over Ana's, her daughter's fingers feeling tinier and more fragile than ever. Her heart pounded in her chest, stomach churning, and it was all she could do not to burst into tears herself.

"I'm so sorry," Karen said, tears in her eyes, though she was doing her best to put on a brave face. She just wasn't succeeding as well as Jordan or Domi. "She was playing well on her own, and we started talking, and Jordan was showing me something on their phone, then the next thing we knew, we heard Ana scream and fall..."

"It's not your fault," Domi said automatically, as another wave of sick fear and worry through her stomach.

My poor baby.

It could have been worse, though.

Thank God, it wasn't her neck.

"I'm sorry, Mommy, I'm sorry." Ana started to cry again.

"It's okay, baby," Domi said automatically, wanting to comfort her daughter, but it really wasn't okay. If Ana had fallen and hadn't hurt herself, Domi would want to wring her neck, but because she *had* hurt herself, it didn't seem right to rub that in. Still, she never wanted Ana to do this again. "Now you know why Mommy or Aunt Rae always want to be with you when you climb. No more climbing on your own in the future, okay?" She said it as gently as she could, and pure relief shot through her when Ana did nothing more than nod.

The sound of sirens caught her ear, getting louder as they came closer, and Jordan jumped up.

"I'll go direct them back here."

Karen patted Domi's back. She was so glad they were there to help her keep from totally falling apart when Ana needed her. She would fall apart later once Ana was taken care of.

MITCH

Familiar, bouncing curls caught Mitch's eye in the last place he'd expected. His heart did a little double thump inside his chest, lifting up in happy anticipation. It sank just as quickly, worry rising up to replace it.

She was walking next to a stretcher the EMTs were bringing in, her entire focus on whoever was on it.

Mitch was on the move before he realized it, blinking with shock when the child, whose hand Domi was holding, came into view. There was no mistaking they were mother and daughter; they looked exactly alike. The little girl, dressed up in a blue princess dress, had a neck brace, an arm brace, and was resting uncomfortably on a bodyboard, eyes red from crying. His heart went out to her immediately—kids were the hardest.

"Hey, Mitch." Braden greeted him, drawing Domi's attention. Her head jerked up, and her eyes widened when she saw who the EMT was talking to. Mitch gave her his most reassuring smile. "We have a possible fracture. I think her neck and back are okay, but she should be x-rayed just to be sure."

"Of course." Mitch bent over to smile down at the little girl. "Hey sweetheart, we're going to get you fixed up, okay?" He directed another smile at Domi, who seemed shell-shocked, finding him here at the hospital. It also made him realize how little they'd talked about their day-to-day lives when they were together. He'd never told her where he worked, and all he knew about her job was she did it from home. They'd kept their conversations very focused. "Hey, Domi."

"Hi." She blinked as if surprised that she'd spoken.

"You know my mommy?" The little voice piping up was tense with pain but curious.

"Yes, I do. Your mommy and I are friends, so I'm going to take extra special care of you, okay?"

"Okay." The little girl was still looking at him a little dubiously.

Thankfully, things had slowed down after the car accident this morning, and no one had jinxed them again. Mitch was able to smooth Domi's way through everything. He was actually starting to get a little worried about her, the way she was acting like an automaton, but she finally relaxed after they got Ana on pain meds, and the little girl was no longer hurting so badly.

Jane gave him a weird look when he hounded the technician to hurry Ana's x-rays along. Yeah, usually Mitch didn't try to cut the line, but this was Domi... and her daughter.

Which made him understand a little better why she'd been reluctant to get into a real relationship and why she might want something more stable than a fuck buddy.

Oddly, meeting her daughter and finding out she was a single mom solidified things for *him*. It didn't turn him off at all, which was a pretty definitive sign his feelings for her were far more serious than he'd realized. Not that he could focus on that right now or say anything to her about it, but he knew.

"Okay, pretty ladies," he said, breezing back into the room where they were waiting, pushing the wheelchair in front of him. His shift had technically ended fifteen minutes ago, but he wasn't going anywhere. "The doctor has signed off, so you two are good to go. As long as you promise no more monkey impressions."

Ana giggled at the stern look he gave her before sitting up straight with a mock solemn expression.

"I promise," she said, holding up the arm that didn't have a cast on it. Thankfully, it had been a simple fracture. She'd need to be x-rayed again in about a week to make sure the bones had stayed in a good position, but surgery shouldn't be needed. Her shoulder had been jarred, but there was no injury to her neck, back, or head. As things went, it was as good a diagnosis as one could hope for.

"Thank you for all your help." Domi had been quiet, and now she looked drained.

"Of course. Are you two going to be okay getting home?"

"Yeah, I texted Rae, and she's almost here."

"Good."

"Thank you for all your help."

"Of course."

They stood there, looking at each other for a moment. Her face was pale and worried, but her dark eyes were filled with gratitude. Relief. Mitch had done what came naturally to him with Domi— took charge without a second thought. Now, with her looking at him the way she was, it took every ounce of his self-control not to reach down and tug on her curl, the way he did at Stronghold or lean down to kiss her lips and tell her everything was going to be okay.

"Thank you, Murse Mitch." The little voice piping up, with the silly name he'd told her to use, brought him back to reality. Domi blinked as if she'd been affected as well. Mitch turned away before he could do something stupid in front of her daughter. He doubted Domi would forgive him.

"Okay, Queen Ana, let's get you moving," he said, shaking off the spell Domi had him under.

"It's Queen Elsa," she told him primly, resting her arm in her lap.

"Ah, of course, my mistake," Mitch said cheerfully. "Queen Elsa is on the move!" He made a bugling sound that set Ana off in a fit of giggles, and even Domi couldn't suppress her smile.

CHAPTER EIGHT

Domi

"That was Mitch. *Mitch*. Your... our Mitch." Rae quickly changed the pronoun, shaking her head as she pulled away from the hospital's roundabout. Ana was strapped into the backseat behind Rae, and Domi couldn't help but glance over her shoulder every couple of seconds to make sure she was okay. Mostly she looked tired but didn't seem to notice what Rae had said.

Considering Domi had never so much as mentioned Mitch's name around Ana, she wouldn't have been surprised if her daughter was curious, but she was either too exhausted or overwhelmed to take notice. Hopefully, she hadn't noticed the little moment between Mitch and Domi right before they left.

Domi wasn't sure whether to feel relieved or worried about Ana's distraction. She didn't want Ana thinking too much about Mitch—or Murse Mitch, as he'd told her to call him, which had made her giggle —but she didn't like to think that Ana was in too much pain or anything, either.

"Did we know he worked at the hospital?" Rae asked, giving her head a little shake of disbelief. Domi knew just how she felt.

Seeing Mitch in the emergency room had thrown her for a loop.

On the other hand, she'd found his presence incredibly reassuring. He'd taken charge immediately, letting her focus on Ana and trusting him to tell her what to do. Not her normal position anywhere except *in* either Stronghold or Marquis, but she'd been grateful for it. For him.

Argh. Which did not help her feelings towards him. Watching him charm Ana... yeah. And he hadn't treated Domi any differently after finding out she was a single mom.

"No, no, we did not," she answered Rae, keeping her emotions out of her voice. "He's a nurse there."

"He called himself a murse," Ana chimed in from the back seat, proving she actually was listening. She giggled. "For 'man nurse.'"

"It's okay to call him that, but only him," Domi reminded her. "Others might not find it funny." That Mitch not only embraced but encouraged the term was probably the least surprising thing about today.

"He would," Rae said, echoing Domi's thoughts.

"He stayed with us almost the whole time," Ana said. "And helped Mommy."

"Oh, he did, did he?" Rae asked, sending Domi a look as if she wasn't sure she approved. Considering how tangled Domi's feelings were over the man, she didn't blame her bestie for being dubious.

"He was very helpful," Domi said. She sighed, leaning her head back against the headrest. "It was nice having someone there I could trust to explain everything to me." Even though she couldn't see Rae's expression, she could feel the other woman soften.

"Yeah, I can see that." Rae glanced. "Weird to see him there, though."

"Very."

They drove in silence the rest of the way home, neither she nor Rae able to really gossip about Mitch while Ana was in the car. Not to mention, Domi was completely spent, as though she'd been put through the wringer. She heard Ana yawn. Today might be a nap day, which was not Ana's usual anymore.

When they pulled onto their street, Marcus was there waiting for them, standing next to his car in front of their house. Domi blinked. It was almost weird to see him without Julia. She felt a little guilty, being relieved Julia wasn't there, though that was nothing compared to the sick feeling filling her stomach at having to actually face her co-parent after letting their daughter get hurt. She knew it was an accident, and Marcus hadn't sounded angry on the phone, just worried. He'd told her he was going to try to get out of work and meet them at home, but she hadn't heard from him after that, so she'd assumed he hadn't been able to leave work yet.

"Daddy!" In the backseat, Ana perked up when she saw Marcus standing in the driveway. As soon as Rae parked the car, Ana scrambled out of it, wincing when she moved a little too quickly, causing all the adults to wince too. "Daddy!"

"Hey there, who's my brave girl?" Marcus asked, giving her a huge hug and picking her up in his arms. "I'm so sorry I wasn't able to be at the hospital with you."

"That's okay." Ana leaned her head against his shoulder, yawning again. "Mommy was there. And Murse Mitch."

Rae snickered as Domi winced. Marcus just looked amused. *He* didn't realize the significance of Ana's statement. Ack. She wondered how long it would take for Ana to reveal Murse Mitch was Mommy's 'friend.'

Why did that make her feel guilty?

"Let's get you inside, peanut," Domi said, reverting to the nickname they'd used for Ana when she was a baby. Revealing just how tired she was, Ana didn't protest the endearment. She stayed cuddled up against her Daddy, who carried her in.

Turning, she saw Jordan and Karen peering out of their front door.

"I'll go update them," Rae said, giving Domi a little push to follow Marcus and Ana. "You go talk to Marcus."

Sighing, Domi did as she was told. They got a yawning Ana settled into her bed, where she fell asleep almost immediately, then Domi took Marcus to the kitchen to explain exactly how everything had happened and what the doctor had said. She glossed over Mitch's presence, causing Rae to give her a look since she had joined them by then.

Whatever.

She didn't feel like explaining Mitch to Marcus. It wasn't as though he was going to be around, anyway. The encounter with Mitch was probably the only one Ana would ever have.

Too bad, a little voice whispered in her mind. *She liked him. He was good with her. You need a guy like that.*

Yeah, one who actually wants *a relationship.*

Which was not what Mitch wanted.

"How's Julia doing?" Domi asked to change the subject.

"Better." Marcus perked up. "The anti-nausea meds seem to be working well. She's eating again and has more energy. If this keeps up and Julia feels up to it, do you think Ana could spend the weekend with us?"

Technically, Ana was supposed to be at Marcus and Julia's right now, then coming back to Domi's tomorrow, which was Saturday. The tug to be with her baby all weekend and watch over her and her arm was strong, but she knew Marcus would be feeling that same tug, especially since Ana had gotten hurt on *her* watch.

"Yes, of course," she made herself say, her stomach only twisting a little. It's not like Marcus hadn't wanted to spend his full week with Ana.

"I don't blame you, Domi." Leaning over the table, Marcus put his hand over hers, his expression earnest. "It was an accident. They happen."

The little twist in her gut relaxed a little, and she managed to smile back at him. He really was a great guy. Steady. Reliable. Kind. The kind of man she *should* have feelings for... if she was going to have feelings for a guy. Not a commitment-phobe fuck buddy. No matter how great he'd been in a crisis.

MITCH

Feeling even more tired than usual but also extremely satisfied with himself, Mitch headed home, Domi and her daughter foremost in his mind the entire way. Ana was an extremely cute miniature version of her mom, with the same energy and sass. He'd wondered where Ana's dad was but hadn't felt it was his place to ask.

Did he want it to be his place?

That was the question.

He and Domi had always gotten along well at the club. That had never been a problem. But how did he know whether he wanted more?

He missed her.

His friends all called the end of their arrangement a breakup.

But what did it all really mean?

The question plagued him all the way home, then out to Stronghold, where he was meeting up with the guys.

"Mitch. Earth to Mitch. Come in, Mitch." Brian waved a hand in front of Mitch's face, making him jerk back in surprise. "You okay, man?"

"Yeah. Yeah, just tired. It was a long day." Mitch shook his head as if he was trying to shake away thoughts of Domi, not exactly something easy to do in Stronghold, even when she wasn't there. He didn't expect her to show up tonight.

"Are you gonna go play?" Zach asked, tipping his beer bottle toward the Lounge area, where the unattached submissives were gathered. He was leaning on the bar table next to Kincaid. The two of them were standing so close, they were almost touching, but not quite. The energy coming off them was almost enough to distract Mitch from his own thoughts.

Mitch glanced over at the subbies.

Any one of them could do a scene with him, scream for him, come for him.

It wouldn't be the same.

The whisper threaded through his mind, and his chest tightened. Dammit. He didn't want any of them. He wanted Domi.

"Hmmm, looks like Mitch is feeling conflicted." A little smile on his lips, Zach half-turned to address the woman at one of the tables behind him. "Hey Sharon, what's that term you use when a man whore starts wanting only one woman?"

"Magic pussy?" The petite sub half-pulled away from her boyfriend, whose arm was wrapped possessively around her, her eyes lighting up with interest. "Oooh, who got magic pussied?! Is it Mitch? Does Domi have the magic pussy?"

Her boyfriend, Jake, turned with her, eyes alight with curiosity, as were the rest of the group they'd been talking to.

Great. Mitch banged his head on the table. So much for privacy. Not that he had any huge expectations of it in Stronghold or Marquis —gossip central with no gender lines.

"We're pretty sure Domi has magic pussy, though Mitch has yet to confirm," Brian said, chuckling.

"Oooh, yay! Kate owes me five bucks!"

"There is no such thing as magic pussy!" Kate protested. "And he's not confirming... he's banging his head on the table. That's not the same thing."

"You okay, buddy?" Kincaid patted Mitch's shoulder with false sympathy, his tone syrupy. "Do you need more time to come to terms with the magic pussy?"

Mitch straightened up.

"I hate all of you."

"Woo-hoo!" Sharon cheered, and Mitch's lips twitched. She turned back to Kate, pointing her finger. "You so owe me five bucks. I told you magic pussy is real. You are not an anomaly!"

Next to Kate, Andrew smirked, then winked at Mitch. With his fiancé by his side, he looked more content than ever. Would they be one of the couples who made it? Intellectually, Mitch knew not everyone was like his parents, but the odds were pretty stacked against them.

Sharon and Kate fell to bickering about magic pussy, while Zach turned expectantly back to Mitch, raising his eyebrows.

"Can we talk about something else? Literally anything else?" Mitch practically begged. "What about you, Kincaid, any special playmate?"

Kincaid shook his head, eyes dancing with amusement. "Should we try talking about work?"

"My partner thinks his wife is cheating on him, which has been the main thing going on this week," Kincaid said dryly. "Trust me, it's not a fun conversation."

Yeah, didn't sound like it.

"Brian? Work? Women?"

Brian shook his head and took a sip of his beer, his dark eyes dancing with amusement.

Fine. He'd go for the low blow. Zach was the one who had started this, after all.

"Zach, what about you and Amy?"

Blinking in surprise, Zach stared back at him. Beside him, Kincaid stiffened. Yeah, well, he should have helped change the conversation instead of leaving Mitch out to dry.

"What about me and Amy?" Zach echoed.

Mitch shrugged.

"When was the last time you scened with someone other than Amy?" he asked. Zach scowled at him.

"She's *engaged*." Something in Zach's tone, the prim way he stated the fact, caught Mitch's attention. Uh oh. "I'm only scening with her so she can get what she needs since her fiancé isn't kinky."

Shit. He'd only meant to poke at Zach and Kincaid, and whatever was going on between them. He hadn't realized Zach actually had a crush or some kind of feelings for Amy. The man was still scening with her, even though it was purely platonic. Everyone knew Amy didn't do anything sexual at Stronghold.

"Then I guess we're back around to Brian." Mitch grinned easily as if he hadn't realized Zach's intensity meant anything. Kincaid was now eyeing Zach with speculation and worry. *Good job, Mitch.* Brian was going to have to suck it up and share the hot seat instead. "Are you going to find someone to scene with tonight?"

Brian glanced over at the Lounge area. As far as Mitch knew, he hadn't scened with anyone since Rae at Marquis.

"Yeah," Brian said slowly, putting his beer down, not looking away from the subs. It was the first one of the night, which meant he was free to play still. "Yeah, I think I will." Nodding his head, he got to his feet, refocusing on Mitch. "Coming?"

He should.

He really should.

But he didn't want to.

"Didn't think so."

A ghost of a smile crossed Brian's lips.

Zach clapped Mitch on the shoulder and leaned in.

"Magic pussy," he whispered in Mitch's ear. After having accidentally revealed the man's feelings for Amy, with Kincaid right there and who knows what going on between the two of them, Mitch let him have the jab.

Besides, he wasn't entirely sure Zach was wrong.

CHAPTER NINE

<u>*Domi*</u>

Saturday night at Stronghold.

She took Ana over to Marcus and Julia's in the morning, dropping off chicken soup for Julia at the same time, who had gratefully taken it before fussing over Ana's arm. To Domi's surprise and relief, like Marcus, Julia didn't blame Domi for the injury.

Apparently, Domi was the only one who felt she was at fault. Unfortunately, the lack of blame from others did nothing to help ameliorate the guilt that was growing in her stomach. Which was why she'd let Rae convince her to come to Stronghold.

If she could find someone to scene with and let some of her emotions out, she'd feel better. But....

"This is a bad idea," she muttered as she and Rae made their way to the Lounge area of the club. Though it looked like a massive warehouse on the outside, inside, Stronghold was elegantly decorated and had plenty of comfortable spots. After getting through the lobby, the main floor had a huge wooden bar on the right and a cocktail area to the left known as the Lounge before the wall where the locker rooms —the real ones, not like the kinky fantasy room upstairs—and the owner's office were located. Gorgeous black-and-white photographs of domination and submission decorated the walls, adding to the atmosphere, though there wasn't often much scening happening on this floor.

Past the Lounge area, there was a large dance floor in front of a stage, where some people would get a little freaky. The stage was usually reserved for large demonstrations, similar to what Marquis put on but more instructional than for pleasure.

Dominants and couples congregated at the bar, submissives in the Lounge area. She didn't think it was hard and fast, but an unspoken rule everyone seemed to follow. It wasn't a bad thing, though. The Lounge had comfortable leather armchairs and a large, dark red fluffy carpet to cushion knees, so if a dominant came over and demanded the submissive, they were negotiating with, kneel for them.

At the back of the room, next to the stage, were the staircases going up to the private theme rooms and down to the Dungeon, as well as a hall leading out to the gardens. The whole club smelled like leather and was designed to put everyone in a sexy mood.

But tonight, Domi wasn't feeling sexy at all, even though she was wearing one of her sexiest outfits.

Normally, when she went to Stronghold or Marquis, it was like shedding her mom persona and letting her inner self be free. Today, she felt like she was trapped in her own skin. Her corset felt too tight, her boobs and legs too exposed, and instead of giving her confidence, she wanted to go back home, put on comfy pajamas, and watch a bad shark movie.

"You are not going to sit in the house and wallow about what a bad mom you are... because you're not," Rae scolded her, taking Domi by the hand and pulling her toward the Lounge. "We are going to hang out at Stronghold. We're going to find you a nice Dom to scene with. And you are going to get some much-needed stress relief."

That did sound good... except Domi didn't want a nice Dom. She wanted a mean, sadistic Dom who would torment her until she was screaming and crying, then pleasure her until she was screaming and crying some more. After, he'd hold and cuddle her, then say something stupid or goofy to make her laugh.

Basically, she wanted Mitch.

Bad Domi.

Yeah, yeah, she knew. But the heart wanted what the heart wanted —so did her vagina.

Which was why this was a bad idea.

Rae wasn't wrong about what Domi needed. She could really use a scene.

As if Murphy's Law had summoned him, Master Mitch stepped in front of her and Rae, grinding them to an immediate halt. Tall, wearing nothing but black leather pants and a black vest that made his hair look even blonder and his eyes even bluer, and so damn delicious it was freaking unfair. Completely different from how he'd looked in scrubs but just as in charge and far sexier.

MITCH

He didn't know why he'd come back to Stronghold tonight. Last night hadn't exactly been great, and none of his friends were coming in tonight. He was just standing alone at the bar. Last night, he'd spent the entire evening missing Domi and wondering what he was doing there, even when his friends had been there to distract him, and tonight was no better. Being here was like being close to her, and he needed to figure out how to tell her he'd changed his mind about what he wanted. Why should she believe him?

Hell, Kate had gotten engaged to Master Andrew, Stronghold's biggest manwhore, yet she was the one who didn't believe in magic pussy. How was he supposed to convince Domi?

Especially since he hadn't thought Domi wanted a relationship in the first place.

Except now she did.

Wait, does that mean I have a magic penis?

Before he could explore that thought, his eyes were drawn across the bar to the main entrance to the club, where Rae was pulling a reluctant Domi along. Domi looked amazing, of course. A black

89

leather corset made the most of her slim figure, pushing her breasts up and giving her more exaggerated curves. He liked her the way she was, but Mitch knew it paid to appreciate the effort a woman put into her appearance. The short skirt she was wearing made her legs look longer than usual, especially when paired with her high-heel ankle boots.

Mitch had a sudden vision of Domi on her back, wearing nothing but the boots... and being fucked by someone else.

That's what was going to happen. She and Rae were headed for the Lounge, and there was no way Domi would remain unattached once it was clear she was available. Which meant he had to talk to her *now* or risk someone else sweeping her away. What if she decided she liked someone else better than she liked Mitch?

He was up and moving before he realized it, his body reacting faster than his mind.

It wasn't until he stepped in front of her, cutting off her path to the Lounge, he realized he still had no idea what to say to her, no clue how to explain himself and what he wanted.

"Domi." There. Greeting done. Good job, brain.

"Master Mitch." The expression on her face was uncertain. Rae's was much clearer—she was not happy with him.

"Master Mitch. Please excuse us, we're headed to the Lounge." She tugged at Domi's arm as though she was going to pull Domi around him.

"Can I talk to you for a minute?" he asked Domi, deciding to ignore Rae. If Domi wanted to talk to him, she wasn't going to let Rae stop her. If Domi decided not to talk to him... well, then he'd work on sucking up to Rae.

Thankfully, Domi only hesitated a moment.

"Sure."

Rae let out an exasperated sigh but let go of Domi's arm.

"Thank you, Rae," Mitch said, giving her his most charming smile. She didn't want to smile back, he could tell, pressing her lips together hard, although that didn't stop her from giving him a warning look. Rae didn't need to say a word, Mitch knew exactly what that look meant—*hurt my bestie, and I'll kick your ass.* He absolutely believed she would, too.

Taking Domi's hand, he pulled her toward the wall on the opposite side of the room from the bar, near the doors to the locker rooms. Rae settled down in the Lounge, in a chair facing where he and Domi were standing, watching them, even though she wouldn't be able to hear what they were saying.

Once they were standing in place, Domi pulled her hand back, crossing her arms over her chest in a protective stance.

"So, what's up?" Her chin lifted slightly. Such an aggressive little pixie.

Mitch had to stifle the urge to tug one of her curls—he didn't think she'd appreciate it right now.

"I…" He cleared his throat and gathered his courage. "I want to see you. Outside of Stronghold. I don't want to lose you from my life."

Confusion clouded her eyes, and a little wrinkle formed on her forehead. Domi stared up at him as if he was speaking a foreign language. Yeah, that hadn't exactly been clear. This was why he'd wanted to prepare something to say.

"Like, hang out as friends?"

"No." He shook his head. *Use your words, Mitch.* Olivia's voice echoed in his head. Mistress Olivia had been in charge of the class for new dominants at Stronghold, the one he'd taken with Kincaid, Zach, and Brian. She'd also been the lead instructor for the submissives when Mitch had met Domi. One of the things she'd hammered into Mitch's head during both classes had been the importance of clear communication. "I want us to date. I mean, I want to take you out on a date."

———

Domi

She didn't know whether to be bowled over by Master Mitch's adorable awkwardness or bang her head against the wall. Why was he doing this?

"*You* want a date?" She asked in disbelief. Mr. No Commitment, Mr. I Only Scene, Mr. Don't Get Attached... wanted to date *her*?

"I don't want to just date. I want to date you, specifically. No one else." He cleared his throat again, shoving his hands in his pockets. Something vulnerable about his demeanor tugged on her heartstrings. Mitch *was* a commitment-phobe, and she hadn't heard about him ever asking anyone out on a date before. No wonder he didn't seem very confident.

Part of her worried this was a road to certain heartbreak, but another part of her had to wonder—how strongly must he feel if he was willing to break his usual M.O.?

"I like you," he said when she didn't say anything right away. "I like spending time with you. I liked your daughter, though I'll understand if you don't want me to spend time with both of you right away. After you broke things off, it made me realize I've gotten used to having you in my life and I like you there. I missed having you there when you weren't."

It wasn't the most romantic speech she'd ever heard, wasn't the most practiced, but it very well might be the most honest. Domi melted... just a little.

"I..."

"You don't have to decide tonight," he said hurriedly. "I know I'm springing this on you. If you want to think about it..." Soulful blue eyes begged her not to think too long. It was almost painful to see this earnest side of Mitch rather than his classic joking demeanor. Definitely not the confident, swaggering Dom she was used to, but it didn't diminish her attraction to him. If anything, it made him seem more real.

"I'll think about it," she found herself saying. This wasn't a Mitch she could turn away with a smile and a joke. This was a more serious Mitch. Similar to the one she'd seen yesterday at the hospital, but not the same. Serious, but open in a way she'd never seen him before.

A brilliant smile was her reward. Damn, if he smiled at her like that all the time, she wouldn't be able to resist him.

"Do you want to play tonight? With me?" he asked hopefully.

"Sure." Yup. Definitely a bad idea, but how was she supposed to say no right now? She wanted to scene with him. She'd wanted to scene with him even before she'd known he was there, and now that he was not only there but saying he had missed her and wanted to try dating her...

If she'd thought his smile was brilliant before, it was even better now. Blue eyes sparkled with anticipation as he straightened up, pulling his Dom persona around him like a cloak. Hands no longer in his pockets, he held one out for her to take, and Domi slipped her fingers into his.

She almost swore she could hear Rae's inaudible groan.

Yup, I'm over here making poor choices. You can scold me later. Right now, I'm gonna go get laid.

Turning, Master Mitch pulled her into position along his side, wrapping her hand around his arm like an old-school gentleman. Domi couldn't help but giggle.

"Let's see what's open in the Dungeon," he said with a wink, walking toward the stairs. No, walking wasn't the right word. He was strutting, and Domi couldn't keep the grin off of her face.

He might be terrible at dating—probably would be—but he wanted to try. That meant something to her. Wasn't it at least worth trying? Not that she was going to give him a yes right now, but they could at least scene together. She'd give him her answer after she'd had some time to think about it.

Even though she was already pretty sure she was going to say yes.

CHAPTER TEN

MITCH

Thankfully, one of the nooks along the far wall of the Dungeon was open, with hanging chains and cuffs, providing all sorts of fun possibilities once he got Domi restrained. Leading her over to the nook, he dropped his play bag on the bench beside it and smiled down at her. She looked back at him, bemused since he was escorting her like they were on their way to the theater or something.

"What kind of scene would you like to have?" he asked. Domi raised her eyebrows. Usually, he took the lead, but tonight, he wanted to make sure she got what she needed, but she didn't seem to understand why he was asking. "Is there anything special you need after yesterday?"

Comprehension flashed in her eyes.

"Stress release." She made a face. "I know I shouldn't feel guilty about Ana being hurt, it was an accident, but..."

Domi was the type to take the blame for things outside her control. Must make being a single mom difficult. He wondered who took care of Ana when Domi was at Stronghold... Not his business, though he hoped they'd be able to talk about their actual lives soon. Maybe when he took her out on their first date.

This wasn't the time to ask. She needed time and space to be herself and have her own needs met. Stronghold was a place to escape reality for a little bit, not sit and talk about it.

"You were not at fault," he said firmly, reaching up to grip her hair and pull her head back, forcing her to look up at him. Her lips tightened, her expression turning mulish, and he knew she wanted to argue with him. "Accidents happen all the time, especially to kids. I see the aftermath of it all the time at work. It means the kid is actually living their life, which is a good thing. So, I'm not going to punish you for Ana getting hurt. I am going to punish you for blaming yourself."

Domi's eyes widened, and Mitch grinned, leaning down to plant a firm kiss on her lips.

Was it just him, or did it feel different this time? Her lips hadn't changed—they weren't any softer, she tasted exactly the same—but somehow, it felt like there was more to it, as though he *felt* more.

Sweeter. More intimate. More meaningful.

It was their first kiss after he'd told her he wanted her—the first kiss after he'd admitted his feelings for her. He hadn't expected anything would really change, but it had, even if he couldn't describe it.

When they broke apart, he couldn't tell if she felt the same way. He hoped so.

"Alright, Domi Darling." Reaching up, he tugged a curl, then trailed his finger down her shoulder to the center of her breasts, giving them a quick tap. "Let's get you out of these clothes."

Domi

Something had changed between them. Scenes with Mitch had always been satisfying, always hot, but now it felt like something *more*. There was tension between them, in a good way, that hadn't been there before.

His hands felt the same as he smoothed out the lines the corset had left on her skin, but his gaze was more intense. More intent.

Though she kind of wanted to kick him for *why* he was going to punish her. They both knew this wasn't going to be a real punishment scene, but it still meant something.

Being punished for blaming herself. Argh.

He has a point.

Not that she would have long to dwell on it.

Tugging the hanging chains into position, Mitch secured Domi's wrists in the leather cuffs on the end, then pulled her arms over her head. She was naked from the waist up, arms stretched upward, and already feeling squirmy. Being restrained, knowing she couldn't go anywhere, allowed her to relax in her bonds.

Like yesterday, she was trusting Mitch to take over, but instead of trusting him to handle all the hospital stuff, she was waiting for him to make her feel good, to pleasure both of them.

After he tortured her a little, of course.

"Very pretty," Mitch said, giving one of her nipples a little pinch. Domi squeaked in reaction, the tiny bite of pain only a fraction of what she craved. "But I think they could use more decoration."

Yes, please, and thank you.

Instead of getting right to it, Mitch cupped her small breasts in his hands, leaning down for another kiss as he fondled her. Domi moaned against his lips, rocking forward and thrusting her chest into his hands. He dug his fingers into her flesh, trapping her nipples between his thumbs and palms, squeezing them tight enough, she whimpered. The little buds throbbed in his grip, craving more.

The increasing discomfort made her squirm even more, her pussy creaming in anticipation.

Pulling away from hers, he bent down to kiss the budded tips. Long fingers plucked and twisted one nipple while his teeth and lips pulled at the other. The sensation shot straight through to her core, leaving her writhing against him. She pressed her thighs together as her pussy pulsed needily, hungry for stimulation. Mitch switched breasts, going back and forth between them until she was whimpering from the need growing inside her.

"Master Mitch, please," she begged—she knew he liked it when she begged. "I need more."

With a chuckle and one last little nip that made her gasp, Mitch straightened and went over to where he'd left his bag. Her body hummed with anticipation of whatever toy he was looking for.

MITCH

Damn, he wanted Domi bad. After playing together for so long, they knew just what the other liked, and he knew she was pushing him a little by begging. She wasn't trying to top from the bottom exactly, but she knew he would give her more of what she wanted if she begged. Was it his fault she sounded so nice when she was whimpering and pleading?

Picking up a nasty pair of clover clamps and an adjustable spreader bar with ankle cuffs, Mitch returned to his beauty-in-distress. Her dark eyes lit up when she saw what he was holding.

Such a sweet little pain slut. His cock twitched, throbbing against the inside of his leathers.

Unfortunately, it was going to have to wait. One thing about kink—there tended to be a long build of anticipation, but the payoff was always worth it.

Cupping her breast in his hand, Mitch looked into Domi's eyes as he closed the silver clamp on her tightly budded nipple.

"Take a deep breath," he instructed her. The look she gave him made him chuckle. By this time, she knew what to do.

Not breaking eye contact as the pain hit her, he watched her pupils dilate in response to the clamp's harsh pinch. Just as quickly, he closed the second clamp over her other nipple and let the chain hanging between them drop. Domi keened a high-pitched moan that left her panting as she adjusted to the pain.

Mitch watched every nuance of her expression, every shudder of her body, his own arousal climbing as he watched her take the pain for him and turn it into her own personal pleasure. If he dipped his fingers between her legs, he knew he'd find her soaking wet, but she'd like that, so instead, he teased her even more by dropping to his knees in front of her and attaching the cuffs of the bar to her ankles. Then he pushed them apart, and Domi sighed. She'd been pushing her legs together, trying to get a little stimulation.

Looking up from his position, he enjoyed the view of her slick pussy and the silver gleaming around her crushed dark red nipples. He reached up and gave the chain a little yank, making Domi squeal. Clover clamps were fun because they tightened every time they were pulled on. They also couldn't be left on for *too* long for the same reason, so he'd better get on with it.

"Was it your fault Ana got hurt?" Mitch asked, getting to his feet.

Domi hesitated, and he tugged on the chain again, hard enough to make her yelp.

"No!"

"Tell me."

"It wasn't my fault, Master Mitch." She said the words, but her tone was more questioning, as if she wanted confirmation from him.

"That's right, it wasn't your fault." He ran his fingers over the tip of her nipple extruding from the clamp. Domi shuddered, sucking in a little breath at the sensation. "Now say it like you mean it."

"It wasn't my fault." That was more like it.

"Good girl." He ran his finger over her other nipple and leaned down to brush his lips over hers. "I'll go get the strap."

DOMI

Some people might think a leather strap was a real punishment, but it was Domi's favorite implement. Supple with a nice thuddy quality and just enough sting, and he hadn't said where he was going to use it.

Probably not her back or ass unless he turned her around.

Her breasts? Maybe. Her already tormented nipples seemed to throb harder at the thought.

Thighs? Definitely a possibility.

Her pussy?

Oh, please.

She needed something there—something to help soothe the itch she couldn't scratch.

Turning back to her, leather strap in hand, Master Mitch gave her that utterly wicked smile of his that did all sorts of crazy things to her insides. Fear, anticipation, and an erotic heat swept through her body, leaving her tingling and eager. Her nipples throbbed in their confinement, the blood trying to force its way through to the clamped flesh and becoming trapped. Fuck, it was starting to really hurt in such a good way.

"Sweet Domi Darling," Master Mitch said. "Such a good girl."

She flushed with pleasure, then braced herself when he positioned himself in front of her before swinging the strap.

Thwap.

It slammed against the tops of her thighs, and she cried out, wrists jerking, the sounds joining with the others in Stronghold's Dungeon. An erotic symphony of accompaniment to her own squeals and screams, lending her voice to the chorus.

Thwap.

Another, across the same spot, and Domi screamed at the sudden rush of delicious pain burning through her, making her pulse race. She moved her hips, pushing them forward as if begging for more, begging him to strap her higher, across more sensitive flesh... and wasn't she?

A third snap over the same welted area made her scream again, more tension leaking out of her as tears rolled down her cheeks. Fuck, that hurt! She could hear her pulse pounding in her ears, her nipples throbbing in time with it. The tortured buds felt as if they were about to burst from the force of her blood trying to push into them.

Letting her head fall back, she gasped for breath, shuddering as heat and need swept over her.

The leather strap came up between her legs, landing squarely on her pussy, and Domi's entire body jerked in reaction. Her clit screamed with ecstatic agony, pussy lips swelling from the blow. Another blow slapped against her pussy with a wet sound, some of her arousal having transferred onto the strap during the first blow. It was exactly what she needed, the pain balancing out that of her nipples, overwhelming her senses and pushing out any lingering guilt and fear from yesterday.

Her legs were lifted, skirt rolling up to her waist, revealing her lack of underwear. Master Mitch ducked under the spreader bar, pushing her back against the hard surface of the wall, taking some of her weight while the rest of her hung from her wrist restraints. Lips came crashing down on hers, swallowing her screams as he lined up his cock with her slick pussy and thrust in hard.

Domi squirmed against him, his chest rubbing against her abused nipples, still imprisoned by the clamps, sending new sparks of pain twisting through her, even as her pussy spasmed with pleasure around his cock. He felt so good inside her, thrusting and pumping, filling her over and over again while she quivered around him.

She moved against him, arching to help his cock slide home as he fucked her up against the wall. The hard surface behind her didn't matter, neither did the twin sparks of fiery pain on her chest when the chain between the clamps bounced. When he thrust home, grinding his body against her abused pussy and clit, the pain was rapturous.

This was exactly what she had wanted. Needed.

When Mitch lifted his head, she screamed out his name in utter ecstasy, clenching and shuddering around his cock. Groaning, he pressed himself against her, fully inside her, and she felt him begin to throb. Writhing against him, the tips of her nipples abraded by his chest hair, her punished pussy crushed against his groin, Domi let the sensations carry her away.

Mitch whispered her name in her ear, emptying himself as they came together until they were both completely spent.

CHAPTER ELEVEN

With Domi insensible and cuddly on his lap, Mitch rubbed his cheek against her unruly curls. The aftercare corner in the Dungeon had a few others sitting in it, but they were mostly private with a couch to themselves. For the first time in days, since she'd ended their arrangement, he felt as if he could breathe properly again. It was a relief to have her with him, in his arms. He didn't want the moment to end.

The worry was still there, of course. Eventually, the moment would have to end. Then what?

Is that when things would start to fall apart?

Probably not yet. Maybe not at all.

Huh. He hadn't ever expected to feel optimism about a relationship, but then, he hadn't had Domi in his life before. She was the first person to make him want to try, and it would probably be a little weird if he didn't feel at least a little optimistic.

There seemed to be an awful lot of successful relationships around Stronghold. Maybe kink was the hidden factor. BDSM definitely required a level of communication and trust he hadn't seen in the vanilla world. His eyes skimmed over the Dungeon, falling on Walter and Marianne. As far as he knew, they were the oldest members of Stronghold.

He had no idea how old they were, but he'd guess in their seventies, maybe eighties. They never played at the club, but they came to be part of the community and occasionally to watch the scenes. They were happy. So was the couple they were watching scene with the spanking bench, Master Adam and Angel. Fairly new parents, they'd recently started coming back to the club on a semi-regular basis.

Just past them, using one of the St. Andrew's Crosses, were Master Michael and Ellie, a sadist and masochist like him and Domi. Like Domi, she'd had a reputation for never getting into a relationship—hell, she wouldn't even accept a club contract or a regular playmate... until Master Michael had come along.

Magic penis, a little voice whispered in his head. It sounded a lot like Sharon's voice.

Domi shifted in his arms, wincing when her arm brushed over her breasts. Her nipples were back to their normal shape after being brutally crushed by the clamps, though they were still much darker than usual. That little jolt of pain must have been enough to bring her back to herself because she sat up a little, and he could almost feel her becoming more focused.

Crap.

What did he say to her? Did he ask her out on a date now? Did he wait and call her later?

Why was this suddenly so complicated? Thankfully, she kept him from making a total ass of himself by speaking up first.

"Is that Rae with Master Eric?" she asked sleepily.

Turning his head in the direction she was looking, Mitch sighed. Yeah, that was Rae being strapped down over a spanking bench with Master Eric. There was nothing wrong with Master Eric, per se, but he wouldn't be Mitch's first choice. Even if Brian wasn't available for the pairing, he didn't think Eric was particularly compatible with Rae.

There definitely wasn't a spark between them. Even from a distance, he could see Eric was going through the scene methodically, paddling her ass with calculated rather than truly interested precision.

Again, nothing wrong if that's what both parties wanted, but Mitch knew Rae tended to need things far more hands-on and cuddlier. Even though things had never become sexual between them when they'd scened during classes, they had been physically affectionate. It was practically a requirement of scening with her.

"Why does she do that?" he asked before he thought about the question. Domi wasn't the only one flying high after the scene, and his verbal filter wasn't at its normal level.

Domi didn't ask what he meant.

"Hey, she wasn't even the one who wanted to join the club in the first place, she only came for me. I don't think she expected to like it. It's hard enough to feel like a feminist when you want to be tied up and spanked, admitting you want someone to take care of you for more than sex stuff..." Domi shrugged. "Plus, she still calls her actual dad 'Daddy,' so I think that weirds her out, too."

"Do you think it would weird her out less if she could call him something else?" They both knew he was talking about Brian.

"Maybe, but I don't know if she could let someone take care of her, and that seems to be a Daddy Dom thing. She's pretty independent."

She wasn't the only one, though Domi had no problem submitting at the club or in the bedroom.

"So, ah..." Mitch cleared his throat, feeling awkward but determined. "I'd like to take you out sometime soon. Whenever you're free."

DOMI

Wow, so they were really doing this. He'd said it, but there had still been a small part of her wallowing in disbelief, thinking maybe he would change his mind after the sex. He hadn't. A rush of happiness swept through her.

"Ana is going to be at her dad's the next few days. I'll have her Wednesday through Saturday, then she goes back to her dad's Sunday morning." When Mitch blinked, his eyes going a little blank as he tried to figure out the complicated schedule, Domi grinned. "Her stepmom was having really bad morning sickness earlier this week. Normally, we alternate weeks, but she had to come back to stay with me unexpectedly, so next week is going to be a little odd, then we'll be back to our regularly scheduled program."

Mitch chuckled, his expression clearing.

"You have a good relationship with her dad?"

"I do. It was an accidental pregnancy from a one-night stand, but he's made a great co-parent, and his wife is a wonderful stepmom to Ana." Domi smiled. Even though Julia didn't like Domi, she was polite about it, and Domi knew things could be so much worse. She felt lucky they all had the relationship they did. Mitch's body relaxed under hers.

"That's good. I know having to come to the hospital can bring out the worst in people, but I've seen some things…" His voice trailed off, and he shook his head before giving her a wink. "I could tell you stories that would curl your hair."

Domi laughed. He was such a goof, but at the same time, she was sure he was telling the truth.

"I'm not sure my hair can handle much more curl."

"There is that." He tugged on a loose piece, grinning down at her. He did love tugging her curls. Usually, Domi hated when people touched her hair, but with Mitch, she'd never minded—which probably should have clued her in to her feelings long before she'd figured them out.

"How about Tuesday? I have off that night."

"Perfect." A couple of days for her to adjust to the idea of going out on a date with him—and figure out what she was going to wear—and he took it as fact, she wouldn't be going out with him while she had Ana. Domi liked that he didn't try to push his way in immediately, even though he'd already met her daughter.

They sat, cuddling and watching the rest of Stronghold's goings-on. They'd done this before, but it had never felt like this… as though they were a couple, and it wasn't just aftercare.

When Rae and Master Eric were done, and it was time to go, Mitch walked them out to the car and gave Domi the sweetest kiss.

Once they were in the car, Rae gave her a look.

"You sure you know what you're doing?"

"Do you?" Domi retorted. "I thought you said Master Eric was nice but didn't really do anything for you."

Something she hadn't shared with Mitch, of course. She'd known he was fishing for information to bring back to Master Brian, and she hadn't objected because she *knew* Rae had a thing for him, even if she wouldn't admit it. Domi wasn't going to go around spilling secrets.

"He doesn't, but…"

"But?" Domi prompted when Rae hesitated.

Sighing, Rae brought the car to a stop at a red light, turning to look at Domi.

"You know that bitchy sub, Caroline? Well, she made sure to make a big deal out of the fact Brian was at Stronghold last night and scened with Alina. For some reason, even though I don't want him, it still pissed me off, so when Master Eric asked, I said yes." Rae's lips twitched. "It might have had a little something to do with Caroline trying to get his attention before he asked me."

Woah. Damn. Still, Domi couldn't help laughing.

"You scened with him, so she couldn't?"

"I am, one hundred percent, that petty." Rae grinned, turning her attention back to the road when the light turned green. "It wasn't a bad scene."

"It just wasn't as good as scening with Brian."

The grin faded from Rae's expression, and she sighed. She didn't need to say it wasn't; they both knew it was true.

"What if you didn't have to call him Daddy?"

One shoulder lifted. From the side, it was harder to read Rae's emotions, especially since she was clearly trying to keep her face blank.

"It's still what he is. What he wants to be. And he needs to have his needs met, too. Which means he needs to find a submissive who wants that, and that submissive is not me… no matter how good our chemistry is." Even keeping her face neutral, she couldn't disguise the sadness in her voice. Damn. The situation sucked.

Everyone knew Brian and Rae had a thing for each other, but Rae was right. If she couldn't give him what he needed, it was better to let it go and find someone who would—could.

Domi hated seeing her bestie down.

"I have a date with Mitch on Tuesday."

"What?!" Rae shrieked, slamming one of her hands on the wheel. She shot Domi a quick glance, shaking her head, and her braids danced around her shoulders. "Girl! And you didn't lead with that?"

"I feel weird about it." Unable to hide her grin, happiness bubbling up inside her, Domi half-shrugged. "We've been..." She tried to think of the right word.

"Fucking for so long, dating seems strange?"

"Yup. That." Both of them cracked up.

It did feel weird. Not like a step backward, exactly... but a step she hadn't ever intended to take—one from which there *was* no coming back. Still, they could take that part of things slowly. It wasn't as if they'd needed to be dating for her to develop feelings for him.

Heck, maybe the more she got to know him, the fewer feelings she'd have. Maybe part of her crush was because of the mystery. A week ago, she hadn't even known what his job was.

Depressingly, that seemed more likely than anything else.

Still, it was better to try than to sit around and wallow, right?

CHAPTER TWELVE

MITCH

The phone woke him on Sunday morning with his mother's ringtone—Kylo Renn's theme from Star Wars. His dad's was Darth Vader's. Usually, it amused him, but it was an unsettling way to wake up. He'd been having a very nice dream about Domi, but the ringtone killed his erection in record time.

Sitting up, he pulled his sheets up to his chest before answering. He always felt weird talking to his mom when he was naked, but somehow covering up with the sheets helped.

"Hello?"

"Hi, sweetie, did I wake you up? I'm sorry."

"No, it's okay. I was getting up soon, anyway. It's..." Mitch pulled the phone away from his ear to squint at the time. A few minutes before nine o'clock, which is when his alarm would have woken him up. Of course. He fell back against his pillow. Those few minutes probably wouldn't have made much difference. "Almost nine o'clock. What's up?"

"I was just calling to see how you're doing. I haven't heard from you in a couple weeks." There was a slight chiding tone to her voice, the kind that never failed to make him feel guilty.

"I sent you some texts," he said, even though he already knew what her answer was, and that she was right. He'd been dropping the ball between work and Domi, then Domi breaking up with him and him realizing he didn't want her to.

"I know, but I like to hear your voice. Been busy at work?"

"Yeah, work's been pretty crazy. I've been hanging out with my friends, too."

"Oh, that's good," she said and almost managed to sound as though she meant it. She would have much rather he'd stayed closer to home, but he got the job offer in D.C., which was only a few hours away. Close enough to visit for a weekend but far enough, she couldn't stop by whenever she felt like it. "I'm glad you're making friends. Have you made any *special* friends down there?"

Which was her way of asking if he was dating anyone. Despite the way her relationship with his dad had gone down in flames, she still had the normal mom desire for her only offspring to be married. Or maybe she was just hoping for grandkids.

"No, Mom." His standard response, complete with exasperation, was out before he thought about it. Though once he did have a moment to think about it, he didn't want to change his answer. Things with Domi were too new, and he wasn't sure where they were going to go yet. If he told his mom about her, when he'd never had any woman to tell her about, her expectations and hopes would go through the roof. It was better to keep her in the dark until he and Domi were more settled. See if they even had staying power.

Right, because seeing each other for literally months means there's no staying power.

It's not the same, he told the little voice in his head. They'd been seeing each other for sex. Now they were actually going to get to know each other.

"How have you been?" he asked, much preferring to talk about her. He let her ramble on, responding in the appropriate places when she paused, slowly relaxing when she didn't bring up anything with his dad. That was good. Unfortunately, he relaxed a little too soon. Right when she was winding up, she snuck it in there.

"You'll probably be hearing from your father soon. He's going to be in D.C. in a couple weeks."

Closing his eyes, Mitch pinched the bridge of his nose as if the moment she said the words, a headache formed.

"How do you know that, Mom?" It wasn't an accusation, more a weary inquiry. He didn't understand why his parents couldn't stay away from each other. Normally, he didn't ask, but right now... well, he couldn't help himself. Maybe because Domi was on his mind or relationships in general, but he wanted to know why his parents continually put themselves through the pain of being in each other's company.

"He told me so," she said matter-of-factly as if it wasn't a big deal. Mitch's back molars ground together.

"Why are you two even talking? I thought you said you were never speaking to him again."

"Yes, well." She paused. Sighed. "I'm sorry, honey, I know our unusual relationship is hard on you. We don't mean for it to be."

"I don't understand why you two are a 'we' at all." It was something that had bugged him all through high school, especially when his mom would come home and cry in her room. Mitch always knew it was because of his dad, even if he hadn't known exactly what the man had done in any particular instance.

It wasn't that he didn't like his dad, but he hated the way his parents were when they were together. It was better when they were apart, other than the constant anxiety of waiting for them to be drawn back together. Every time, his mom said the same thing, *Just because we can't live together doesn't mean we don't love each other.* She said it as if it explained everything.

That wasn't the kind of love Mitch had ever wanted. Which was why he'd eschewed relationships.

Until now.

This was going to be different. He'd seen it at the club. BDSM made for stronger relationships, which was the most logical explanation he could think of. Communication was better, the bonds between people were better, even the sex was better. Granted, that last was just his opinion.

The sex was better, the relationships were better... made sense to him.

"If you say so," he said, which was how he always responded.

"One day, you'll find out," she said as if that was a good thing. He never had the heart to tell her the last thing he wanted was to end up like her and his dad. "Alright, I'll let you go. Love you, Munchkin."

Another good reason to stay away from Pittsburgh—no one around here knew his mother's nickname for him. Mitch liked a good funny nickname, but there was a line.

"Love you too, Mom, bye."

For another long few minutes, he laid on his bed, his heart hurting for his mom... and his dad. Though his mom more. His dad tended to take everything stoically, whereas Mitch had seen his mom's pain far too often, even though she tried to hide it. Although she wasn't as good at it as his dad, Mitch knew his dad was hurting, too.

And his mom thought he'd want to get married after watching them? Have kids?

Not like them... but maybe like Marjorie and Walt. Andrew and Kate. The others at Stronghold.

Maybe like them.

Maybe that's what he could have with Domi.

Domi

There was nothing as nerve-wracking as a first date.

When the doorbell rang, Rae went running for it while Domi nervously swiped her hands on her yoga pants, bending down to check on the pizza in the oven. She could hear Avery and Rae greeting each other, then a moment later, they came into the kitchen, Avery carrying a bottle of wine.

"Hey, how are you?" Avery said. She looked just as nervous and Domi and Rae. Domi couldn't even remember the last time she and

Rae had tried to make a new friend. Which just made it even harder—they needed to prove they could. And not make her feel like a third wheel while they did their usual thing so she would want to hang out with them again. On the other hand, after this, going on a first date with Mitch would probably be a breeze.

A lot less pressure.

"Good! Still trying to figure out what to wear on Tuesday."

"Do you know where you're going?" Avery asked, handing the wine bottle over to Rae. "That should breathe before serving, but it'll go well with the pizza."

Oh, right. Shit. Avery was a chef... who they'd invited over for pizza. In their heads, it had seemed like a good idea to invite her over to a good old-fashioned girls' night/date planning dinner, but was DiGiorno going to be good enough for her?

"Uh, right." Rae glanced nervously at Domi, looking as though she was having similar thoughts. At least they were all dressed the same. Rae had on a pair of leggings and an oversized shirt, while Domi and Avery were both in yoga pants and t-shirts. Avery's had the Marquis restaurant logo on it, and her hair was up in its usual ponytail. Seeing their expressions, Avery looked uncertain.

"It's a good wine," she said as if she was trying to reassure them.

"I'm sure it is, I just... I just realized we're serving a chef frozen pizza." Domi gave her a lopsided grin, hoping she took it in good fun. Thankfully, Avery laughed, leaning her hip against the counter, and some of the tension leaked away from the room.

"Trust me, I'm no food snob," Avery said, grinning. "Half the stuff I make for myself at home is microwavable. Cooking for other people all the time doesn't really leave me in the mood to cook for myself."

"Well, next time you come over, we'll cook a real dinner for you," Rae said, pulling the wine key out of their junk draw with a flourish. She cut the foil and peeled it off with practiced movements before starting to screw the opener into the cork. It had been a while since they'd had wine that didn't come with a screw cap, but some skills were never forgotten.

Avery's expression brightened at the idea. "That would be

wonderful."

That seemed to break the ice, and by the time they sat down to the pizza and wine, it almost felt as though Avery had always been part of their little group. She clicked with them in a way neither Morgan nor Samantha had.

"So, did you ever talk to Olivia about becoming a member of Stronghold?" Domi asked. Olivia was the manager of Marquis—the upstairs kinky part—and also the instructor for the new submissives class. A badass both on the streets *and* in the sheets, she was the kind of Domme nobody wanted to tick off. She was also incredibly protective of 'her' subs, which included almost every submissive to walk through a Stronghold or Marquis' door, and not just her actual submissive and boyfriend, Luke.

Avery made a face, looking down at her pizza.

"No," she sighed, taking a big bite of pizza and chewing as though it was comforting. Heck, it might be. Pizza was one of Domi's comfort foods. She wasn't sure why not talking to Olivia would get this kind of reaction. "I uh... well, Nick and I have been flirting a lot more, then this weekend... he kissed me, and..." She was turning beet red as she spoke, but she didn't look entirely happy about the situation. "It was hot, and he's very take-charge, but... I don't think he's kinky."

"Is kinky a requirement?" Rae asked, glancing at Domi. Rae hadn't completely sworn off the idea of a vanilla guy, though she'd prefer to find a kinky one, especially once she'd figured out where to look. Which was how they'd ended up at Stronghold in the first place. Domi hadn't wanted a guy—at all—but now she couldn't imagine herself with someone who wasn't at least a little into the same things.

She didn't need wild, kinky sex every time, but she couldn't imagine giving it up entirely now.

"Maybe?" Avery shrugged. "It's been so long since I've even had sex, I don't know if I care."

Ouch. Domi knew how that felt.

"So, your dry spell may be affecting your judgment," she teased. "Maybe you should come to Stronghold with us and get laid before making a decision."

"I don't know when I'd have the time," Avery said ruefully. "Marquis has only been open a few months, and I'm *needed* Wednesday through Sunday. Even though I can get the occasional Sunday night off, Friday or Saturday would be impossible, and by the time the restaurant closes, it's way too late for me to go out."

"What if you asked for the time off, super far in advance?" Rae asked. "Maybe on a Thursday night or something. And we could go to Marquis instead of Stronghold and watch a show. That way, you won't have to travel, and it might give you a better idea about whether you want to hold out for someone kinky."

Hope lit Avery's eyes, but she still looked conflicted.

"I'm kinda smelly at the end of a shift..."

"We won't care," Domi reassured her. "We can just spritz you with body spray or something."

They all laughed.

"Okay," Avery said happily. "I'll see if I can get a night off sometime soon. It might not be for a few weeks."

"No problem. We'll make it work. The reservations usually fill up several weeks in advance, anyway." Rae grinned at her, then changed her focus to Domi, as they were all finishing up their dinners. "So... Domi. Where are you and Mitch going on Tuesday? Has he said?"

"No." Domi glanced down at her phone. "I texted him to ask. He said it's a surprise, but to dress casually and so I can move."

Rae and Avery blinked, nonplussed. Clearly, they had as little clue as Domi did what Mitch might be thinking.

"Casual and so you can move? What does that mean?" Avery asked. Since she only knew what Domi and Rae had told her about Mitch, she had the least to go on.

"Knowing Mitch, it'll be something memorable." Rae picked up her glass of wine, which was only half-finished, and got to her feet. Domi and Avery followed suit.

Trying on clothes right after eating pizza might not be the best idea... but hey, he was the one who told her casual. Domi was going to take him at his word.

"Rock climbing, maybe? Trampoline park?"

"Is that the kind of thing he's into?" Avery asked, bemused, as she followed Rae and Domi to Domi's room.

"No idea. I'm not sure when the last time he dated someone, if ever. He's not exactly Mr. Commitment." Domi smiled wryly, heading to her closet and flinging the door open. "Hmmm… maybe I shouldn't try too hard."

"So, what am I looking for then?" Rae asked, rolling her eyes. "Something with holes in it?"

"My clothes don't have holes in them."

"Maybe something tacky… some mismatched accessories…"

"You're an accessory," Domi muttered.

"Thank you," Rae said breezily. "I consider that a compliment."

"I didn't say you're a pretty one."

"Bitch, please."

Avery started cracking up, and Domi and Rae winced, exchanging a look. Oops. They'd almost forgotten she was there. Yeah, they needed to be better about that.

"You guys are awesome," Avery said, lifting her glass in tribute. Domi smiled back at her, relieved she didn't seem upset at being left out, but she and Rae were still going to work on including her more.

"What do you think?" Domi asked, pulling out one of her favorite shirts. Cute, dark blue with big pink and white flowers on it, and incredibly comfortable, not something she'd normally wear for a date, but it would still look good. Also, it was worlds away from what she'd usually wear to Stronghold.

"Oh, that's cute," Avery said, stepping into the closet with them and reaching out to touch the material. "Oooh, soft."

"So, he'll want to get his hands on you," Rae said, grinning and nodding. Domi rolled her eyes.

"Like his hands haven't already been all over me." They were doing the relationship thing a little backward, but that was okay. At least she didn't have to worry about whether the sex would be good.

Just whether or not they could do anything other than the sex.

Yup. No big deal.

CHAPTER THIRTEEN

DOMI

"Fuck, fuck, fuck, fuck," Domi panted, ducking down behind a large wall, pressing her back against it. A moment later, Mitch slammed into position beside her, the lights on his chest blinking ominously.

Glancing at them, she snickered.

"Quiet," he said defensively. "You're a much smaller target than me."

"Should have thought about that before we got in here," she told him with a smirk. She wasn't the one who had chosen laser tag for their first date. "Besides, I warned you I was awesome at this."

He flashed a quick, hot grin and winked.

"Which is exactly why I chose it. I wanted to see you in action."

As first dates went, it wasn't exactly ripe for conversation, but Domi was still learning a lot about Mitch. He was competitive but a good sport. He wanted to win but accepted defeat gracefully. He was also a show-off and a goof, even in the middle of trying to win.

"I have to admit, I'm not doing as well as I usually do." Domi groaned as she pushed herself into a crouching position, a spot in the small of her back aching slightly. "I'm getting too old for this shit."

"Okay, Murtaugh," Mitch said, laughing. He bumped her shoulder, leaning down to sneak in a quick kiss that sparked some heat, even though it couldn't go anywhere. He was turning out to be a tease. "You're only what, three years younger than me? I'm thirty."

"I'm a mom," Domi countered. "That means the last five years have operated more like dog years. Now, move it, old man." She leapt into action rather than letting him kiss her again, sprinting across to the next barricade, shooting in the direction of the other team.

The birthday party of ten-year-olds were far more vicious opponents than any adults could be. They were smaller, faster, and didn't have any hesitation in throwing themselves in any and all directions, whereas Domi kept worrying about throwing out her back. Yeah, yeah, she knew she wasn't *that* old, but it was times like this when she felt like it. At least half of the birthday party was on her and Mitch's team, even if that half didn't seem super happy about it. Kind of demoralizing to realize they were the weakest link.

It was still fun as hell... especially since she was kicking Mitch's ass. Maybe he'd spank hers later to make up for it.

MITCH

Last place. Not second to last, that spot belonged to Domi. Nope, full-on last place. Most number of times killed and injured, least number of hits on anyone else. Embarrassing. Mitch put his hand over his heart as he looked up at the board, shaking his head mournfully.

"This is the last time I play laser tag with a bunch of people half my size."

"Hey, I'm not that short!" Domi elbowed him in the side, making him grunt.

Chuckling, he wrapped his arm around her. As petite as she was, she tucked in nicely next to him. She was more like two-thirds than half his size.

"What was that?" he asked, leaning down. "I couldn't hear you all the way down there."

"I will end you," she threatened, but she was laughing and jabbing her fingers into his side, trying to tickle him... or something. Mitch tensed his stomach muscles, blocking her attempt. "I don't have to stand here and take this."

"That's right, you could bend over the table and take it." He curved his fingers around her ribcage just under her breast, feeling the softness of her breasts before she wiggled away.

"Mitch!" she hissed, half-laughing, half-aghast. "The kids!"

"They aren't watching... or listening," he said, glancing around. The kids were involved in their own little party world. The only ones looking at him and Domi were the ones who had been on their team and weren't too happy about losing. Pretty clear who they blamed. "Come on, let's go get dinner. I'm starving."

Then she wouldn't be able to scold him about anything else filthy that fell out of his mouth. What could he say? He had a one-track mind when she was around, especially with the shirt she was wearing. His fingers stroked down the sleeve. It was so soft.

"So, is laser tag a normal date for you?" Domi asked as they walked out of the building. Mitch steered her down the sidewalk. The restaurant he'd chosen was on the other side of the shopping complex.

"Wouldn't know." Mitch shrugged. "I haven't been on a date since high school. I did laser tag and paintball fairly regularly then, but it was always with a group of friends, so I don't know that you could call it a date, even if my girlfriend was there."

When Domi came to a halt, Mitch had to as well or risk knocking her over. She stared up at him in surprise. "You haven't been on a date since high school?"

"Nope." A bit of anxiety welled up at the reminder. Hmmm, he hadn't felt anxious while they were running around the laser tag arena. Shaking her head, Domi started walking again, and Mitch's stomach twisted in anxious worry. What must she think of him right now? Shit. He needed to give her some kind of explanation. "My parents had a really nasty divorce my freshman year of high school."

She turned her head to look at him, her expression a little softer.

"That convinced you that you should never have a relationship?" There was a dubious quality to the question as though she didn't understand why that would be enough.

"Sort of. It wasn't the divorce so much. Hell, by the time they separated, I was relieved. I think they stayed together for too long, thinking they were doing it for my sake, but it was awful living with them while they were fighting all the time. Then they divorced, and I thought it would be better... but it wasn't." He shook his head, trying to shake off some of the dark emotions creeping in at the memories. "They couldn't stay away from each other, even after the divorce was final, and *not* because of me."

"What do you mean?" she asked when he paused, bewildered. Yeah, it didn't make sense to him either.

"Mom always says just because they can't be together doesn't mean they don't love each other. I came home freshman year of college to find them going at it on the kitchen counter." Mitch winced exaggeratedly, and Domi laughed. "They were always doing that. I could always tell when they were seeing each other on the sly and when they fell apart again."

Domi's arm wrapped around his middle, squeezing him in a half hug. She pressed the side of her head against his chest, warming him against some of the cold beginning to creep in.

"I'm sorry," she said softly. "I can't imagine how hard that must have been."

"It sucked. Gave me a pretty skewed view of love. Went to college, and... well, I didn't want to try. Didn't meet anyone who made me want to try." Winking down at her, he tightened his arm to give her a little squeeze back. "Now, I look at everyone at Stronghold now and start thinking... maybe BDSM helps make a difference."

"There do seem to be an awful lot of happy couples, doesn't there?" Domi mused. She grinned when Mitch turned to the left, putting Pasta Plus directly in front of them. Despite its cheesy name, it was damn good Italian and one of his favorite restaurants. "Please tell me we're going to Pasta Plus."

"Well, now that you've expressed your wish, how can I possibly say no?" Mitch teased. "But yes. It's my favorite restaurant."

"One of mine, too. Ana chose to come here for her birthday the past two years. We both love their rose sauce."

"Then that's another thing we have in common." Mitch grinned, his heart lifting. See, nothing to worry about. This was working out really well already. Dating wasn't so hard.

Domi

As first dates went, Domi couldn't remember when she'd had a better one. Granted, she hadn't had any in recent memory, but she hadn't been as closed off as Mitch before she had Ana. She'd had *some* first dates.

There weren't any awkward silences through dinner—only delicious ones after their food came. She stole some of the ravioli in rose sauce from his plate, and he returned the favor, going after her baked ziti in rose sauce. They were both starving from all the running around. It was light, easy conversation, a little banter about who had chosen the better meal, some teasing about the laser tag. Domi didn't bring up his parents, though she did tell him a little about hers and more about how she co-parented with Marcus and Julia. In return, Mitch told her some of his funnier ER stories.

Kind of funny how they'd ended up together. Domi wouldn't call herself commitment-phobic, just apprehensive about dating, and Mitch clearly felt the same way. From what he said about his parents, she got that. It sounded as if he'd been given a pretty skewed view of what marriage looked like, whereas she'd always had her parents' loving example.

The fact he'd decided to take a chance on her...

No pressure, right?

When they pulled up to her house, Domi had no doubt Rae was peeking out the front window, waiting inside for an update. She pressed her lips together, amused. Rae was going to have to wait a bit longer.

Mitch walked her to the door, his hand wrapped around hers. His blue eyes twinkled before he leaned down to kiss her. Lips pressed against each other, parted, opened. She leaned into the kiss, her body rousing in anticipation. Playing laser tag hadn't been particularly erotic, neither had dinner, but knowing how much fun they could have together? Yeah.

Her lips curved as he began to straighten. Hands pressed against his chest, she curved her fingers slightly, hooking them into his shirt.

"Do you want to come in?" she asked sultrily, teasingly, knowing he would say yes.

"Not tonight." He pressed his lips against hers, a quick kiss as she stared up at him with shock.

"Not tonight?"

"Now, Domi, you can't expect me to put out on the first date. I'm not that easy." Mitch stepped back, pulling away from her and smoothing his hands over his shirt where she'd wrinkled it.

Domi scowled at him. Seriously?

"We've been fucking for months!"

"That was when we weren't dating," he said breezily over his shoulder, making his way back to the car in the driveway.

Fuming, Domi still found herself checking out his ass as he went. What? He had a really nice butt, and it looked good in jeans.

"You suck," she called after him.

"Sadist, remember?" Opening his car door, he winked at her, leaning against the opening. "Speaking of, don't you dare get yourself off. I'll know."

"And what, you'll punish me?" Yeah, she knew she was bratting, but hey, she was disappointed. She'd had a really great first date, a really great end of the first date kiss, and had been looking forward to some really great first date orgasms.

Hmmm.

Wait... does this mean I'm easy?

"I'll tie you to a spanking bench with your legs spread far apart and use a vibrator on you until you're begging me to cum... and I still won't let you." A wicked grin accompanied his threat, and Domi's horror rose even as the words sent a shot of lust straight to her pussy. Her body was so messed up sometimes. The picture he painted was hot as fuck but also sounded awful. She couldn't decide whether or not she actually wanted him to do it.

Would it be worth it?

Probably not.

Sadist.

One who had already proved very adept at knowing exactly how to punish her—and not in a *fun* painful way.

Giving her a jaunty wave, Mitch closed the car door and got his seat belt buckled. Domi crossed her arms over her chest and scowled at him, still disbelieving he was going to leave her standing there, sexually frustrated. Sure enough, he gave her another wave and drove away.

The rat bastard.

Stomping into the house, Domi flounced to the couch where Rae was sitting. The expression of surprise on her bestie's face didn't help anything.

"Was it bad?"

"No." Domi bit off the word. "It was really good! But apparently, Mr. Manwhore doesn't fuck on the first date."

There was a long moment of silence, then Rae burst out laughing.

No love. No love from anyone.

CHAPTER FOURTEEN

MITCH

It turned out, liking someone and enjoying their company actually made dating pretty easy. The only downside was she wasn't ready to introduce him to Ana as Domi's boyfriend yet, which he totally understood and respected, but they weren't able to get together when she had Ana. Since Mitch's work schedule wasn't exactly normal, it worked out.

They texted every day, and when he got to sleep at a normal time, he called her before going to bed. They made plans for a second date on Sunday after Ana went back to her dad's.

It felt kinda like when they were fuck buddies at Stronghold, except they were making plans to actually see each other instead of having sex. A little different, but not in a bad way.

Truthfully, Mitch was feeling a little awkward about how to have sex with her again. Did they do it at his house? Hers? At Stronghold or Marquis? Probably Marquis, which seemed more special if it was going to be the last option. They were dating now, and he was making her wait for the third date... he should make it special, right? That was the kind of thing people who were dating did.

Being nervous about having sex with a woman he'd already fucked many times in every position he could think of was a little weird, but there it was. That's exactly what they'd been doing—casually fucking, with no intentional meaning, though obviously, feelings had slowly crept in, anyway. He'd been fucking in ignorance, unaware of the change, but now that it had been acknowledged...

Well, there might be some performance anxiety.

Not that he'd admit that to anyone. Just thinking about trying to explain it made him cringe.

"Mitch? Mitch?" Jane's voice finally punctured his reverie, and he jerked upright to a standing position, nearly fumbling the clipboard he was holding.

"Yes?" He pressed the clipboard down on the counter he'd been leaning on, pretending as if he hadn't been lost in his own little world. "Were you saying something?"

Jane smiled up at him, a little shyly, a coy look in her eye, and a little alarm went off in the back of Mitch's brain. He'd honed the instinct to know when a woman was interested and when she wasn't. Jane had never set off any signals before that he'd noticed, but now she was. He shifted back. Jane leaned forward. Yup. Definitely interested. His reflexes were slow, his brain too caught up in everything else to get him out of there before she spoke again.

"Shift is almost over. I was wondering if maybe you'd like to go grab a drink?" She tilted her head, clearly expecting a yes.

"Oh, ah..." Shit. Her invitation could be interpreted as a normal co-worker invite, but Mitch could tell it wasn't. He also knew from experience, turning down a date when the woman hadn't phrased it as exactly that could be harrowing. He also didn't want to leave an opening for later. Then a thought occurred to him—a reason he'd never been able to use before because he'd never *had* it to use before. "Sorry, Jane, but I gotta get home and call my girlfriend. We didn't really get the chance to talk last night."

Wow. He'd expected that to feel weird, but it actually felt pretty nice. It was the first time he'd called Domi his girlfriend, and a weird sense of possessive pride swept through him. Domi was his girlfriend.

Jane blinked.

"You have a girlfriend? You've never talked about a girlfriend before." Her tone was almost accusatory.

"It's kinda new. Well, the girlfriend part." A stupid, wide grin had taken up space on his face, and he didn't seem to be able to make it go away, not even in an attempt to spare Jane's feelings. "We've been seeing each other for months but never really made it official. Until now. Now, we're official."

"I see." Jane looked disappointed but not crushed, which was perfect. "Guess you should get on home and call her then."

"Yup. Have a nice time out." Picking up the clipboard, Mitch headed to drop it off at the nurses' station, then get out of there. He had a girlfriend to talk to.

DOMI

"Mommy, who are you texting?"

"Ah, no one. I mean, no one you know," Domi said, putting her phone down and directing the smile that wouldn't quit at her daughter. Ana squinted at her suspiciously, and on the other side of the couch, Rae raised her eyebrows, clearly guessing who Domi was texting. But really, what was she supposed to tell her daughter?

The first date I've had in years.

Your new daddy.

The guy I've been banging and now have been on one date with.

Yeah, none of it really parsed down well for a five-year-old's understanding. Domi wasn't even sure she *should* tell Ana she was dating, especially since Ana had already met Mitch and liked him. What if she wanted to see him, too? What if she got attached, and things didn't work out? What if she decided she *didn't* like him?

It was too new, and Domi wasn't ready yet. Though the conundrum also reminded her why she'd avoided dating in the first place. Ana came first. Always. That was why having a fuck buddy had been so perfect, right up until her emotions decided to ruin everything.

Stupid emotions.

On the other hand, things were going really well with Mitch. He'd kept in touch, even though they hadn't been able to see each other. Domi worried a little about how unconcerned he was about that, even though she was grateful. His job kept him really busy, which didn't hurt.

Eventually, she'd tell Ana she was dating. Once things were a little more settled. When she was ready to let Ana hang out with Mitch. She knew Ana would want to. She'd already asked if they were going to see "Murse Mitch" again when she went in for her checkup and had been very disappointed to be told they'd be going to her regular pediatrician instead.

"But who is it?"

"Don't worry about it, sweetie, it's no one," Domi said, causing Rae to cough. Ignoring her, Domi leaned in toward her daughter, nodding at the television where *Frozen* was playing for the eleventy millionth time. "Are you bored with the movie? We could do something else."

"No!" Ana looked aghast, but the little trick worked. She immediately turned back to the television, concentrating intently to prove she wanted to keep watching. On the other side of her, Rae shook her head.

Domi stuck out her tongue at her bestie. It wasn't the right time to tell Ana. It was way too soon. She and Mitch had only been on one date.

MITCH

Second date success.

Dinner and a movie, at the same time, thanks to the new theater's recent upgrade. Sure, the food was expensive as hell, but it was fun. Much better than eating dinner and then going to the theater, only to buy a massive bucket of popcorn. He needed to eat in a movie theater; he didn't know why… it was like a compulsion. Thankfully, Domi felt the same way. They chatted through their appetizers, and the main meal came right before the movie started.

About halfway through, Mitch discovered the theater had also upgraded the seats. Pulling up the chair arm between him and Domi, Mitch grinned as he pulled her in. She squeaked and elbowed him in the side. Even though they were in the back row and the theater was pretty empty since it wasn't a new release, they weren't alone.

"You'd better not be thinking what I think you're thinking," she muttered under her breath, eyes never moving from the screen.

Mitch made a noise of insulted affront, snuggling her in closer.

"Please, you're the one who tried to have your way with me on the first date," he whispered back, making her giggle. "This is only our second date, so I'm pretty sure I only get to go to second base. Maybe third if I'm *very* lucky."

His cock was not super happy about his plan for restraint, but a little abstinence wouldn't kill him. Besides, he enjoyed torturing Domi. This was a bit unconventional, as erotic torture went, but it worked. There was a part of him that got off, knowing they were both sexually frustrated.

Palming her breast over her shirt, hearing her soft intake of breath, there was something very appealing about taking their physical relationship slow, even though they'd already had sex. This was like a fresh start.

Knowing they weren't going to do more than fool around was a sweet torment of its own.

"Mitch..." She hissed out his name as he squeezed her breast, plumping the soft flesh through her shirt. He could feel her nipple hardening into an aroused bud, and she did nothing to actually stop him. Anyone looking back at them wouldn't see anything, but a couple cuddled up against each other. Well, probably. His hand *was* above her shirt—something easily fixed.

He slipped his hand down and under her shirt before sliding it back up. Domi gasped, squirming in her seat.

Leaning down, Mitch whispered in her ear, "You know your safeword if you want me to stop."

His fingers pinched her nipple through her bra, and she whimpered, the sound easily covered by the car chase on the screen. Mitch's cock jerked as he nibbled on her earlobe before pulling her closer to him. One hand on her breast, the other touched her leg, right at the hem of the skirt she was wearing. It was much longer than the skirts she wore to the clubs and more flowy, allowing him to easily slide his hand between her thighs.

"Keep watching the screen," he whispered, nipping her earlobe again. "Don't look away."

Like the cinema gods had been gifted with foresight, the car chase ended, and the hero and heroine ran off, exuberantly. Mitch's hand continued sliding up Domi's skirt, his other hand caressing her breast as the pair on-screen ended up in a hotel room. They looked at each other, attraction and heat sizzling across the silver screen, then came together in a hot, passionate kiss. Mitch's fingers reached Domi's wet heat and slipped between her folds.

DOMI

Oh, fuck...

While no longer a stranger to the exhibitionism of the kink clubs, what Mitch was doing to her in the middle of the movie theater was wildly outside her realm of experience. When she'd been in high school, she and her friends had giggled over the idea of doing something like this but had never actually *done* it.

Mitch had one hand up her shirt, fondling her breast, the other up her skirt, stroking her pussy. Domi thought she might spontaneously combust. Her body was thrumming with need, nerves tingling from the sensations and the heady excitement of knowing someone could catch them.

Her hand drifted over, settling on his lap and his incredibly hard cock, and he moaned softly in her ear. On-screen, the characters were already ripping each other's clothes off, the sexy music, sights, and sounds adding to what Mitch was doing to her. It was sexy as fuck, in a heart-pounding, adrenaline-producing, anxiety-ridden kind of way.

If someone looked back at her and Mitch right now, would they realize what was happening in the back row? Would they know? Would they care?

Would they watch?

Domi mewled, resting her head against his shoulder and spreading her legs wider as Mitch slipped his fingers inside her. Her own fingers tightened around his cock, rubbing the stiff shaft through his jeans. Panting for breath, her inner muscles tensed as the heel of his palm pressed against her clit, trapping the sensitive bud between his hand and her body as fingers plucked her nipples.

On-screen, the couple tumbled into bed, and Domi shuddered. Dammit, she wanted to be in bed with Mitch. Up against a wall. Anywhere she could get his cock in her.

Yet the forbidden taboo of touching each other in a movie theater, knowing they *couldn't* go farther, contributed to her excitement in a way she hadn't expected. It was wickedly hot. Mitch's fingers pressed deeper, the base of his hand rubbing her clit in slow circles, driving her wild as pleasure shot through her.

A bite of pain nipped at its heels when he twisted her nipple, harshly enough to delight her masochist side.

"Be quiet, Domi," he whispered, hands moving, fingers probing, pinching. "Absolutely silent."

She bit her lip and arched her back, closing her eyes as ecstasy rose higher. The fingers inside her stroked and pressed, his hand rocking against her clit, and Domi shuddered with the hot rapture of forbidden bliss that blasted through her body. Fingers gripped Mitch's cock hard through his pants, her other hand digging into the seat beneath her as she barely managed to keep from crying out.

Mitch kept caressing, stroking until he'd wrung every last spasm of her orgasm from her all-too-willing body, leaving her limp from the pleasure. She opened her eyes, turning to look at him. Their eyes connected for a brief moment, then his mouth was on hers, hungrily kissing her.

The hand between her legs slipped away, and a moment later, he broke off the kiss and pushed her head down.

Somehow, he'd managed to get his pants open enough to free his cock. It stood up from the center of his lap, eagerly awaiting her lips, and Domi did not disappoint. Her body still humming from her climax, she felt dizzy as she took him between her lips.

Humming with pleasure around the thick shaft, she swallowed him deep, happy to have him inside her, even if it wasn't exactly what she wanted. Domi *liked* giving head. She especially liked it when the man took control, the way Mitch did now, his hand on the nape of her neck, holding her down as his hips thrust up, pushing him deeper.

Her tongue flicked along the shaft, her throat working as he slid in. Mitch groaned, but it blended into the moans still coming from the screen. Domi's hand gripped his thigh, squeezing, and she sucked hard.

A few more bobs of her head, slicking the length of his cock as she moved up and down, pausing only to tease the bulbous head before sliding her lips back over him, and she felt his fingers tense. His hand pressed down harder, pinning her in place, his cock deep in her throat.

Hot liquid pulsed, and she swallowed, still sucking in long, hard pulls until he was completely drained, and she was dizzy from the lack of air.

When he pulled her upright, cuddling her in his arms, she was giggling from the wild glee of having fooled around in a movie theater. Reaching up, she tried to pat and twist her curls back into place but was pretty sure it was a fairly useless attempt.

"Good girl," Mitch murmured in her ear, kissing her temple.

Worth it.

Their clothing set to rights, her hair still mussed, and her lips swollen, but otherwise normal, they watched the rest of the movie, cuddled up in their double seat.

It was definitely the best second date she'd ever had.

CHAPTER FIFTEEN

MITCH

"You are so lucky you didn't get caught," Brian said, shaking his head, with what Mitch assumed was reluctant admiration.

"Would have been worth it even if we had." Mitch grinned. The element of danger, the excitement of knowing someone could have caught them... it's not like there had been kids in the theater. Besides, the important point was they _hadn't_ been. No harm, no foul.

Suppressing a smile, Kincaid shook his head. He was the only one Mitch had been a little nervous about telling. While Kincaid was incredibly tolerant of a lot of shenanigans, he _was_ a police detective.

"Tell me you never did anything of the sort before," Zach said, arching an eyebrow at Brian. "Also, hurry up and finish shuffling."

Chuckling, Brian gave the cards one last shuffle before dealing them out. As game nights went, gin rummy wasn't exactly intensive in Mitch's opinion, but he'd grown up in an extremely nerdy household. Still, he liked that it didn't require his full concentration and was easy to set up, take down, and he didn't have to remember anything for the next time they got together. Much easier than the games he'd grown up playing.

"I might have gotten a little handsy in a movie theater, but that was in high school." Brian gave Mitch his stern look, one that would have sent the baby girls of Stronghold and Marquis swooning. "Maybe once in college. Not as an adult."

"Well, I didn't date much in high school and not at all in college, so there ya go. I'm making up for lost time." Mitch grinned, picking his cards up from the table to sort through them.

"It might be kind of fun to try as an adult," Zach mused, earning himself an intense look from Kincaid, he didn't seem to notice. Brian and Mitch both focused on their cards, pretending they hadn't noticed, either. Whatever was brewing between the two men seemed to be making its way to the surface more often lately.

"Anytime you want to go see a movie, just let me know," Kincaid said silkily, using the same tone he did for submissives. Zach went beet red, but he didn't protest Kincaid's flirtatious statement. The tension in the room seemed to ratchet up another notch, and not only the sexual tension between Kincaid and Zach. They seemed to be waiting for Brian and Mitch's reactions.

"Are you two official now?" Brian asked.

Zach and Kincaid exchanged another look, then Zach nodded. He was still beet red but apparently, determined to see the confession through. "We're... seeing each other. Officially."

"Cheers!" Mitch said, lifting up his beer. "About fucking time. What are you doing about the whole neither of you being submissive and Kincaid not being a masochist?" Zach had finally admitted he had feelings for Kincaid, which seemed like the biggest roadblock ahead of them. Zach was a sadist. Kincaid dominated. While Kincaid could get everything he needed by dominating Zach, and Zach had always been more switchy than dominant, he was still a sadist.

"Keep playing at Stronghold and Marquis," Kincaid said, smiling at Zach, the look in his eyes almost tender. Damn, that was cute. "There are enough unattached masochists willing to scene without a relationship. Sometimes, we'll even pair up."

Oh, now that was interesting. Mitch wondered exactly how that was going to work when Zach definitely had a crush on Amy. Not his business, though. He just hoped it didn't blow up in their faces.

"Well, ten out of ten would recommend a trip to the movie theater," Mitch said, giving them a thumbs up. Zach blushed harder, and Kincaid grinned.

"If y'all want to be in public that badly, you could sign up to be one of the stage shows at Marquis." Brian grinned at their reactions. None of them were against some exhibitionism at the club, but being the center of attention on a stage was a step none of them had taken yet.

"I'm taking Domi to Marquis on Thursday," Mitch said, his inflection heavy with meaning, before picking up his beer to take a sip.

"Ah, taking her back to where it all started for your third date," Brian said, his voice going a little higher and taking on a dreamy tone. "Then you'll take her into one of the back rooms and do filthy, depraved things to her."

They all cracked up, and Mitch pointed his finger at Brian, winking.

"Exactly."

Granted, he planned on making it a little more romantic than that. Even though he'd never dated much, he'd watched enough movies and his friends' relationships to know some of the basics. He'd already talked to Freddy to get it all set up.

Domi

She couldn't count the number of times she and Mitch had been at Marquis together, but this time felt decidedly different. Maybe because instead of wearing his leathers and nothing else, Mitch had on an actual shirt with buttons, and he'd insisted she wear a dress instead of her regular fetwear.

Granted, it was a helluva sexy dress, but it was still something she could have worn to a regular club. It did make her feel more date-like, though.

A little smile played on her lips as Mitch escorted her through the restaurant and to the stairs at the back. Third date. The sex date. At least, it better be the sex date. She was pretty much assuming it was, and she was so, so ready.

The hostess, a submissive named Tracy, escorted them to their booth, which was the same one where they'd agreed to become bondage buddies. Domi ground to a halt, her eyes widening in surprise. Though all the booths were gorgeous on their own, the tables were usually left mostly bare to make it easy for the servers to clear them before the show started. They didn't normally have flowers as a centerpiece, much less a large array of red roses in a crystal vase.

Beaming at them, Tracy winked at Domi before walking away, leaving her feeling somewhat bemused.

"For me?" Domi asked, giving Mitch's hand a squeeze. "But how are you going to throw me on the table to have your wicked way with me?"

His dark chuckle stirred her insides.

"Who says I'm going to have you on the table? Patience, Domi Darling." He patted her ass, far too gently, directing her into the booth.

Grr. Patience was the *last* thing she was feeling. More like wet, hot, and ready for action. Other than at the movie theater, she hadn't had an orgasm since they started dating—cruel and unusual punishment. Still, she was a good girl and scooted into her seat without protesting because she knew damn well being a bad girl was only going to delay her reward.

Dinner was delicious and completely unerotic, with Mitch acting like a proper gentleman, much to her annoyance. She was pretty sure he was just doing it to get under her skin, so she did her best to hide it... and also tease him back.

Putting her hand on his leg while they were ordering dinner, fingers massaging his thigh and moving closer to his groin until he covered her hand with his own and asked how Ana's arm was doing.

Made sure to lean into him, giving him a good view down the front of her dress.

Licking the bearnaise sauce from her steak off her fork enticingly, drawing his attention to her mouth. His wicked grin demonstrated his appreciation for her efforts, but that was all. Dammit.

The server came by to clear the table, leaving them with the roses on the table. Domi eyed them a little anxiously.

"Aren't those going to get in the way?"

"Nope. I told you, you need to be patient. We're not having sex on the table."

Domi narrowed her eyes. "But this is the sex date."

"Is it?" he asked innocently, then laughed when she glared at him. "We're going to one of the private rooms, Domi. I booked us a stay for the night."

She blinked, her lips dropping open in surprise. The rooms were incredibly expensive, and a stay in them was *not* part of the general membership.

"You did?" Her voice squeaked, then she glanced down at her dress in dismay. "But... You didn't tell me! I didn't bring clothes for tomorrow! What about—"

Mitch put his finger to her lips, hushing her. She pressed them together, stifling the urge to bite him.

"Rae packed a bag for you, and I dropped it off earlier today, along with mine. They're waiting for us in our room. You're all set. Just sit back and enjoy the show."

As if he'd timed it, the lights dimmed with his last sentence. Squirming in her seat, Domi thought *fuck it*, and bit his finger. Hard.

Chuckling and seemingly impervious to her teeth, Mitch tugged his finger away from her and pulled her against him.

"Naughty girl," he whispered in her ear, his fingers stroking oh so gently down her arm, sending goosebumps crawling along her skin. "I *was* going to play with you, but now we're just going to watch the show."

Dammit.

Mitch

Naughty Domi. Mitch could hardly wait to get her back to their playroom. The anticipation was killing him, but it was also hot as hell. Maybe he was a bit of a masochist... or so sadistic, he even enjoyed torturing himself? Either seemed possible.

In the dim light, two men and a woman walked out. Of course, Mitch recognized them from Stronghold—there were a few polygamous relationships at the club, but these three were there the most often. Jessica went to the middle of the stage, waiting for her two husbands, Masters Justin and Chris. They were all friends with Master Andrew and the club owners.

Beside Mitch, Domi stirred with interest, leaning forward.

"What?" he murmured questioningly. The three got set up, a long chain descending from the ceiling right above Jessica's head.

"I didn't realize they'd *both* be here with her," Domi whispered back, sounding fascinated. Sudden understanding swept through Mitch, along with a wave of jealousy. Did Domi like the idea of being shared? Was that something she wanted to try?

It wasn't an uncommon fantasy, neither was sharing in other ways. Hell, last year Mitch had enjoyed a seriously hot scene, erotically torturing a submissive while her husband watched, for his pleasure. He hadn't thought about sharing Domi. Now that he was, he wasn't sure he wanted to.

Still, if it was something she wanted to try, shouldn't he provide that for her as her Dom?

Or should he protest it vehemently as her boyfriend?

A few months ago, he would have happily arranged a scene for her and found someone he trusted. Not Brian, of course, since Brian had a thing for her best friend. Kincaid probably. Or Zach. Though now that they were officially together, that was probably out of the question unless he wanted to invite both of them in... His brain balked at the idea of *two* more penises being involved. One more was bad enough.

Onstage, either Justin or Chris—both of similar build and coloring, so it was hard to tell them apart when their backs were turned—took Jessica's robe, leaving her completely naked, while the other stepped forward a moment later to lift her hands above her head and attach the cuffs around her wrists to the hook at the end of the chain above her.

With her hair in a high bun, abundant curves on display, chin lifted in anticipation, she looked both vulnerable and excited as the lights brightened to their full display, and a throbbing bass filled the room. The music was low but audible, there to enhance the scene rather than distract from it.

Justin and Chris prowled around her, touching her with their hands, leaning down to whisper things in her ears. A tweaked nipple and a little slap on her ass, both eliciting little gasps that could be heard above the music.

Domi took a deep, shuddering breath.

"Does the idea of two men turn you on?" Mitch whispered in her ear, his fingers stroking her midriff over the silky material of her dress.

She turned her head slightly toward him, giving him an arch look.

"*Two* of you? I can barely handle one. I don't know how she does it." Domi shook her head, making her curls bounce.

Feeling slightly reassured, Mitch couldn't stop his mind from working in the background while Justin and Chris stepped back from Jessica and went to retrieve identical floggers. One behind her, one in front, at a nod from Justin, they raised their arms and let the leather strands fall, striking her breasts and her ass simultaneously. Domi sucked in a quick breath.

Watching the flogging, thinking about how he was going to alter his plans for Domi after this, Mitch reached to tease her breasts through her dress. She wasn't wearing a bra, allowing him to use the silky material to rub against her hardening nipples, teasing her without giving her any of the pain or satisfaction she'd be craving.

His cock throbbed in time with the music, pulse racing with the floggers while the erotic tableau in front of them heated up. Jessica was moaning, crying out, thrusting her ass back and her breasts forward for punishment. Domi's body moved in sympathy with the tormented submissive. She'd be craving the punishment, and Mitch could tell his gentle caresses were frustrating her more than anything else.

Smiling sadistically, he began to give a little of what she needed... but only a little. Harder pinches to her nipples interspersed between the other caresses. Tiny twists, then right back to the gentle massage, his hands plumping her breasts.

He didn't touch her pussy at all.

By the time Justin and Chris let their floggers drop, walking up to Jessica and sandwiching her between them, Domi was practically on Mitch's lap. Her hand reached down to grip his cock, likely thinking rubbing him through his pants would make him change his mind about doing her on the table. Justin and Chris pumped into Jessica's pussy and ass, filling her completely, while she cried out between them.

Watching them while Domi gripped his erection from the exterior of his pants, giving enough pressure and stimulation to make his balls tighten, Mitch had to pull her hand away or else embarrass himself. The music came to a crescendo, encouraging the voyeurs to join the trio on stage in erotic culmination.

"Please," Domi begged, turning her head toward him.

Instead of answering, Mitch caught her lips in a kiss, keeping hold of her hands and pushing them behind her back to capture her in place. She whimpered and opened for him, kissing him back desperately.

When they came up for air, the music was fading away, and the trio on stage was leaving, but Mitch didn't bother looking at them.

"Skip dessert and go check out our room?" he asked in a low voice.

"Yes, please, Sir."

CHAPTER SIXTEEN

<u>*Domi*</u>

On fire with need, the tops of her legs felt slippery from her cream as Mitch led her down the hallway. Her pussy felt plump and swollen between her legs, and she had a feeling her underwear wasn't protecting her from a wet spot on her dress at this point.

She couldn't help but laugh when they reached their door, though.

"Really? We're playing doctor again?" she asked, raising an eyebrow and teasing. "Should I be worried about you having a medical fetish while you're working in a hospital?"

"I am a *nurse*," he said, stressing the last word as he opened the door for her. "I am far more useful than a doctor." It was said in one of those joking, not joking ways.

"But you like playing doctor?"

"I do with you. Now get in there, Domi Darling." Mitch's hand came down, giving her a short, sharp swat on the ass that got her moving and left her gasping. The spot tingled, the burn from the impact making her almost lightheaded with the ache throbbing between her legs. She'd heard it could feel like all the blood was rushing to a man's dick when he got hard—was this the feminine

138

equivalent? His voice had changed, going from date-Mitch to Master Mitch in a single sentence.

The room was the same, set up like a doctor's office, though the table came with restraints, and the cabinets were filled with sex toys, alongside any real medical equipment. Marquis' hotel rooms were set up with the theme room first, then a room right behind it set up like a gorgeous—traditional—hotel room. Domi glanced over at the door on the far wall. When they'd been here for classes, the door to those rooms had always been locked. She'd always wanted to see what the hotel rooms looked like... but right now, having an orgasm was the bigger priority.

Behind her, she could hear Master Mitch closing the door and a rustle of fabric indicating he was picking up the provided lab coat. She grinned. He absolutely liked playing doctor. Maybe because real doctors at his hospital would be horrified at the idea. That seemed very Mitch.

"Welcome back, Miss Ortiz," Master Mitch said, his voice a little deeper than usual. "I'm glad to see you're taking your health seriously."

Turning to face him, Domi put one hand on her hip and lifted her eyebrows. He winked at her, though when he was in Dom mode, he somehow managed to wink but be serious at the same time. She knew from previous experience how devious he could be with medical equipment, and her heart was already beginning to race with anticipation.

"Since you've been here before for a checkup, I think we'll take time to run some tests this evening." The sadistic twinkle in his eyes, combined with the wicked smile on his lips, did all sorts of things to her insides. Everything felt fizzy, tingly, and achy with the desire to be touched, to be hurt.

"Please undress."

Mitch

Watching Domi undress out of the corner of his eye, Mitch took out a square blue cushion from one of the cabinets. Since the room was set up like a doctor's office, it had the usual hard tile floor, not at all conducive to putting a subbie on her knees for a long period… unless she was being punished. Mitch was going to be a gentleman and provide something for Domi to kneel on while she sucked his cock.

She looked at him curiously before her eyes sparked with understanding when he dropped the cushion on the floor. His lips twitched with amusement when she took her neatly folded dress, underwear tucked inside, over to the chair on the side of the room and put them down. Though he could have stopped her, he took the moment to appreciate how beautiful she was naked.

Petite and slim but with gentle curves. She'd recently told him she sometimes wished she had more curves, but Mitch didn't think she was lacking in any way. Women in all their shapes and sizes appealed to him for different reasons, and he thought she was perfectly proportioned. The hard brown nipples tipping her breasts looked swollen and ready to be played with, as did the puffy pussy lips between her legs. He could see a thin sheen of gloss on the tops of her thighs, a testament to how turned on she was after the show.

"Come here, Miss Ortiz," he said, gesturing to the cushion in front of him, hands going to the front of his pants to free his cock. "I need to check your gag reflex."

"With your tongue depressor?" she joked, though her eyes lit up with interest. Man, he loved it when a woman got him. He also loved when a woman enjoyed giving head as much as Domi did.

Dropping to her knees in front of him, she started to reach for his dick when he stopped her.

"Just your mouth, Miss Ortiz, this is an *oral* examination. If you need something to do with your hands, you may play with your breasts and get them ready for their exam."

Grinning, he slid his hands into her curls, pulling her head forward and enjoying the sight of her cupping her own breasts as her lips parted to take his cock between them. The wet heat of her mouth, her tongue sliding along the sensitive mushroom head, then down the vein on the underside, felt fucking fantastic. Mitch moaned, watching, fascinated as she took him in with enthusiasm lighting up her eyes.

Sucking hard, she bobbed her head down then back up, hands already massaging her breasts. Mitch could tell how worked up she was by how hard she was kneading the soft flesh, pinching and tugging her nipples. He thrust his hips forward, working with the rhythm of her head, sliding his cock deeper into her mouth until the head pressed against the back of her throat, and she gagged.

A soft mewl, another thrust, and he pushed past her gag reflex, burying himself in her throat, her lips pressing against his groin. He shuddered, savoring the sensation, then backed off enough to let her gasp for air before plunging back in again. Her whimpers vibrated along his cock, her throat muscles working around the tip every time he pushed all the way in.

Tears gathered in her eyes, spilling over and sliding down her cheeks, taking some of her eyeliner with it. Fuck, that was hot. Mitch stared down at her, fingers tightening in her curls as he forced her head down on his cock faster, thrusting forward again as he did so, using her mouth for his pleasure. She whimpered louder, squirming and rubbing her thighs together, fingers so tight on her nipples, the poor little buds were crushed while she let him face fuck her.

With his own excitement already at its peak, it was a shamefully short time before he couldn't hold back his orgasm and groaned, pushing her head all the way down. His muscles spasmed, cock pulsing with ecstasy while her throat worked, pulling every last spurt of cum from him until the sensation was almost painful.

"Stop, Miss Ortiz," he said, using her hair to pull her away.

She went, reluctantly, panting, still abusing her nipples.

"Hands by your side," he ordered. Defiance flashed across her face, but only lasted for a brief second, then she lowered her hands while Mitch tucked himself back into his pants. He didn't doubt he'd be hard as a rock again very shortly, but he'd also be able to last a lot longer now that he'd taken the edge off his desire.

Poor Domi, on the other hand, was still eager and needy... and would stay that way for a bit longer. She wiped away the few tears that had fallen and most of the eyeliner from her cheeks. Too bad. But there was plenty of time to ruin the rest of her makeup.

"Your gag reflex is working perfectly," he said in a pompous tone, holding out his hand for her to take. "Stand up, and we'll continue the examination."

DOMI

If she'd been on fire before, she felt as if she was about to combust now. The sweet torment was becoming actual torture if she didn't get to come soon. Hell, she'd been almost there just from rubbing her thighs together while Master Mitch fucked her mouth.

By 'continue the examination,' he'd better mean examining her pussy. Though it was no surprise, he'd gotten off first. The only reason it didn't bother her was she knew he was going to make her orgasm multiple times tonight. Otherwise, she'd probably be pretty ticked off.

"Hmm, self-abuse to the breasts," he murmured, cupping her breasts far more gently than she'd done. Domi blushed. She'd gotten a little carried away with her nipples, which were throbbing in protest. "Not bad, though. Let's see how much more they can take."

Trepidation swept through her, followed swiftly by arousal. There was always the small part of her brain that protested—*that shouldn't be hot*—but she'd learned to ignore it. She liked what she liked, and she wasn't going to apologize for it.

"Up on the table, Miss Ortiz."

Curious to see what he had up his sleeve—with Mitch, it was never what she expected—Domi did as she was told. She did grumble a little when he spread her legs apart, putting them in restraints the same way he did her wrists, so she couldn't rub her thighs together anymore, although it wasn't like she was actually going to be able to get herself off that way. Probably. But putting pressure on her throbbing pussy had helped with some of the relentlessly growing need.

Which, she knew, was exactly why he'd taken that bit of relief from her. Sadist.

Squirming against her restraints, her eyes widened when he went to what she'd always thought was a closet-type cabinet on the side of the room and wheeled out an odd-looking contraption she'd never seen before. It looked like medical equipment... sort of.

"What is that?" she asked, her voice going up in a squeak. Rolling it next to her, stopping at her torso, Mitch's lips spread in a wickedly sadistic grin.

"This is a heavy-duty vacuum pump, Miss Ortiz." He picked up two large suction cups attached to the machinery by long, clear tubes. "For your breasts."

"Holy fuck." The words slipped out before she could stop them, her body cringing away. It didn't matter she was also wildly curious about how they would feel—they looked scary, and she didn't know what to expect.

Master Mitch's eyes lit up at her reaction, full of happiness and growing arousal. A quick glance at the front of his pants confirmed he was already getting hard again, just at the idea of torturing her with the vacuum.

All tied up and unable to escape, there was nothing Domi could do but squirm as Mitch carefully placed the large suction cups over her breasts.

"Hold still, Miss Ortiz, or I may not be able to place these correctly," he said sternly. Body throbbing, apprehension growing, Domi bit her lower lip and forced herself to remain still. Apparently satisfied with the placement, Mitch held them in place with one hand—his thumb on one, fingers on the others—and reached back to flick on the machine.

Domi gasped at the sensation, the tingling pull as the suction cups latched on to her sensitive flesh. It didn't hurt and wasn't a very strong pull, but she could see how it could get there.

"There are smaller suction cups for just nipples," Master Mitch said conversationally. Out of the corner of her eye, she could see him sliding something on the machine, and the suction increased, making her arch her back in reaction. "I've ordered some for us to try sometime."

Imagining that kind of localized suction made Domi squirm, but this time, Mitch didn't scold her. He didn't need to. The cups firmly latched onto her breasts, pulling them into the cups and making them look bigger. Her nipples stretched higher, being pulled along with everything else.

It felt odd but incredibly good.

"Oh!" She threw her head back against the table when Mitch made another adjustment, increasing the suction. Now it was beginning to hurt, in a good way, her breasts throbbing and pulsing in the cups, feeling swollen and tight. They looked even bigger, and the sensation left her panting and her pussy creaming.

"Good girl, Miss Ortiz." Master Mitch smiled, moving away and leaving her with her breasts suctioned into the cups, body quivering with need. "Now, we'll see how that goes while I examine the rest of you."

CHAPTER SEVENTEEN

MITCH

From the way Domi's juices were dripping down into the crack of her ass onto the paper on the table beneath her, it was clear she was intensely aroused. She wasn't the only one. It didn't matter that he'd already had a blowjob. As he predicted, his cock was hard and ready to sink into her all over again. Going to the counter, he quickly pulled on a pair of medical gloves and grabbed a bottle of lube before returning to his panting, squirming beauty.

Her breasts looked even larger and were tinged with pink, slowly getting darker, nipples more swollen than ever.

"Master Mitch... I mean, Doctor... is that supposed to be happening?" She eyed her breasts a little worriedly, and Mitch chuckled.

"Absolutely. Don't worry, Miss Ortiz, you're in good hands." He waggled his fingers at her before pouring lube over them. Too far gone to giggle, Domi looked at him with lust-filled eyes, eager and waiting for his next move.

Standing between her splayed legs, Mitch appreciated the pretty sight she made. When he did take the suction off her breasts, they were going to be more sensitive than ever, and he would enjoy turning her over and pressing her weight down onto them.

First things first, though.

Pressing two well-lubed fingers against her pussy, he easily gained entrance. He probably hadn't needed the lube, but since he planned on stretching her out a little, he'd wanted to be extra careful.

Moaning, Domi's hips lifted, and her head thrashed back and forth.

"Please," she begged, the heartfelt plea going straight to his cock.

"More?" he asked, pulling his fingers out, so he had room to add a third before pushing back in. She moaned again as he pumped all three fingers into her tightly grasping pussy, easily feeling the heat and clench of her muscles around the digits through the gloves. "Don't worry, Miss Ortiz, I plan on stretching you out a bit."

Her eyes widened as he pulled his fingers away again and began to push four back into her, a much tighter fit. He had to work a little while Domi gasped and tugged on her restraints, squirming away from him rather than toward him.

"Mitch!"

"Don't worry, sweetheart, I'm not going to fist you... tonight." She squeaked, but her pussy clenched around him, quivering in reaction to the threat. *Promise.* It was both. He would love to fist her, but they'd need to work up to that. For tonight...

He pushed his fingers in deeper, up to the knuckles as she thrashed against her restraints. The fingers on his other hand were already slick as he pressed one up against her ass.

"Fuck! Master Mitch—Doctor—that isn't going to fit."

"It will, Domi Darling. It will." He pushed against her tiny pucker, ignoring the resistance, watching the pain and pleasure play out across Domi's face as her ass was invaded. "Did you wonder what it might be like to be Jessica tonight? One cock in her pussy, one in her ass? Well, now you have a bit of an idea."

Domi

Heat and shame flushed over her.

She had wondered. Had imagined. Even though she'd told Mitch he was more than enough—he was—but, of course, she'd *wondered*. What woman wouldn't?

The fingers in her pussy pulled out, not all the way, but enough, so Mitch had space to push two fingers into her ass. The tiny hole stretched, burning in a similar manner to the way her pussy was. The sensation of being completely filled was overwhelming, an exquisite agony that left her feeling breathless, as if there wasn't enough room inside her for both air and all of Mitch's fingers.

Hell, there probably wasn't. His hands weren't exactly small. Which made her think about him fisting her, and her body did another absurd little jump of excitement. Part of her wanted to tell him to do it now, to see how far he could push her, but she was too scared. *One day*, her mind whispered, and the fantasy was enough to push her closer to orgasm.

He pumped them rhythmically, the four in her pussy pushing in deep as the two in her ass retreated, then trading places. She could feel his eyes on her, observing her, examining her with heat and a critical eye, purposefully driving her higher and higher. The throbbing in her breasts was beginning to hurt more and more, adding the necessary dash of spice for her to truly enjoy her pleasure.

When he leaned down and swiped his tongue over her swollen clit, Domi went off like a rocket, her body spasming in ecstasy. She cried out as his tongue circled the swollen bud, fingers still pumping and moving inside her. The thrusts felt rougher, harder, filling her completely and sending her into paroxysms of rapture that encompassed her entire body.

"Mitch! *Fuck*, Mitch!" She thrashed uselessly against her restraints when he sucked her clit into his mouth, sending her flying, her muscles shuddering as the tension uncoiled, leaving her utterly spent.

And they hadn't even had sex yet.

MITCH

Sliding his fingers from Domi's clenching holes, Mitch straightened, smiling as she slumped, breathing heavily. The paper beneath her ass was a mess of liquid, and his hands were coated in her juices—proof of a job well done. Not that *he* was done.

She was all stretched out and ready for the next part.

Quickly turning off the pump and releasing the suction from Domi's breasts, Mitch leaned down and gave her nipple a quick nip, making her gasp.

"A little more sensitive than usual?" he asked innocently, enjoying her aghast expression.

"More than a little." Some of the lustful haze in her eyes cleared, anticipation and apprehension rising—exactly what he liked to see. Mitch chuckled, setting the suction cups aside and moving down to her feet to release her ankles. For the next part of their activities, he wanted her on her stomach, so she could really appreciate just how swollen and plumped her breasts felt.

Turning her onto her stomach, he enjoyed her gasp as her chest pressed down, her spine arching to lift some of the weight off her chest. He didn't immediately correct her posture, though. Dropping the lower section of the table, he left her legs dangling against the padding while she was bent at the waist, putting her in the perfect position to be spanked or fucked.

"Oh!" She wriggled in surprise, twisting and arching, her bottom lifting, legs kicking slightly. So completely helpless.

"Perfect," he murmured, running his hands over her ass. His cock jerked in anticipation. Lifting one hand, he gave her bottom a short, sharp smack, and Domi moaned, squirming even more in response. Between her cheeks, the little star of her anus winked at him.

Domi had never crossed that line during any of the Submissive 101 classes nor with Mitch since then. Anal play? Plenty. Anal sex? Zero.

Stroking his finger down the center of her crease, Mitch grinned when his fingers paused on the crinkled hole, and Domi froze. At the very least, she had to have a suspicion of his intentions.

"Have you ever had anal sex, Domi Darling?" he asked, dropping the doctor persona. He didn't want to be someone else for this, didn't want to roleplay anymore. While that was fun, especially with the room set up, he wanted it to be clear this was between the two of them.

"No, Sir," she said softly, turning her head slightly and trying to crane her neck to see what he was doing. Pushing his gloved finger into her again, it sank in easily since he'd already stretched her out, but this time, there was nothing to distract her from the sensation. Well, other than her breasts, but nothing else below her waist.

"Why not?" He'd always wondered. Granted, he hadn't pushed the issue before tonight, but he'd had the sense she wouldn't welcome it. While anal sex had never been stated as a hard limit, he'd instinctively shied away from it with her. He moved his finger back and forth inside of her, mimicking what he was planning to do with his cock once his question was answered.

One shoulder lifted. Her curls hid most of her features, but from what he could see, she looked sheepish.

"Anal seems so… intimate. It seemed like a big deal, like something I should do with someone…" Her voice trailed off.

"Anal means commitment?" He couldn't keep the amusement out of his voice. That was one he hadn't heard before, and it was cute as hell.

"Maybe." There was a touch of defensive testiness to her tone. Mitch pushed a second finger into her ass, making her gasp and lose some of the attitude, reminding her who was in control.

"Well, it's a good thing we decided to be committed because I'm going to fuck this pretty ass tonight." He pushed his finger in deep, and she whimpered, her head falling down to rest against the table, body shuddering in response. "Unless you want to safe word, you're about to lose your last virginity, darling."

Another whimper, but no protest. Her response was music to his years.

"Yes, Sir." Her voice was breathless.

Oh fuck, oh fuck, oh fuck...

It wasn't as if things going in her ass was something new. She hadn't met a Dom who didn't want to play with her ass, even if they didn't do it for every scene, and Mitch was no exception. But none of them had pushed for sex as if sensing her hesitation, somehow knowing it was off-limits. She'd noticed good Doms seemed to have a keen sense for avoiding things that would get a hard no.

Somehow though, the idea of actually having anal sex... well, like Mitch said, it was her last virginity. She'd lost her virginity in high school at prom with her high school boyfriend like a terrible cliché. Not that she regretted it. It had been nice. Sweet. He'd done his best to make it romantic.

But this... this suited who she was now. Mitch had added some romance, in his own way, but there was also the pain, the kink, the dizzying heights of pleasure. Her breasts felt extra swollen and sensitive beneath her, pressed against the padded table. The more weight she put on them, the more they tingled painfully, but in her current position, she couldn't exactly keep her weight off of them.

Something slid up her legs, then straps tightened around her thighs. Mitch lifted her hips a little to get them in the perfect position. Soft, rubbery, it pressed against her clit, and Domi moaned. She recognized the sensation. Mitch had strapped a butterfly vibrator to her. It could be fluttering, teasing torment or intense stimulation, depending on the setting.

A flip of the switch and fluttering, teasing torment it was, humming to life against her swollen clit. The tiny bud felt more sensitive than usual after her previous orgasm. She squirmed in place, unable to escape the tiny vibrations, which tickled more than pleasured at the moment.

Hands grasped her hips, and something hard, hot, and slick pressed against her anus. Domi froze.

"Good girl." Mitch's deep, approving tone filled her with warmth head to toe.

He began to push in.

It was similar to the toys she'd had inserted in her ass, yet utterly different. The tight ring stretched, burning with discomfort as he pushed in. The butterfly buzzed against her clit, but it barely served as a distraction from the slick sensation of his cock sliding deeper inside her. Unlike a plug, there was no notch for her sphincter to settle into. Unlike the plastic dildos and probes, he was not cool or even warm. He was hot, pulsing inside her in a way a toy could never replicate.

"Oh, fuck…" She clenched around him as he pushed even deeper, filling her far more than any of the toys. Her opening was widening even farther, muscles stretching to accommodate his girth. Did his cock get thicker as it went?

"That's it, sweetheart." Hands massaged her ass, no longer wearing gloves. She knew he was looking down at his cock in her ass, appreciating the view of splitting her cheeks with his dick. He finally bottomed out, groin pressed up against her body, the front of his thighs against the back of hers. Domi dropped her head against the table, panting for breath.

Even though her pussy was empty, she felt even fuller than she had when he'd used his fingers to impale both of her holes. His cock felt bigger than ever in her ass, and she swore she could feel him throbbing against the sensitive walls. The sensation was excruciatingly intimate and incredibly arousing.

Just when she was beginning to adjust to the massive intrusion, she felt Mitch shift behind her. The vibrator kicked into high gear, pulsating against her sensitive clit and sending her careening straight toward orgasm. Less than a second later, Mitch was pulling back, his cock sliding out of her, and the sensation of retreat was even more intense than that of insertion, making her channel feel raw, extra sensitive. She clenched hard in reaction, only for him to drive back into her with a hard thrust that made her cry out.

Hands slid under her body and hard fingers curved around her swollen breasts, closing down on them hard. Domi's legs kicked as Mitch fucked her ass hard, using her breasts as leverage. The butterfly sent waves of ecstasy reverberating through her to mix with the sparks of pain from Mitch's rough handling and a confusing clash of both pleasure and discomfort as he pillaged her ass, a devastating assault on her senses.

Tears filled her eyes as the first orgasm crashed into her. She screamed his name, rocking back against him, shuddering and clenching around him. His rhythm never faltered as his cock drove into her ass over and over. The mercilessly relentless hum of the butterfly against her swollen clit quickly became agonizing as the pleasure became too intense for her body to bear.

MITCH

Feeling Domi come apart beneath him, his plan to ride her ass long and hard was rapidly collapsing. She was too hot, too tight around his cock, her screams of pain and pleasure too exciting.

"Mitch! Please! Fuck!" she babbled, twisting and fighting against the intense pleasure he was pouring into her. The butterfly vibe was doing its work, keeping her high, her muscles convulsing in wave after wave of inescapable orgasm. The sob in her voice drove him harder, faster.

Ecstasy pulsed. He slammed home, hands tightly gripping her tormented breasts, cock buried deep in her ass, his body resting against hers and pushing her hips against the table, pressing the vibrator even more firmly against her clit. He could feel every twitch, every wriggle, every tiny movement of her muscles as she tried to escape the intense assault of sensation. He felt when she passed out, just as the hot spurts of rapture faded, leaving him sated.

Quickly removing the vibrator, he got the table back in place and turned her over to give her a quick check over—a real one.

Her racing pulse was slowing, breathing normalizing… nothing wrong as far as he could see. Mitch allowed himself a grin. Damn. She'd come so hard, she'd passed out. Like he wasn't going to be proud of that.

Undoing the restraints on her wrists, he gathered her in his arms, feeling as protective as he was satisfied. Time for aftercare in their hotel room.

DOMI

Cool water slipped through her lips.

An insistent voice said she needed to eat something.

Domi slapped the hands, trying to rouse her awake.

She wanted to sleep.

A soft chuckle.

"Okay then, Domi Darling."

Warmth wrapped around her.

Sighing happily, she fell back into the darkness.

CHAPTER EIGHTEEN

MITCH

Waking up next to a woman he didn't feel the immediate need to sneak away from was a new experience. Actually, being cuddled around Domi was pretty nice. She was tucked into his body, her head resting on his arm, curls tickling his nose, and her ass pressed up against his morning erection. The sweet ass that was all his.

Grinning, Mitch bent his head to press a kiss to the back of her neck. Not to try to wake her up—he doubted he could, and she'd been very clear last night how she felt about that—but because he couldn't *not* kiss her right now. This felt too good. He felt too happy. He needed to show it.

She stirred against him, then came awake with a jerk.

"Where... Oh." She relaxed.

Mitch chuckled. "Forgot where you were for a minute?"

"Yup." Squirming onto her back, so she could look at him, she only winced a little. Mitch stroked his hand down her stomach, caressing. His erection prodded her thigh, but he ignored it while Domi blinked up at him. In the morning light, which was coming in through a crack in the curtains, she was adorably rumpled. "I'm not exactly used to waking up next to a man."

"Me, either." Mitch grinned. "Or a woman. Or anyone, really."

Giggling, Domi groaned, putting her hand over her eyes. "It's too early in the morning for bad jokes, Mitch."

"It's never too early. Or too late."

"Mmm." Rolling toward him, she snuggled into his chest, and Mitch tightened his arms around her. "Hmmm. I forgot about this happening in the morning." Dainty fingers wrapped around his cock. Mitch groaned, thrusting his hips forward.

Didn't matter how much wild kinky sex they'd had last night, his dick still wanted more. Knowing she'd still be feeling the aftereffects of last night's activities, that she'd be a little sore, only turned him on more.

"You're two seconds away from being rolled onto your back if you don't let go," he warned. Her fingers tightened. Pumped. She squealed as he rolled her onto her back, exactly as he'd promised.

It wasn't wild, kinky sex. It was softer, more tender, though not exactly gentle. That wasn't what he or Domi wanted. She whimpered and moaned as he fondled her breasts, leaning down to suck and nip her hypersensitive nipples, his cock sliding in and out of her wet pussy as she wrapped her legs around him. Hands pressed her wrists into the mattress above her head as he pumped in and out of her, riding her to mutual ecstasy.

DOMI

"You look happy." Rae plopped onto the couch next to Domi. Ana was in the dining room, working on her 'homework' for the weekend, making a poster to show off in class. Domi had been staring off into space, remembering her time with Mitch. It wasn't until Rae joined her, knocking her out of her reverie, she realized she'd been doing so, with a big, stupid grin on her face.

"What's not to be happy about? My daughter's home and feeling good, my bestie is here and feeling good..."

"And you had multiple orgasms this week..." Rae added in a low voice.

Even so, Domi glanced over her shoulder to make sure Ana wasn't paying attention to them. The little girl didn't look up from the poster she was decorating. Domi had offered to help but had been roundly rejected. Ana wanted to do it on her *own*. Probably so Domi wouldn't limit her use of glitter.

"That never hurts anything." She grinned. Her body still had a few small aches and pains, but it had been... glorious. Did that seem over-dramatic? It was how it had felt, though. She hadn't even been mad at Rae for keeping Mitch's plan for an overnight at Marquis a secret from her. There was still a little bundle of nerves hiding underneath her happiness, some pessimistic part of her waiting for the other shoe to drop.

"So, what's next? You had *the* date, now what? Is it time for sleepovers? Introducing him to Ana?" Rae prodded.

Glancing over her shoulder again, her daughter was still oblivious to the conversation. Turning back to Rae, she shook her head. Rae leaned back against the cushions, giving Domi a questioning look, almost challenging.

"I guess that means he's not coming to Ana's birthday dinner?"

Rae's tone was bland, and Domi couldn't tell what her friend thought. Was it a mistake not to invite him? Ana's birthday, when Domi and Rae would take her out to dinner with Marcus and Julia, was only a few weeks away. That felt too soon.

"Ana already met him, but I'm not ready to have him come around while she's here. I think the birthday dinner might be a little much. But... I thought I might introduce him to my parents. You know, over a call." Since her parents had moved to Puerto Rico a few years ago to take care of her grandparents, they wouldn't be able to meet in person any time soon, but she video chatted with them regularly, usually when Ana was around, though obviously, she'd wait until Ana was at Marcus and Julia's to introducing Mitch.

Somehow, introducing Mitch to her parents didn't seem as big a step as introducing him to Ana, but it was still a step. A significant one, though she'd already let him do butt stuff with her, which was a pretty big step. Heck, in some of the romance books she read, butt stuff was basically an engagement ring—and often led to one.

Not that she was expecting that. Nope. They were so not anywhere near there yet. In fact, just thinking about it made her queasy. She was just acknowledging how significant giving up her last virginity to him had been.

That was a step.

Introducing him to her parents would be another step. She hadn't introduced a guy to them since Marcus, and obviously, that had been done with Julia by his side. Hopefully, this would get her *mami* off her back.

"Hoping this will satisfy your mom for a bit?" Rae asked as if she was reading Domi's mind. Sometimes, their closeness could be a little unnerving.

"Hey, she's been wanting me to date... I'm dating. She'll like Mitch. As long as we're dating, she'll stop bugging me about dating, and if things don't work out, I'll probably still get a break for a while."

"And if things do work out, she'll be thrilled."

"Right." The little weight of uneasiness in the pit of her stomach grew a little more. If she and Mitch worked out, would they end up with... marriage? More babies? They hadn't talked about any of that. Did he even want kids?

"What?" Rae asked, poking Domi's arm. After she repeated her thoughts, Rae sat back with a thoughtful expression. "You two aren't that serious yet, but you should probably talk about it. Soon. Before you get in deeper."

"What if I don't know my answers?" Domi really didn't know what she wanted. For so long, she'd seen her future as taking care of Ana and making sure her daughter didn't want for anything. Somehow, she'd always envisioned being here, in this house, with Rae and Ana, while having her a life separate from her daughter when Ana was with Marcus and Julia.

The idea of joining that separate life with her daughter's life...

scared her. So many things could go wrong. She could handle her own heartbreak but wasn't sure she could handle her daughter's.

"Then take some time to think about it." Rae shrugged. "There's no rush."

Right. There was no rush. She'd figure it out.

"Mommy, Aunt Rae, come look! All done!"

"We're coming," she and Rae chimed together, glancing at each other and laughing. There was no rush. Right now, she had everything exactly the way she'd always pictured it, except better—Rae and Ana at home, and her own life when Ana wasn't there. A life that included a boyfriend. While she hadn't pictured that before, she'd grown. Changed. It fit. She and Mitch worked together this way.

She didn't need to combine her worlds yet, not when everything was going so well as it was.

MITCH

"It was very nice to meet you, Mr. and Mrs. Ortiz." Mitch gave Domi's parents his most charming smile. *I'm a totally normal young man. I definitely didn't spend last night clamping your daughter's nipples, plugging her ass with an expanding, vibrating plug, whipping that ass, then fucking her raw.* Domi's mom beamed back at him through the computer screen, though her dad seemed a little more suspicious.

From everything Mitch had heard, that was normal. Dads were protective of their daughters, especially when they were dating. It was impossible to tell size on a computer screen, but he got the impression Domi's mom was petite like her, while her dad was taller and bulkier. Domi definitely got her hair from her mom, who had similar corkscrew curls.

He was relieved his first time meeting the parents was a video chat introduction. It was much less intimidating than meeting in person, though he'd be ready when the time came for that. At least Domi's mom liked him.

"It was wonderful to meet you, too, Mitch. We're so happy Domi has such a nice boyfriend. *Si, Enrique?*" Because of the screen, it wasn't possible to see exactly what she did, but Mitch was pretty sure she'd elbowed her husband.

"Uh-huh," Domi's dad said unenthusiastically. Mrs. Ortiz elbowed him again. "I mean, nice to meet you. I look forward to meeting you in person when we come up to visit in a few months." He sounded more dubious than sincere.

"Me, too, Sir." A few months was plenty of time to prepare. Besides, if he wasn't mistaken, Mrs. Ortiz was the dominant personality in their relationship, and she was thrilled to meet him. Hopefully, she'd be able to convince her husband.

"Alright, *adiós mami, adiós papi. Les hablo luego gracias por el video chat,*" Domi said, leaning forward. Thanks to the video chat, Mitch could see her bemused expression clearly. High school Spanish had been a long time ago, but he understood enough to know she was saying goodbye and thanking them for the chat.

"*Adiós, cariño te quiero!*"

"*Yo también tequiero.*" Domi clicked off the call and leaned back. "Well, I think we can call that a success."

"Me, too." Mitch pulled her in for a short hot kiss he had to end far too quickly. "If I didn't have to get to work, we could celebrate."

"When you get off work, I could come over, and we could celebrate then," she suggested, watching him get to his feet. She leaned back, giving him a sassy look, then winced as she shifted her weight on her welted ass. Mitch grinned in appreciation.

"Sounds good to me." Sliding his fingers into her hair, he tugged her head backward, dropping another kiss onto her lips. Fuck, he loved kissing her, spending time with her, and he was flying high, knowing he'd passed the parent test.

They'd only been official for a few weeks, but it felt good. Easy. *Right.* Like the other relationships at Stronghold.

Brian had asked if Mitch was worried about Domi not introducing him to Ana as her boyfriend yet, but he and Domi had talked about it, and he understood she wasn't ready yet. Yeah, sure, there was a part of him that was impatient, but only because he understood what a big step that was. An important step and a necessary one if they were going to have a future together.

She was a single mom doing her best, and he was the first boyfriend she'd had since becoming a single mom. He also had a bit of a track record. He wasn't going to blame her for being cautious. They'd get there.

Meeting her parents was proof of that. One step at a time.

He was halfway to the hospital when his phone started playing the Imperial March. Sighing, Mitch answered using the car's system.

"Hey, Dad."

"Hello, laddie, how are ye doing?" His father's Scottish burr was as strong as ever. No matter how long he'd lived in the states, it never seemed to let up. Mitch suspected it was a deliberate choice on his father's part since women went nuts for the accent. While Mitch could do the same and sound completely genuine, he'd always preferred not to follow in his dad's footsteps in any way.

"Not bad, but I'm on my way to work. What's up?" His dad wasn't the talker his mom was, the opposite in fact.

His dad cleared his throat.

"I'm going to be in town next week for a few days and was hoping I could spend some time with you. Maybe get dinner."

"Yeah, sure, that sounds fine." Mitch's brain was already jumping ahead. "Are you free on Wednesday?" Domi always had dinner with Ana, Ana's dad, and stepmother on Wednesdays, and Mitch had off, so that would work out well.

Unless... did he want to introduce Domi to his dad? No, not really. They'd have to meet eventually, but it would be better if he introduced her to his mom first. Otherwise, it might hurt his mom's feelings. Unlike Domi's relationship with her parents, things were always a bit awkward between Mitch and his dad. He didn't want her seeing that right after he'd charmed her parents.

"Wednesday is good. I'll see you then. Also, you should talk to your ma soon, she wants you to come home for Passover. Bye, Son." The phone clicked off, hanging up before Mitch could respond, so he wouldn't have to answer any questions about how he knew what Mitch's mom wanted.

It wasn't a surprise his mom wanted him home for Passover. It was one of the bigger Jewish holidays, but the only reason his Catholic dad would be saying something was *she'd* said something to his dad. Which meant they were talking again. Typical. Scowling, Mitch shook his head. Yeah, he wasn't ready for his parents to meet Domi yet. Introducing her to that dysfunction could wait.

CHAPTER NINETEEN

Domi

"This one, mommy," Ana said, tugging on the skirt of a dark purple dress Domi almost never wore. In fact, she was pretty sure the last time she'd worn it was for a friend's wedding before Ana was born.

"That's a little fancy for Pasta Plus, sweetheart," Domi said, hesitating. When she'd agreed to let Ana pick Domi's outfit for her birthday dinner, she hadn't expected her daughter to go straight to the back of her closet where her cocktail dresses were hanging. All three of them. Of course, Ana had picked the flashiest one with lace and tiny sparkling gemstones. Since they were going to the same restaurant Ana always chose when she had the choice, Domi didn't know why her daughter suddenly wanted her to look so dressy.

"You said I could pick." A mulish expression Domi recognized settled onto Ana's face. She was not going to be easily talked out of this.

"You did say that," Rae said from her spot on Domi's bed, amusement in her voice. Domi shot her a dark look.

"Are you going to pick out something similar for Aunt Rae?" Domi asked in an innocent tone, even though Rae hadn't offered to let Ana pick. If Ana said yes, it wasn't like Rae would be able to tell her no. It was Ana's birthday, which was why Domi already knew she was going to end up wearing the purple dress.

"Aunt Rae looks fancy all the time. You never do."

Ouch. That hit her where it hurt. Going by the way Rae's eyes widened, her lips forming an 'o' even if she didn't make the noise, she felt the same way. The brutal honesty of children could be unintentionally vicious.

On the other hand, Ana wasn't wrong. Rae didn't dress extra fancy for work, but she did have to wear business or business casual, which included dresses. Since Domi worked from home, she tended to go from her pajama pants to her yoga pants. She tried to remember the last time she'd dressed up—that wasn't for Stronghold. Or her third date with Mitch since Ana hadn't seen her then. Thankfully *that* dress was tucked away in a box at the top of her closet with her other super sexy clothes and fetwear—where her daughter couldn't find it.

Damn. It had been a long time.

"Alright, birthday girl, you win." Domi reached over Ana's head to pick up the hanger. The little girl clapped her hands in excitement. She'd been clapping a lot lately, thrilled to no longer be hindered by the cast.

"Yay! Now you can look nice and get a boyfriend."

"Excuse me?" Domi froze, blinking in shock at her daughter.

"Mama Julia says that's how you get one."

Domi's jaw dropped open. She had absolutely no idea what to say to that. From the bed, Rae cackled madly.

MITCH

Making small talk with his dad was always awkward, even when they hadn't seen each other in a long time. It was funny because his dad ran a bar and actually excelled at conversation with the strangers who came through there, but with his own son or his ex-wife…

"You look good," Mitch said, giving him a hug, which his dad returned. Hugging was good, taking up time that didn't feel like an awkward silence.

"So do ye, lad." His dad thumped his back before releasing him. Stepping back, his dad looked Mitch over, grinning. "Chip off the ol' block."

Mitch snorted, but he couldn't deny he could do worse than look like his old man. While he didn't want to emulate his dad in other ways, his dad was what the women at Stronghold called a 'silver fox.' Only an inch shorter than Mitch, he was still in extremely good shape, and his mostly grey hair made him look more distinguished than when it had been dark brown. His blue eyes twinkled with good cheer ninety percent of the time. The silver beard was new since the last time Mitch had seen him, but it looked good.

Wearing jeans and a blue button-down that matched his eyes, it was no surprise when more than one woman gave him a second glance as they walked past, even those closer to Mitch's age.

"Hope you're hungry," Mitch said, gesturing for his dad to precede him down the sidewalk. "Because I'm starving."

"Enjoy the carbs while you can. Eventually you'll need to slow down," his dad said, patting his stomach as they walked to the front door of Pasta Plus. There really wasn't much more to say as they entered the restaurant and were seated before busying themselves with their menus. Mitch delayed asking any questions until after they'd ordered and had the feeling his dad was doing the same. They needed to hold on to whatever conversation they could to get them through a whole meal together.

"So." Mitch cleared his throat once their server walked away with their menus. "What brings you to D.C.?" Hopefully, some kind of project that would be long and involved.

"Oh, ye know, business." His dad rubbed the underside of his beard, a sure sign he was being cagey.

"What kind of business?" Mitch didn't really care that much. His dad had never really wanted Mitch around the Outlands, the bar and club he owned, as if he thought Mitch would either make trouble or would fall prey to bad influences if he were there too much. He'd even refused to hire Mitch as a server or bartender, even after Mitch turned twenty-one. At one point, Mitch had had a vague idea of them working there together until his dad eventually retired and turned the bar over to Mitch, but since he'd never been allowed to work there, that idea never turned into anything more.

"I'm meeting with another club owner down here. Later this evening, in fact, so I can take a tour of his place. We're going to talk business. Trade some tips. You wouldna be interested. What's new with you?" His dad shrugged, picking up his glass of water and taking a drink. The lilt of his Scottish brogue had seemed slightly more intense than usual, which was one of the few reliable indicators of his dad's emotions.

Mitch narrowed his eyes. For some reason, the fact his dad didn't want to talk about it just made him even more curious and determined to find out. He was an adult now, and his dad couldn't keep him out of Outlands business forever. Unless he was planning on selling it?

"Are you planning on selling the Outlands?" He had trouble imagining that.

His dad blinked in shock, putting the glass down with a thud.

"Hell, no!" He shook his head. "I... No, it's just to talk about a business venture and find out some more about a new space they opened. I've been thinking about expanding, and I want to know how it's going for them."

That made a lot more sense.

"What club down here?" Mitch asked. "Maybe I've been to it."

His dad chuckled. "I doubt it."

Rolling his eyes, Mitch sat back in his chair.

"I do go out, you know. What club?"

"It's called Stronghold."

Time skidded to a stop—except it didn't. It was Mitch's brain that stopped. Froze. Time, the rest of the world, it all kept moving. Their server appeared at their table with the crusty bread he loved so much and the beers they'd ordered.

"Here you go," she said cheerfully while Mitch and his dad stared at each other across the table, his dad's expression slowly changing as he realized Mitch knew *exactly* what Stronghold was.

"Stronghold? And Marquis?" Mitch's voice sounded odd. Strangled.

Did his dad look paler? He nodded. "Aye. I ah... I take it you know of them?"

"I'm a member." His brain felt as if it was exploding. Suddenly, his dad's reluctance to have him anywhere near the Outlands took on a whole new meaning. "Does this mean... you and Mom?" Of course, his mom was part of it. His parents had owned the Outlands for years before Mitch was born. They'd gone out every weekend on dates before things started to break apart. Sometimes, even after things had started to break apart.

Back then, Mitch hadn't understood why they kept going out together when they did nothing but argue at home. Now... fuck. He'd had more than one thought lately about how hard it would be to go back to vanilla sex. Not that he wanted to think about his parents getting their needs met, especially kinky needs, but... fuck. It all made sense—too much sense.

His dad's chuckle was a pale imitation of his usual hearty laugh. "Ye really are a chip off the ole block, eh?"

Mitch's stomach sank like a brick.

Which, of course, was when Domi and her family walked in.

DOMI

Meeting up with Marcus and Julia in front of the restaurant, Domi was trying not to seethe. For some reason, Ana was completely invested in finding Domi a boyfriend and was convinced the purple dress was the way to do it. Ana had dressed up in her fanciest dress as well—her Elsa costume—so Domi wouldn't feel so alone. Which was very sweet. Rae thought the whole thing was hilarious, and Domi could tell from her bestie's significant looks, she thought Domi should tell Ana about Mitch.

But it was Ana's birthday, which was definitely not the right time.

"Daddy! Mama Julia!" To everyone's surprise, rather than running to her father's arms, Ana went straight for Julia, stopping in front of her and pushing her face up close to Julia's stomach. "Hello, baby!"

From the expression on Julia and Marcus' faces, Domi wasn't the only one who melted at the sight, and she could hear Rae let out a soft little sigh beside her. Damn, the kid was cute. She was going to be such a good big sister.

Wedging herself between Marcus and Julia, Ana grabbed both of their hands, pulling them forward.

"Come on, come on! Time for my birthday dinner!"

"Wow." Marcus' eyebrows went up in surprise when he saw Domi's outfit, and Julia looked a little stunned. They were both dressed nicely but far more casually, Marcus in slacks and a dress shirt, while Julia wore a long-sleeved blue dress with a belted waist to emphasize her curves. It also hid any sign of a bump, if there was one yet. Rae had also gotten away with a dress and a sweater for when the evening got cooler. "You look nice."

"Thanks," Domi said, smiling with a smile that wasn't really a smile. "Apparently, this is how I get a boyfriend."

"Yes! Mommy is dressed up." Ana did a little happy dance that killed some of Domi's ire, though it brought up a whole host of other emotions.

Marcus' brows drew together, but Julia lifted the hand that wasn't holding Ana's and covered her lips, sudden mirth filling her eyes.

"Oh, dear," Julia said, clearly trying not to laugh. The expression on her face was friendlier than it had ever been, though, which was something. "I think something might have gotten a little lost in translation. One of the characters on a show we were watching got all dressed up to go on a date, and Ana had some questions."

The anger Domi had been fighting drained away when she saw the pair's reactions. Ana hadn't been very clear on exactly how the topic of Domi getting a boyfriend came up. Obviously, it hadn't. Her daughter had gotten the *idea* of a boyfriend in her head and decided Domi needed one.

Great. Was this a good segue to talk about Mitch?

No. Not tonight. Later. When she'd had some time to prepare what she was going to say and how to explain to Ana, she shouldn't get too attached. Just in case. As if that was optional.

Sighing, Domi looked down at her daughter with loving exasperation.

"Yes, well. Let's go inside and get dinner. Who knows? Maybe I'll pick up a boyfriend while we're here," she joked.

Famous last words.

The moment they walked into the dining room, something—she didn't know what—drew her eyes to the left of the room, even though the hostess was walking to the right, and she met Mitch's blue gaze. Something about his expression was very *off*. Shocked, Domi ground to a halt as the man sitting across from Mitch turned to see what he was looking at. At the same time, Ana grabbed onto Domi's waist, looking around her mother to see what *she* was looking at.

"Murse Mitch!" Ana squealed gleefully and was off and running before Domi could react.

"Ah, the famous Murse Mitch," Marcus joked, sliding around Domi.

He didn't seem to realize anything was wrong, though Domi could hear Rae muttering behind her, her words reflecting Domi's thoughts exactly.

"Oh, shit."

With Ana already at Mitch's table and Marcus and Julia following right behind, there was no choice but to join them. A helpless glance at Rae didn't provide any answers. Her bestie looked as nonplussed as Domi felt. She shrugged at Domi, dark eyes filled with sympathy, but it wasn't as if there was anything she could do.

Groaning internally, Domi followed the train to Mitch's table, where Ana was holding introductions.

"This is my Daddy and my Mama Julia. She has a baby in her belly that's going to be my little sister or brother!"

Mitch smiled at Ana, but it wasn't his usual smile. It didn't light up his face. Was he worried about seeing her now when he knew Domi wasn't ready to introduce him to Ana as her boyfriend yet? Or had something been going wrong before she'd even walked into the restaurant? The way he'd looked had been weird, but that might have just been surprise at seeing her.

The man across from Mitch was beaming down at Ana. He was a total silver fox, complete with a grey beard.

"Well, aren't ye a cute wee one?"

Holy crap, that Scottish accent was killer. Domi blinked and gave herself a little shake, and she could see Julia doing the same. The man was twice Mitch's age but lethal with that accent and those looks and seemed to have a lot of the same charm as Mitch. Actually... she blinked again. The beard had thrown her for a moment, but the man looked a *lot* like Mitch.

"I'm Ana. Who are you?"

"Murse Mitch's father," the man said, confirming Domi's suspicion. He held out his hand to Ana. "Gavin Craig, missy. Pleased to meet you." The fact his last name was different from Mitch's threw Domi for another loop, but that was hardly the thing to focus on right now.

"Nice to meet you, Mr. Craig." Ana beamed as he shook her hand like a real adult, then turned her head toward Domi and reached out her hand. "This is my mommy. She and Murse Mitch are friends."

"Are they now?" Mr. Craig gave her a curious look as he released Ana's hand and held it out to Domi. "And what's your name, lass?"

"Domi, Sir," she said automatically, reacting to the authority in his blue eyes. Shit. She wondered if he was a Dom. Was that genetic or something? Mitch's father had the same commanding aura Mitch did when he was in Dom mode.

He also had no visible reaction to Domi's name. A sick feeling started to churn in her stomach as Mitch sat there silently while she met his father, who clearly had no idea who she was to his son.

CHAPTER TWENTY

MITCH

He was going to be sick.

Everything was happening too fast, right after his dad had hit him with a serious blow. He needed time to process everything but didn't know how to get it. Not with Ana, adorably dressed as Elsa, right there with Domi, and her co-parents, who seemed only vaguely interested in him. Which was surprising, unless Domi hadn't told *them* she was seeing him. Or maybe she'd only told them a vague 'someone.'

Whatever. It didn't matter. What mattered was that his parents were kinky. *Kinky.* Hell, his dad owned a BDSM club. Was meeting with Stronghold and Marquis' owners to talk about *their* clubs and expanding his own club.

All this time, Mitch had thought…

Fuck.

BDSM, kink, it wasn't the saving grace he'd thought.

He didn't doubt for one second his dad was a good Dom, which meant the failure in his parents' relationship still happened despite BDSM.

I can't breathe.

"Excuse me," he said suddenly, standing up with the same abruptness. "I need to use the bathroom."

Splash some cold water on his face. Figure out what the fuck was going on. What he was going to do next. How this changed things.

He stumbled away from the table.

The revelation did change things, didn't it? Hell, it changed everything. Not that he thought BDSM would be some kind of magic bullet, a guarantee things would work out with him and Domi, that he wouldn't end up in a relationship like his parents... but he'd thought it gave them more of a chance. He'd seen the happy couples around Stronghold and thought it meant something.

But everything was still a crapshoot.

"Mitch... Mitch!" Domi caught up to him before he could reach the safety of the men's room. Grabbed his arm. He turned around reluctantly, emotions simmering and bubbling under the surface, barely contained. "What's going on?"

"I need a minute, Domi." His voice came out distant, harsh, and she flinched, but he couldn't do anything about that. It was all he could do to keep his emotions under control, which meant locking them down entirely.

"Fine then, just one question." Her dark eyes flashed with hurt. "I introduced you to my parents, but your dad clearly doesn't know who I am. You didn't tell him about me, did you?"

Fuck. No, he hadn't, but he wasn't going to stand here in the hallway and explain things to her when she was supposed to be eating dinner with her family.

"No. I didn't. Did you tell Ana's dad and stepmother you're seeing someone?" It came out more accusatory than he meant. Domi took a step back. From the way she pressed her lips together, guilt tingeing her expression, he knew he was right. She hadn't mentioned him to *her* family either. Sure, he'd met her parents, but they were far away, weren't they? It wasn't a big deal to her. She hadn't even asked him *why* he hadn't told his dad, just jumped on him about not doing so. "You're here having family dinner, all dressed up, and I wasn't invited, was I? Because I'm not part of the family."

He knew he was venting his frustration about his own parents on her, but he couldn't seem to stop. Hell, he wasn't even sure he should. She'd followed *him* when he'd clearly needed space and had been ready to throw accusations at him.

"If I'd known you were going to be here, I would have told you," she said, clearly trying to keep a hold of her temper. For some reason, that made him even angrier.

"Why? So, I would take my dad for dinner somewhere else?"

"No... I mean... I don't know." She clenched her fists by her side. "It's Ana's birthday, and she wanted to come here—" She cut off as a cold, resigned laugh burst from Mitch's lips.

"I didn't even know it was Ana's birthday." He closed his eyes and shook his head. "This was a bad idea."

"What was?" Hesitancy crept into her voice, but it was too late.

"This." He opened his eyes, sweeping out his arm. Hell, he was never going to be able to come back to this restaurant without thinking about tonight. His favorite pasta place was going to be tainted forever. That's what relationships did. They got people all hopeful, then they shit on everything, ruining it by association. "All of it. You, me. Probably everything. I didn't even know it was your daughter's birthday. I have no idea if you were ever going to tell her or your co-parents about me. I didn't tell my dad about you. Maybe that's for the best. Makes it easier."

"Easier?" she repeated, staring up at him as though she didn't understand what he was saying. Fuck. Was this what breaking up was like? This sucked even more than he'd ever thought it would.

But it was the right thing to do.

"I'm a bad bet, Domi, I always was. We should end this now, while our lives are still separate. Go back and celebrate your daughter's birthday. You should be there with her, not over here with me. You weren't even supposed to see me tonight, remember?" He whirled away from the shocked expression on her face, shoving his way into the men's bathroom where she couldn't follow.

At least, where she shouldn't follow. There was a small part of him that worried she would, anyway. Another part that hoped she would.

Standing in front of one of the sinks, he stared at himself in the mirror, gripping the porcelain and waiting... but no petite firecracker came storming through the door to yell at him. Hell, he wasn't even sure what he would say to her if she did. It really was better this way.

Wasn't it?

DOMI

In shock, feeling completely hollowed out on the inside as if she was an empty doll, moving through space because someone had wound her up and set her into motion, Domi turned away and started walking back to the table. The table she had sent the others to while she'd chased down Mitch.

She wished she hadn't.

Except...

Was he right? Was it better this way?

Hell, if it was going to happen anyway, better sooner than later, right?

That's why she'd broken off their arrangement in the first place. To end things before her emotions got involved.

Too late for that now.

She should have been angry, furious, but she couldn't summon the emotion. She felt like someone had frozen her from the inside out. As she reached the table where her family was sitting, she also realized that wasn't the worst thing in the world. She pasted a smile on her face for Ana and sat down. The other adults looked at her with worried expressions, Rae more so than the others.

"Is everything okay?"

"Yeah, Mitch isn't feeling well," she heard herself say as though from a great distance as though someone else was using her mouth to speak. To smile. She was on autopilot. "Hopefully not something he ate."

They all laughed, Ana a beat later than the others because she didn't actually get the joke, but Rae still looked worried. Thankfully, Marcus and Julia seemed to accept her explanation at face value.

Out of the corner of her eye, she saw Mitch returning to his table, but he didn't sit down. He leaned down and said something to his dad, giving the older man a quick hug, then walked out the front door. He didn't look in her direction. Didn't even glance.

The inside of her chest felt like it was starting to rip open. Her emotions were coming back into focus.

"Mommy?" Ana's voice pushed them down again, leaving her once more in control.

Smiling, she looked down at her daughter. Her joy. Her constant.

"Yes, sweetie?"

"Can I have the ravioli *and* the macaroni and cheese?"

"Sure, baby, it's your birthday," Domi said automatically. "You can have whatever you want."

Ana should have whatever she wanted. One day, she wouldn't be able to have something she wanted. One day, she would want something more than she'd ever wanted anything else in the world, but it wouldn't be within her power to get it. It would have to be given... by someone else. That person might decide not to give it to her. They might run away at the first confrontation, leaving her bereft and hurting.

Until that time, Domi was going to make sure her daughter had any small thing she wanted.

Domi, too. Tonight, she was going to want Rae and Ben and Jerry. First, though, she had to get through this dinner, then get Ana to bed.

"Excuse me." The charming Scottish accent made Domi jerk her head up. Mitch's dad smiled down apologetically at her, holding out his hand, and she automatically took it. This time he didn't shake it, just held her fingers in his warm palm. "I wanted to say it was verra nice to meet you. I upset my son before you came in, and he wasna able to give us a proper introduction, but I can tell he cares about you verra much."

"Thank you," Domi said robotically.

"G'night then." He nodded his head, returning to his table to pick up a to-go bag of food, then following his long-gone son out the door.

Domi realized everyone at her table was staring at her.

"Uh, Domi? Was… is… are you seeing…" Marcus' voice trailed off, and his eyes darted to Ana, who looked concerned but also very confused.

Mother fucker.

"Let's talk about it later, shall we?" She pushed her smile back onto her face, pretending she didn't see the look Marcus and Julia exchanged as she focused back on Ana. "Dinner tonight is all about Miss Birthday Girl here."

"Yay!" Ana beamed at her. "Can I have pudding *and* cake for dessert?"

"Sure," Domi said. She had a feeling she was going to want to binge on her daughter's leftovers later tonight. Ben and Jerry's might not be enough to cut it.

MITCH

After leaving the restaurant, Mitch drove without really thinking about where he was going or even looking at the road. It was a freaking miracle he didn't get into an accident.

Somehow, without thinking about it or meaning to, he ended up at Marquis. There was even a parking space right in front of the building as if it was waiting for him to arrive. Staring blankly at the front of the restaurant, Mitch wasn't sure he really wanted to go in.

On the other hand, he didn't know where else to go and could seriously use a drink. Somewhere to sit. Driving more probably wasn't a good idea.

His stomach rumbled.

Food would be good. He'd left without getting his dinner, unable to stay in the restaurant and around his dad or Domi for one minute more. Food, a drink, and some time and space to think.

To hurt. Fuck. He'd broken up with Domi.

Mitch rubbed his chest, then started moving, getting out of the car, and going into the restaurant. He figured even if his dad came here with Master Patrick and the others, it wouldn't be until later, and hopefully, they'd come in the back door.

Huh. He wondered if Patrick got the idea for Marquis from the Outlands. Mitch had never known Outlands was anything other than a regular restaurant during the day and a dance club at night. The idea seemed horribly possible.

Waving off the hostess, he headed straight for the bar, where there were thankfully still several open seats. Sliding onto one, he waited for the bartender, Shane, to notice him. He was an older gentleman who bartended because he liked it. He'd once told Mitch he enjoyed talking with all the different kinds of people who came by, though he wasn't a fan of Mitch's puns and bad jokes.

Bald with a salt and pepper goatee, broad shoulders, and a permanent half-smile on his face, he had the kind of aura that made people feel immediately comfortable around him. Seeing Mitch sitting down, Shane took one look at his expression and raised one eloquent eyebrow. He didn't even ask what Mitch wanted, just turned around and started mixing.

Staring at the rows of liquor bottles above Shane's head, Mitch wondered when his life had gotten so out of control. Had it been when he couldn't let Domi go the first time she'd tried to end things between them? Had it been halfway through their bondage buddies' arrangement when he hadn't realized he was falling for her? Or was it from the very beginning, when he'd asked her to be his bondage buddy?

A multi-colored drink slid in front of him. Mitch stared at it.

"What is it?"

"Does it matter?" The half-smile on Shane's face lifted slightly, turning a little fuller. "It's a whiskey sour with a little something extra."

Sour was exactly how Mitch felt. He hadn't had one before, but he trusted Shane. The man was a master at mixology, and the few times he'd ignored Mitch's usual preference for beer, he hadn't been wrong.

Lifting the straw to his lips, Mitch took a sip, and flavor burst over his tongue. Sweet, sour, and a bit of a kick that spread warmth through his chest, loosening some of the tension there.

"Damn." Mitch blinked. Shane's smile widened. Lifting the glass in acknowledgment, Mitch took another long drink that emptied half the glass in one go. Shane's smile slipped.

"I'll be right back." Shane stepped away, heading down the bar to someone else who needed his services.

That was fine. Mitch wasn't sure he'd wanted the company, anyway. He was probably better off alone. That was why he'd broken up with Domi tonight, right? Alone. Party of one. The Playboy Dom.

So, why did it hurt so much?

Another long sip of drink. Sure, it had no answers, but it tasted good. All it needed was a little umbrella and a maraschino cherry, and it would be perfect.

A hand landed on his shoulder, making Mitch jump. Turning his head, he met the cool, grey eyes of Mistress Olivia—manager of Marquis, Domme extraordinaire, instructor of all introduction classes, protector of submissives, and ball buster of Doms. Fuck.

He glanced back over to where Shane was standing, pretending to clean glasses behind the bar. Apparently, he'd decided he needed reinforcements.

Sliding onto the barstool next to him, the intimidating redhead gave Mitch a once-over with a scrutinizing eye. Even in a pantsuit rather than her leathers, she was kinda scary. She sent a little finger wave to Shane, who, despite supposedly being completely focused on the glass he was cleaning, stopped what he was doing and went to the fridge to get her a beer.

The second he came over with it, Mitch gave him a dirty look.

"I can't believe you tattled on me to Mommy." Not that Olivia was into that kink, but she kind of was the mom of the clubs.

Shane shrugged. "You looked like you needed more focused help than I can give tonight." A point proven when another patron down the bar clearly needed Shane's attention, and the man had to turn away.

"So..." Olivia took a sip of her beer. "What's up, buttercup? Tell Mommy all about it."

Mitch's lips twitched. He almost smiled—almost—and then did exactly what she'd ordered and told her everything.

CHAPTER TWENTY-ONE

Domi

Rae called an emergency girls' night.

Which really meant asking Marcus and Julia if Ana could go home with them—which they'd readily agreed to. Thankfully, Ana had thought it was a surprise birthday sleepover switch and was thrilled, especially when told she could stay up to watch *Frozen*. Marcus had even hugged Domi and told her he was sorry, and she'd find someone better. Even Julia had hugged Domi—the first time she'd ever done *that*. That was how pathetic Domi looked.

Ana noticed she was off but accepted Domi's explanation that she was sad at how fast her little girl was growing up. Since it wasn't the first time Domi had said it, and it *was* true—seriously, how was she six years old already—it was believable.

She was grateful to Marcus and Julia for stepping up and taking Ana home with them. It wasn't their week, and they didn't fully understand the situation, but they'd said yes as soon as she'd asked. It wasn't as if she was throwing up or anything, the way Julia had been when Domi had done it for them. Nope. All her issues were emotional.

She had let her emotions get involved instead of following her head. Breaking off with Mitch the first time was the right thing to do. Not giving him a chance. Not setting herself up when she'd known, deep down, this was the only possible conclusion for them. Seriously, what had she expected?

That she would live happily-ever-after with a commitment-phobe? She could change her ways and stop being a commitment-phobe? There was a reason she had written off dating, and this was it, right here. She couldn't be a proper mom to her daughter when she was dating. Tonight, she'd handed her kid off to her co-parents. Thank goodness she had those.

Yeah, she would have coped if she didn't, but she'd been relieved they were there. That they could take Ana with them, so she could wallow. What kind of mom did that make her?

"Oh, good, Avery's already here," Rae said as they pulled into their driveway. Avery sat on the front step, a plastic bag in her hand. Her hair was pulled back in its usual ponytail, and she was wearing her Marquis shirt, so she'd probably come straight from her shift.

To Domi's surprise, she was also happy to see their new friend. Normally, it would be her and Rae cursing Mitch's name to the high heavens. She hadn't thought of calling Avery but was glad to see her.

Hey, look at that. She really had made a friend. That was worth celebrating. Maybe she should focus on that instead of all the ways she'd failed.

"I come bearing frozen gifts," Avery said when they got out of the car, standing and holding up the bag. "I wasn't sure what you would like, so I brought options."

"Seriously, anything sounds good right now." It didn't matter that she'd just eaten a huge dinner and dessert and brought home Ana's leftovers, she wanted ice cream. Maybe if she ate enough, her stomach would hurt more than her heart. That had to be an improvement, right?

Avery's face was sympathetic. "That bad, huh?"

She opened her arms and Domi gave her a hug hello, feeling the first prickling of tears in the backs of her eyes. Pulling away before they could move their way forward, she smiled wryly.

"I've had better days."

"Come on, let's go in. I want to know all the details." Rae passed them on her way to the front door, and Domi finally understood why her bestie had let her simmer in silence on the way home rather than demanding to know everything Mitch had said. She'd thought Rae was waiting till they got home, so if she broke down, she could be comforted. That was probably partly why, but this way, she'd get to tell both Rae and Avery at the same time and wouldn't have to repeat herself.

Not even taking the time to change into more comfortable clothes, Domi took one of the ice cream cartons from Avery, a spoon from Rae, and slumped down on the couch to dig in. Her friends sat on either side of her with their own ice cream, eyes on her, patiently waiting. Well, impatiently waiting in Rae's case.

Sighing, Domi stared at her ice cream and told them everything— catching Mitch before he went into the bathroom, what he'd said to her, what she'd said to him, and his final decision to break things off.

"I didn't want to break up, I just wanted to talk... but he wouldn't *listen.*" She stabbed at her ice cream. That had been the worst part. Mitch had always been a good listener, but he'd suddenly shut her out. He hadn't even looked at her the same way. "The asshole. I don't know why I expected anything different from him. He has the emotional capacity of a trash can."

Avery and Rae were silent for a long moment, so Domi looked up, turning her head between the two of them. Wait... was she the asshole?

"He *was* an asshole, right?" she prodded. They were supposed to be supporting her, but she didn't feel very supported.

"Okay, sweetie... tough love or support?" Rae asked. Domi groaned. The only time she and Rae asked each other that question was when one of them thought the other was in the wrong in some way. Domi always made the same choice because she wanted to know... needed to know.

181

"Tough love." She sighed, mentally prepping herself to hear some things she might not want to.

"He was definitely an asshole," Rae said, but Domi knew not to get excited. That was just the buffer before the real talk. "But he had some good points. You really haven't let him into your life in a real way. You never told Marcus and Julia about him, and that was something you always said you'd do if you dated someone."

"If I was serious about them!" Domi protested, then widened her eyes. Shit. She'd walked right into Rae's trap.

"Exactly." Rae pointed her spoon at Domi. "Which implies you weren't that serious about Mitch. You kept him completely separate from other parts of your life. You didn't even tell him it was Ana's birthday. It wasn't like he needed an invitation, but you can't totally separate your life into segregated pieces and expect it to stay together."

Shit. Rae was making sense. Maybe she had been a bit of an asshole, too. She hadn't meant to… thought she was doing the right thing… but… hell, they had gotten serious, hadn't they? Or it would have felt serious if *she* had treated it seriously. She'd done the bare minimum by introducing him to her parents, and half the reason she'd done *that* was to get her mom off her back.

Not exactly epic girlfriend material.

"What do you think?" she asked, turning to Avery, whose eyes widened when Domi put her on the spot. "Don't hold back, I can handle it. I get Rae has a point, but you're… well, you haven't known me as long, so you have more of an objective point of view."

Avery pursed her lips together, thinking for a long moment.

"You said he left the table when you were talking to his dad. Do you think he was upset about you meeting his dad?"

Glancing at Rae, Domi tried to remember. Her bestie shrugged.

"He was definitely off. I'm not sure it had to do with us being there, though," Rae said. "He had a weird expression on his face from the beginning."

"I thought so, too!" Domi shook her head. "I don't know, though. It might have been because Ana went running up to him, and he knew how I felt about them meeting again."

"Or maybe his dad told him something that upset him. You said you followed him, and you wanted him to listen, but, and I mean this in the nicest way possible, did you listen to him?" Avery asked tentatively.

Mitch's voice echoed in her head.

I need a minute, Domi.

She hadn't given him that minute, had she? Whatever had upset him, whatever had sent him running from the table, she didn't know because she hadn't listened to him. Hadn't given him the very first thing he'd asked for. Instead, she'd pushed him when he was already visibly agitated. Demanded he talk to her when he clearly needed some space.

Fuck. *She* was the asshole.

The tears that had been gathering in her eyes spilled over.

"Support now," she choked out as she curled up, crying into her ice cream.

"Oh, honey..."

Arms wrapped around her from both sides, telling her it was all going to be okay, that Mitch had been a total asshole and fuck him, he'd lost the best thing he'd ever had. That only made Domi cry harder because she suspected that she had as well.

MITCH

Expecting to be castigated by the time he was done telling Olivia about how everything had gone down with Domi tonight and what an ass he'd been to her, it was still a relief to get it off his chest. What surprised him was when Olivia didn't immediately tear into him. She was known for being super protective of the submissives, and while some of that had been extended to him, Kincaid, Zach, and Brian after they'd gone through Dom 101 with her, they knew where they ranked.

Tapping her fingers on the bar, she seemed to be gathering her thoughts.

"Your father is Gavin *Craig?*"

"Yes." Mitch sighed. "I lived with my mom after they divorced and took her name. I didn't want anything to do with him for a while after they separated. I hated how he kept stringing her along."

Olivia's fingers tapped on the bar, amping up Mitch's anxiety every tap. He couldn't even begin to guess what she was thinking. Probably about how big a stripe she was going to take off his back. When she began to speak again, it was in a matter-of-fact tone that got straight to the heart of everything.

"So, let me get this straight. You didn't want to become your dad because your parents had an on-again, off-again relationship that was clearly painful for your mom, so you avoided relationships. You thought BDSM would be a magic bullet for that situation because of the relationships you saw around the club, and when you realized you had feelings for Domi, you decided to act on them."

"Pretty much." Man, that sounded stupid when she said it out loud. Didn't it? It had made so much sense in his head. Or maybe he'd wanted Domi so badly, he'd let himself think it made sense. Raising his hand, he caught Shane's eye, silently requesting another drink. The bartender nodded and moved to grab the necessary bottles.

"Tonight, you found out, not only were your parents kinky, but your dad owns a BDSM club, proving kink can't necessarily save a relationship."

"Yup." A sick feeling churned in his stomach. He didn't know what had gone wrong with his parents, but it didn't really matter. Mitch refused to get stuck in their cycle. They loved each other but couldn't let each other go.

He was going to be different. He'd let Domi go. Hell, she was already gone.

The thought was like a physical punch to the gut.

Fuck, that hurt.

Thankfully, Shane was right on time with the medicine to help push the pain away. More sweet and sour, though truthfully, it was getting harder to actually taste it. Just how Mitch wanted it.

"What do you think was your parents' biggest issue?"

"Lack of communication." Mitch snorted. That was easy. Which made even less sense how they could be kinky. BDSM required communication. People seemed to be better at it in the scene. "My dad isn't much of a talker at the best of times, but anything emotional, he locks down tighter than Fort Knox."

"Mmm… and would you say you communicated well with Domi this evening?"

He opened his mouth to say 'of course'—he had told her what she needed to know, what he needed to get her away from him—but something in his brain pinged a warning. Maybe it was the way Olivia was looking at him expectantly or the alcohol lowering his own defensive barriers, but he suddenly wasn't so sure.

They had talked. Domi hadn't listened to him. He'd lashed out at her, pushing her away… and that was it.

That wasn't communication. Not the way he'd been taught by Olivia.

"If you don't want to be your dad, don't be." She patted his shoulder. "Now, let me get you a ride home. I see someone else in need of rescue."

Turning, she gestured at someone in the dining room.

Squinting his eyes to get them to focus, Mitch was shocked when he saw Brian at a table with a bunch of other people. He was sitting between Morgan and another woman, Mitch didn't recognize. Amy, the submissive Zach was always platonically scening with, was across from him. Her back was to Mitch, but he was pretty sure that was her, which meant that must be her fiancé with his arm along the back of her chair. Next to Amy was Carolyn, another submissive from the club, and another man.

"What's going on over there?" he asked. Had Brian told him he had a date tonight? Mitch didn't think so.

Olivia winced.

"Some kind of group date. I told Morgan not to go out on her own at first, though some of the company she chooses is still pretty terrible. Amy's good, though, and she asked Brian to go with Tr—" Olivia coughed, cutting off whatever she'd been about to say. When she spoke again, there was a curious strain in her voice. "With Marissa, so she would have one of you there to watch over her." Hmmm. 'Marissa' didn't start with a 'tr.' Mitch wondered what Olivia had been able to call the woman. Not important right now, though.

"And Morgan needs to be rescued?" She looked as if she was smiling, and besides, she wasn't the one standing up in response to Olivia's summons.

"No, with Marissa as his date, Brian does. Trust me." Olivia's voice was dry. The woman next to Brian looked up and frowned at him as he stood. She was pretty, with pale skin, a thin face, and long hair, and when she looked where Brian pointed—at Mitch and Olivia—she got the oddest expression on her face before she turned away.

"Maybe he's having a good time." It was hard to tell with Brian since he usually had a smile on his face. He liked to keep people happy and take care of them. Which, now that Mitch thought of it, made him a good choice for an impromptu drive home.

"Doubtful." Distaste dripped from Olivia's voice, making Mitch more curious than ever, but he didn't get a chance to ask before Brian reached them.

"You okay, buddy?" Brian asked, putting his hand on Mitch's shoulder and pushing him slightly more upright. He hadn't realized he was slumping.

"He's totally trashed because he made a big mistake. Can you take him home? He has some serious thinking to do." Olivia patted Mitch's shoulder, hopping down from her seat, not waiting for Brian's answer. "I know you'll make the right decision."

Giving them both a finger wave, she walked off.

"You don't have to take me home, I can call a cab or something," Mitch said. "Olivia thought you needed a rescue. I don't think she likes your date."

"Huh. Well, she doesn't have to worry. I'm only here for Morgan. She wanted to try going on a date with a vanilla guy as practice. Next time, maybe I'll see if Kincaid or Zach is available if she's going with this same group of friends. Olivia might have been right about me needing a rescue." Brian slid an arm around Mitch. "Now, let's get you paid up. I can go back and ditch my 'date' and make sure Morgan's okay to get home safely. Then we can head home, and on the way, you can tell me all about what Olivia thinks you fucked up."

"Oh, goody," Mitch muttered.

CHAPTER TWENTY-TWO

Head pounding, mouth like a moldy sock, for some reason, his chest hurt as though someone had wrapped a bunch of iron bands around it and squeezed. It took him a moment to realize it was because he felt like something was missing. Something big he'd gotten used to being there.

Even though he and Domi hadn't had a ton of sleepovers, he'd thought there would be more. Now there wouldn't be. That was what he felt—the absence of her in his life.

He stared up at the ceiling.

A knock on his bedroom door made him jerk with surprise, but the movement was slower than normal, as if he was trying to swim through thick air.

"Mitch, you up yet?" Brian's voice was muffled through the door. Oh, right, Brian had taken him home last night.

"Yeah." At least, that was what he tried to say. It came out sounding more like "blegh." His tongue felt swollen, and it wasn't working correctly. Clearing his throat, he swallowed and tried again. "Yeah. Getting up."

"Okay, breakfast is ready, and coffee's waiting."

Coffee.

Driven by that one word, Mitch forced his body to start moving. Coffee might not fix everything, but it would help his brain work, and right now, that would be a massive improvement. Last night, Brian helped him get down to his boxers so he could sleep. All he had to do was grab a pair of sweatpants, and he was good to go. Not that Brian would have cared, seeing him in his underwear again, but Mitch would feel weird if Brian was fully dressed.

The sound of multiple voices, speaking in low tones, didn't register until he reached the kitchen.

"What are they doing here?" he asked Brian, staring blankly at Zach and Kincaid sitting at his kitchen table, eating what looked like fast-food breakfast sandwiches. His stomach rumbled in anticipation of grease.

"After last night, I figured I needed reinforcements," Brian admitted, sitting down on the chair next to Kincaid. "You were pretty fucked up."

Yeah. He should probably stop drinking when he was upset. It wasn't healthy. Especially since he'd started off alone.

"Come eat. We picked up breakfast," Kincaid said, prodding Mitch into motion. "Brian updated us on most of it."

Oh, good, he didn't have to relive his heartbreak first thing in the morning while suffering from a hangover.

Heartbreak?

Yeah.

"Shouldn't you all be at work?" he muttered, sitting down.

"My shift doesn't start for another couple of hours," Kincaid said calmly.

"Working from home today." Zach's smile was almost sadistic. Bastard.

"Told them I'd be in late this morning due to a family emergency," Brian said.

A little ball of warmth took root in Mitch's chest. His parents might be fucked up, and they'd never given him siblings—which he'd been both grateful and disappointed about at various times throughout his life—but Brian was right… they were family. If he could choose his own brothers, he'd choose these guys right here.

Proven by the fact they were here for him right now.

"Do you have to work today?" Brian asked.

"Yeah, but not until tonight." Mitch took a long drink of his coffee, which was just barely cool enough. The hot liquid helped clear away some of the fuzziness inside his mouth, and he could almost feel the caffeine hitting his system, helping wake him up.

To his relief, the guys didn't seem intent on hounding him over breakfast. Zach and Kincaid wanted to know about Brian's date last night, especially about how well Morgan had handled it and what he'd thought of the guy. Once they'd been reassured everything had gone well on that front, they wanted to know more about the woman Brian had been with.

"Marissa?" Kincaid cocked his head. "I think I've heard that name before."

"Olivia didn't like her," Mitch said suddenly, interrupting the conversation. He'd been listening but not participating, which wasn't like him, but the guys rolled with it. "I think she almost called her a name at one point."

"Really?" Brian blinked in surprise, his brow furrowing. Both Kincaid and Zach had similar reactions. Olivia didn't like everyone, but it was rare she actively disliked someone. They'd had a total misogynist asshole in their Dom class. Olivia had been perfectly civil to him until she'd kicked him out. "She seemed nice enough."

"Do you think you'll see her again?" Mitch was genuinely curious.

"No chemistry." Brian shrugged. He looked between Zach and Kincaid. "If Morgan wants to go on more group dates with them, and Marissa needs a date, we should probably switch off. I wouldn't want to lead her on."

"What about me?" Mitch asked, frowning. Not because he *wanted* to date someone other than Domi, but he didn't like the feeling of being left out, and he *wasn't* dating Domi anymore. Looking out for Morgan would give him something to focus on.

Three pairs of eyes bore into him.

"Aren't you going to try to get back together with Domi?" Zach asked the question, but it was on all of their faces.

Yes!

The little part of his brain that reacted wanted nothing more... but... was this how it started? Was this how his parents had begun? Knowing they should stay away, but always giving in to the impulse to be together again?

Mitch knew Olivia thought he'd made a mistake dumping Domi. He had a feeling she meant for him to try to win Domi back, then stick with it. She'd been right when she'd told him it was easy not to be his dad—he had to do what his dad had never done and stay away from Domi.

"I don't think so," he said finally, looking down at the breakfast sandwich in front of him. The tight bands around his chest squeezed hard. "It's better this way."

"If you say so," Brian said doubtfully. Kincaid patted Mitch's shoulder. He could tell none of them agreed with him, but they'd support whatever decision he made, which meant the world to him.

DOMI

Staring at the numbers until they started swimming in front of her eyes, Domi finally slammed her laptop shut. She couldn't concentrate, and that meant she couldn't work. A mistake on her part could cost thousands of dollars, even tens of thousands.

She needed to finish her work, but she couldn't do it when all she could think about was Mitch. Who hadn't called... or texted.

Not that she had done either.

She shouldn't... right? He'd broken up with her, so he had to reach out first, right?

Though she supposed, she could reach out and apologize for not listening to him, for not giving him space when he'd told her what he needed. Not with the intention of getting back together, even though part of her wanted to, but she did owe him an apology. She could check in on him, make sure he was okay. Maybe find out what had set him off in the first place.

Argh.

This was madness.

Clearly, Ben and Jerry, though they'd tried their best, hadn't cut it. She needed her *real* comfort food.

Abandoning her laptop and work, Domi headed for the kitchen. Cooking would help her get her head on straight anyway. Even if it didn't, the end result would be worth it.

When Rae got home a few hours later, she came straight into the kitchen, following her nose.

"Oooh, honey..." Rae's voice trailed off as she put her purse down, looking around at the array of food. Ana would be excited when she got home. Domi didn't often take the time to make Puerto Rican food. It was usually a special treat, or they went to a restaurant. Ana also wouldn't realize what it meant, but Rae definitely did.

Using the back of her arm to wipe the sweat off of her forehead, Domi looked around. Maybe it had gotten a little out of hand. She'd ended up running to two different stores to get everything she needed —the first store hadn't had quite enough plantains for both the *mofongo* and the *tostones*.

"I couldn't concentrate on work," Domi said, wringing her hands.

"It smells amazing. Ana will be thrilled. It's been months since you made *tostones*."

"I made *alcapurrias*, too."

Rae's eyes lit up. Those were *her* favorite. What Domi really wanted was the Asopao de pollo she'd made. Once she got the idea in her head, she wanted the food her mom made her when she was a kid, suffering some kind of disappointment, she hadn't been able to let it go. Which actually reminded her of her mom. It was never enough to make one thing—she had to make a whole feast.

"Too bad Avery has to work. I bet she'd love this."

"I can set some aside for her. There's plenty." That was an understatement. There was enough for ten people. They'd be eating leftovers for days.

The thought made her sad but relieved. She didn't want to feel like she needed comfort food for days, but she was relieved it was going to be there since she was probably going to need it.

Stupid Mitch. Stupid her. She couldn't help but wonder, what would have happened if she hadn't pushed him? What if she'd let him retreat and have his minute instead of pushing things? Would he have still ended things? Would they have been able to talk and work through it?

Was it too late?

Arms wrapped around her, squeezing her tight.

"It'll be okay," Rae whispered in her ear. Squirming around, Domi hugged her bestie back, thankful she had Rae. Sometimes, she thought Rae might be her real soul mate. Not in the romantic way. Platonic soulmates. Sisters by love, rather than by blood.

"I know," Domi replied. It might not feel like it right now, but eventually, it would be. Though she didn't think she'd be exploring dating again any time soon.

MITCH

After his friends left, Mitch sat on the couch, wondering if it would do him more harm than good to take a nap. Maybe he should go in early and see if he could get a Vitamin IV. It wasn't a 'cure' as such, but it sure helped speed up the recovery time and would make him feel less nauseous. The grease from breakfast had helped a little, but his gut still felt all twisty and unsettled.

Maybe that's because you know you fucked up, and it has nothing to do with all the alcohol.

Thanks, brain.

That was exactly his fear.

As if to punctuate his misery, Darth Vader's theme began playing on his phone. Mitch groaned. The temptation to let it go to voicemail was strong, but... he had some questions only his dad could answer.

"Hey." With only a single word, he sounded tired.

"Hey." His dad was quiet for a long moment. Mitch was too tired to try to think of something to say, so he waited for his dad to say something. "I ah... I'm sorry about last night. I didn't mean to make you uncomfortable."

"It wasn't that. I mean... it was... but..." Mitch scrubbed his face. "I really don't want to know about your and mom's sex life, but that wasn't why I left."

"Ah." Another moment of silence, though this one didn't last quite as long. "Was it the lass? She seemed verra nice. Unhappy after you left, though."

"What did you say to her?" The words came out sharper than he intended, but there was also a weird little feeling of... craving? He wanted to know what she had done. If she'd been okay.

"Told her it was nice to meet her, and it was my fault you were upset. I hope that was all right." His father's voice turned a little quieter than usual. Mitch blew out a long breath. Could have been worse. Could have been better.

"That's fine. What did she say?"

"Thank you."

It took Mitch a moment to realize that was what Domi had said. Sounded like her. Polite even when she was upset. Holding it all inside. She held far too many things inside. Which was why she loved scening and was always lighter afterward.

"Did the two of you have a tiff? Do you want to talk about it?" The oddly hesitant way his dad asked brought Mitch out of his reverie and made him blink. These weren't the kind of conversations he and his dad had. They didn't talk about feelings or what had happened. That was his mom's arena. When his dad asked how he was, Mitch knew he wasn't really asking, but this... this was a clear offering for something more.

"Are *you* okay?" he asked, some of his sense of humor trickling back in. "Who is this? Did the aliens finally get you? Tell me your D&D alignment, so I know it's really you."

His dad snorted.

"Still lawful neutral, lad. I've been..." His voice trailed off, and he cleared his throat uncomfortably, his brogue thickening as it always did when he was emotional. "I've been seeing a therapist."

"Okay, well, the first answer was right, but..." If Mitch hadn't already been sitting down, he probably would have fallen to the floor in shock. He couldn't count the number of times his mom had begged his dad to go to couples' therapy, but his dad always scoffed at the idea. "Are you going with Mom?"

"By myself, for now. Eventually, I'd like to go with her. If she'll have me."

Holy shit. His dad sounded uncertain. His dad never sounded uncertain.

"What brought this on?"

"A gentleman and his wife came to Outlands this past fall to reconnect. Got me thinking..." There was a wistfulness to his dad's voice, shocking Mitch even further. His dad was never this open with his emotions. "I never stopped loving your mom, lad. I just wasn't very good at showing her that. While there was one place, we *could* communicate—"

"Don't wanna hear about that," Mitch murmured, making his dad chuckle. Another shocker. Man, his father really was loosening up in his old age or maybe thanks to the therapist.

"I didn't try outside of that. I thought as long as we had it, that was all that mattered. I didn't take the time to listen to what she was saying or wanted from me. I didn't give her the little things she asked for. I didn't think it should be necessary. We loved each other, and that shoulda been enough, right?" His short, sharp bark of laughter held no humor. "But tis not. I should have chased after her every time we argued. Talked through it. Got to the root of why she was angry instead of focusing on the single incident that set her off and got me going my merry way. Apologized where I was wrong and made it up to her."

"You apologized a lot." That was something Mitch definitely remembered. He always knew when his dad had fucked up.

"Nah, I made excuses. I didn't actually apologize. I sure as hell didna change." His brogue had thickened with emotion.

"Do you think you can now?" The question was as much about being a protective son, worried his mom might get hurt again as it was for himself.

"I can try. I want to. So, I hope this old dog can learn some new tricks and impress your ma." There was another small moment of silence. "What about you and this lass, son? I could tell she means something to you, or you wouldn't have been so upset."

To Mitch's surprise, he found himself telling his dad everything. Unlike with Olivia, where it was more a purge of negativity or his friends when he'd been torn between anger and frustration, now he was just sad. He'd liked having Domi in his life. Hell, he'd been falling in love with her.

Did he love her?

Hell, he didn't know. If he didn't, it was something close.

When he got to the end of it, telling his dad what had happened last night in the hallway to the bathroom, his dad was quiet for a moment. Mitch hadn't spared him. He hoped he hadn't hurt his dad's feelings, but it had also been a chance to let his dad know how Mitch had felt seeing his parents' back and forth over the years while the man was actually listening.

"Your Olivia is right. Terrifying woman, by the way. I met her last night. Your ma would like her. If you don't want to be me, don't be. I never chased after your ma the way I should have. I was too high in my pride, too afraid she'd reject me. I always waited for a sign from her. Then once I had her again, I took her for granted, thinking she'd always come back... Now, it might be too late, but for the first time, I'm going to try."

The determination in his voice was encouraging, and for the first time, Mitch found himself hoping his dad could actually do it and make his mom happy.

"Don't make the same mistakes I did. Go after your lass. Apologize. Listen. Show her what she means to you. And don't try to keep all the communication confined to the scene. That's no way to run a relationship."

Hell, his dad was right. Last night, he'd done exactly what his dad had always done to his mom—run away without talking, made a unilateral decision about their relationship for both of them. Not because it was what he wanted, but from a place of fear and pride.

"Thanks, Dad," he said, meaning it.

"Any time, laddie." The warmth in his dad's voice seeped into his chest, giving him a bit more courage. "I'm proud of you, Son. Even if she turns you away, at least you'll know you tried."

Yeah, but he really hoped she didn't turn him away.

CHAPTER TWENTY-THREE

Domi

The entire house smelled like her childhood, even though dinner had been over hours ago, and Ana was long in bed. It smelled delicious but unusual enough to be a reminder of why it smelled that way. She wished she could pretend it was just one of those days when she got a hankering or had planned out a menu to share with Ana and Rae. She'd cooked what her heart had needed because it had been hurt. Bruised. *Broken.*

Ana had been excited about the elaborate dinner and thought it was a special birthday surprise for her. Which was what it should have been if Domi had thought of it.

"Hey, stop it." Rae poked her in the side, hard.

"Ow! I wasn't doing anything!"

"Yes, you were. You had your 'guilt' face on, which means you're thinking about something you think you did wrong. Probably something that wasn't your fault, or the only person who thinks it would be a big deal is you."

Domi rubbed her side, scowling. "I was just thinking tonight should have been a special dinner for Ana and wishing it hadn't been a wallowing dinner."

"And feeling guilty you hadn't thought about making her a special birthday dinner, even though we took her out last night, right?" Rae asked dryly. Dammit. They really did know each other too well sometimes.

"Shut up. What are you doing?" she asked, leaning over. Rae had been scrolling through something on her laptop for the past few minutes, but now that Domi actually looked at it, she could tell it wasn't social media. When Rae immediately tried to shift the screen away so Domi couldn't see, it made her even more curious. "What is that?"

"Nothing." Rae's shoulders hunched defensively. "I mean… it's a website. A blog."

"Yeah, what's the blog about?" Domi reached for the laptop again. "Does that say self-publishing?"

"Maybe. Yes."

"You're finally going to do it?" Domi squealed, clapping her hands together.

"I'm *thinking* about it. Maybe. I'm looking at what's involved *if* I decide to do it."

That was more than she'd been willing to do in the past. Domi knew Rae would eventually end up giving in. She was going to make sure of it. Rae was a great accountant, but it wasn't her passion. At the very least, she could do *both* things. She was always afraid of putting her work out there, afraid of failing, but Domi believed in her.

"Do it, do it, do it," she whisper-chanted, making Rae giggle. They both froze when Domi's phone went off with the unique text message sound she'd assigned to Mitch. Slowly turning her head, Domi looked where her phone lay on the coffee table as if it was a snake about to strike. It laid there, quiet and still, totally innocent looking.

"Are you going to pick it up?" Rae asked. "I can read it first if you want."

No. That was the coward's way out. Which was probably why part of her wanted to ask Rae to do it, but she should look.

"We can do it together." Picking up the phone, she leaned back against the couch, Rae setting the laptop aside so she could move right next to Domi and see the phone's screen. Domi's stomach twisted with a nauseating combination of hope and anxiety, but with Rae's comforting presence snuggled up against her, she made herself turn on the phone and check the text.

Hey, Domi, I'm sorry about last night. It was a bad night and a bad time, and I took it out on you when I shouldn't have. Can we get together and talk?

"Oooh... that's a pretty good apology," Rae murmured. "Do you think he wants to get together, so he can try to get *back* together?"

"I don't know." Domi chewed her lower lip, conflicted. Part of her was jumping for joy, he'd finally reached out, but another part of her worried he wanted to get together to apologize, then explain more about why he'd dumped her... and she'd remained dumped. "I hate it when someone says they want to 'talk.'"

"Kind of hard to have an in-depth conversation over text message," Rae pointed out, turning over to reach for her own phone.

"What are you doing?"

"Calling Avery. She should get the latest update." Rae pressed the screen and put it on speaker, so Domi could hear the phone ringing.

Shaking her head, Domi stared back at her own phone, trying to interpret the few words on the screen. Why hadn't he called? Did he not want to hear her voice? Was he trying to respect, she might not want to hear his? Was he trying to manipulate her into actually seeing him if she wanted to talk?

"Hello?" Avery whispered into the phone. "What's up? It's almost the end of my shift, but it's still busy, so I only have a few minutes. Is Domi okay?"

"I'm here, I'm okay," Domi said. "Mitch sent me a text message." She repeated it for Avery.

"That's a pretty good apology." Like Rae, Avery sounded fairly impressed. "Are you going to meet him?"

"That's what we're trying to figure out," Rae told her. Turning to Domi, she lifted her eyebrows, holding the phone between them, so Avery would be able to hear them both. "Do you want to meet him?"

Shit. Yeah. She did.

"Yeah," she sighed. "If only to find out what was going on that he acted like that."

"Curiosity killed the cat," Avery said, but the warning in her tone was playful.

"And satisfaction brought it back." Rae grinned, finishing the saying. It was one she often corrected people on, probably because she'd heard it so often. Rae was always curious. "Do you want to get back together with him?"

Yes! That was the part of her brain that got her into this in the first place, but this time, Domi wasn't jumping ahead to listen to that part of her brain so quickly.

"I guess it depends on what he has to say." She pressed her lips together. "I can't meet him till this weekend at the earliest. Ana doesn't go over to Marcus' till Saturday morning."

"Oooh, come to Marquis for brunch," Avery said immediately. "I can make sure you're seated near the back hall, and Rae and I can listen in. You know, in case you need moral support. He won't even know we're there."

"Yes." Rae nodded decisively, making Domi snort. Of course, she'd like that idea. "Do that."

It wasn't the worst idea. That way, if Mitch crushed her again, her friends would be right there.

"Okay, fine. I'll tell him Saturday at eleven at Marquis..." Her fingers were already moving to reply when they heard a man's voice bark out Avery's name.

"Avery! What are you doing?"

"Taking a smoke break," Avery yelled back at him. Her voice was slightly muffled when she whispered into the phone. "Oops, gotta go."

"You don't smoke."

"Then I'm taking an air break. Chill out, Nick." The line cut out, leaving both Domi and Rae hanging.

They looked at each other.

"Did not expect her to be a brat," Domi said before returning her attention back to her phone.

"Maybe he brings it out in her," Rae suggested, dragging her laptop back atop her thighs and giving Domi an idea.

"You know, I'm thinking maybe I gave in a little too quickly," Domi said, putting down her phone without sending the message. "How about... I'll meet with Mitch on Saturday at Marquis if *you* self-publish a book."

"What if I don't care if you meet up with Mitch?" Rae asked, crossing her arms over her chest, her expression even more stubborn than usual.

"Oh, no, I'll still meet up with him, but not at Marquis, where you'll have Avery to help you overhear everything. I'll go somewhere you have to watch from a distance and guess what's going on."

"Oh, you're good," Rae muttered, frowning down at her laptop. She stared at it for a long moment before shaking her head. "Okay, fine." She moved the mouse and clicked. "Done."

Domi blinked. "Wait, seriously?"

"I've had it set up for about two weeks now, I just hadn't pressed publish," Rae admitted sheepishly.

"What?! Rae, that's amazing!" Domi was about to throw her hands up in the air and hug her friend when Rae pointed at her.

"Set up your date with Mitch, then celebrate with me."

Sighing, Domi settled back down into her spot and pressed the send button.

"It's not a date." She tossed her phone back onto the coffee table and tackle hugged her bestie. "I'm so proud of you!"

Hell, if Rae could do something as scary as finally self-publishing her work, Domi could have brunch with the guy who had broken her heart.

MITCH

Nervous as hell, Mitch waited in the booth the hostess had escorted him to. He was fifteen minutes early and extremely uncomfortable. Suits weren't his thing. He'd actually had Zach and Kincaid go shopping with him last night, which was crazy but... he was feeling a little crazy.

After talking to his dad, Mitch realized he was right. He had to do something his dad would never do. At least, his dad never would have done in the past, though he might now.

Reach out.

Talk.

Grand gesture.

Still working on that last one, but Mitch had watched enough romance movies with his mom to know he was going to have to do something big to make it up to Domi—something that wasn't flowers. The new suit was part of that gesture, though it wasn't exactly grand, more like uncomfortable. At least Zach had let him get away with not wearing a tie or a vest. Zach's personal style was a little too GQ for Mitch.

He did look damn good today, though, in a grey suit that fit his shoulders and a button-down blue shirt exactly matching the color of his eyes. He'd wanted to dress up a little, so it wasn't only his words showing Domi he was serious, but he *looked* like he was taking this seriously.

Never taking his eyes off the door, he saw her the moment she walked in and jumped to his feet. To his surprise, Rae wasn't with her. He'd figured he'd be facing both of them together.

Wearing black pants, a red shirt, with her makeup and hair done—though not as dark as she would for Stronghold—Mitch knew she hadn't dressed up for him. She'd dressed up for herself. This was Domi with all her armor on, and it made his chest ache. She looked beautiful but distant, without her usual warmth.

Part of him wanted to pull back, to hide his own emotions... but that's what he'd done wrong before. He'd held back without realizing it, thinking everything would fall into place, *then* he could be all in. But that wasn't how it worked.

After Wednesday night, Domi had good reason to fear being hurt, to hold back. If Mitch was going to show her, she didn't need to be, he was going to have to give her a little more of himself.

The hostess waved her over, and Domi's eyes widened when she saw him, her gaze flicking over his body. Appreciation glimmered in her expression before she hid it. Mitch preened.

Yeah, she liked the suit.

"Domi," he said by way of greeting when she reached him, holding out his hand to help her into the booth.

"Mitch." Her tone was a little terse, but she took his hand and let him help her sit down.

"I haven't been here for brunch." Sitting across from her, studying her expression, he tried to get a feel for where she was mentally and got the impression, she was extremely guarded. He couldn't really blame her. He was a little envious, in fact. Right now, he felt very exposed and not in a fun, sexy way.

"Me, either, but I heard it's good." She didn't look at her menu, warily keeping her eyes on him.

Their server came by to get their drink order, and Mitch ordered coffee, while Domi opted for an espresso. She still didn't look at her menu, which was making him nervous. Wasn't she planning on staying to eat?

"Yeah, the menu looks good," he hinted, nodding to where she had her arms crossed over hers. Her plump lips twisted.

"Why don't you tell me why you wanted to meet, and I'll decide whether or not I should bother looking at the menu." Her tone was tart, but there was something in her eyes—Mitch couldn't define exactly what—gave him the tiniest bit of hope.

CHAPTER TWENTY-FOUR

<u>*DOMI*</u>

Damn him for looking so good.

Mitch in a regular shirt? Hot. Mitch in Dom leathers? Sexy as hell. Mitch naked? Total eye candy.

Mitch all dressed up in a suit with a shirt that matched his eyes exactly?

Devastating.

It was all she could do to keep from throwing herself at him. Which was why she hadn't managed to get an apology out yet, even though she knew she owed him one. The suit had thrown her. Knowing her attraction to him hadn't diminished in the slightest— even though she'd cried before going to bed the past few nights— made her defensive. How had he managed to get so far under her skin?

"I wanted to apologize," he said, becoming more serious at her question. There was something different about him today. Not just the suit. She couldn't put her finger on exactly what, but there was definitely something. "On Wednesday... well, my dad and I don't have the best relationship. I've told you about him and my mom's relationship." Domi nodded. "My dad owns a bar that's also a nightclub up in Pittsburgh, the Outlands. He told me he was down here for business, to talk to another owner to get ideas for expanding the Outlands. Right before you came into the restaurant, he told me the club he was visiting down here is Stronghold."

"Oh my God." Domi's hands flew to cover her mouth, her reaction torn between horror and hilarity as the implications sank in.

"Yeah." Mitch's lips twitched with his usual good humor, sparkle beginning to shine in his eyes. "My dad owns a kink club, and I never knew."

"Oh my God," Domi repeated, starting to laugh. "I can so see that. The Outlands... is that like an Outlander reference?" That would make some sense since his dad was Scottish.

"No, it's a Dungeons and Dragons reference. My parents are massive nerds." Mitch cleared his throat, pausing as the server returned with their drinks and asked if they were ready to order. After telling her they needed a few more minutes, Mitch took a sip of his coffee and continued, fingers twiddling with the napkin in front of him. "Anyway. When we started seeing each other, I thought BDSM would make the big difference, guarantee we wouldn't have the same kinds of issues."

"Oh, Mitch." She reached out to put her hand atop his where he was fidgeting with the napkin. "There are no guarantees in life."

"I know, but I don't do well with uncertainty. Especially not after watching my parents go back and forth and never knowing when they'd end up seeing each other on the sly again." He gave her a wry smile, his fingers trapping hers. Domi could have pulled her hand back, but it felt too nice to be touching him again, even in a small way. "So, on top of finding out what my parents get up to in their free time, suddenly wasn't sure what that meant for us. Then you walked in, and it was the worst possible time. I already needed to get away from my dad and think for a minute, but then I couldn't, and yeah..."

"I owe you an apology, too," she said, a sense of relief flooding through her saying the words. "I shouldn't have chased after you, but even after I did, when you asked for space, I should have respected that. I wanted to make you listen so badly, but I wasn't listening to you."

Mitch tightened his grip on her fingers, his blue eyes boring into hers.

"I want to try again, Domi Darling," he said softly. "Not to be like my parents, but because I *don't* want to be like my dad. I want to give us a real shot. I don't want to hold back. I... fuck. The past few days have sucked. I miss you all the time. I hate not hearing your voice at the end of the day. I hate being apart from you."

Tears started forming in her eyes, and Domi blinked rapidly. She'd worn her waterproof mascara, just in case, but that didn't mean she actually wanted to cry. A little ball of unhappiness curled in her chest, pressing down like it was actually trying to crush her heart.

As much as part of her wanted what he was offering, as much as she wanted to try again...

She pulled her hand away.

"I don't know if that's a good idea," she said slowly. Mitch's face fell, which made the ball of unhappiness inside her grow. She felt like the Grinch, with her heart three sizes too small and shrinking. "Like I said, there are no guarantees in life, and... the past few days *have* been awful. I missed you, and it hurt being without you, but there was a part of me also relieved I'd kept my life separate. I have Ana, and even though I felt like half my life was falling apart, *her* life was unaffected. I think... I think you were right, and it's better we end this before we get more involved."

Seeing the hurt, the disappointment on his face was too much for her. She shoved out of the booth as quickly as she could, espresso untouched, and headed for the door, tears already blurring her eyes. This felt even worse than Wednesday. It felt so final.

Turn around! Go back! Part of her head screamed.

Yeah, she was a masochist, but not for this kind of pain.

MITCH

Staring dumbfounded after Domi, it felt like his insides were cracking open, and there was nothing but ice inside. She was walking away. Maybe it was for the best?

No.

Do something, you stupid fool.

Grand gesture.

Tell her how you feel.

What do you have to lose?

Domi. Domi was what he had to lose.

That meant he had *everything* to lose if he stayed silent. In the face of that, what was his dignity worth?

He would hate himself forever if he didn't at least try.

Scrambling onto the booth, Mitch stepped onto the table, barely aware of the clatter of silverware or the coffee that sloshed over his shoe.

"Dominique Ortiz!" Shit. That came out even louder than he'd intended, but Domi whirled around and gasped when she saw him. The restaurant had fallen silent, everyone staring at the crazy man standing on a table in the middle of brunch. If she walked away now, everyone would see her reject him, but it didn't matter.

It was time to face his fears, to *show* Domi he was willing to put it all out there for her.

To tell her the full truth because even now, he'd been holding back, unwilling to make the declaration when he hadn't been sure how she would react... if she would reciprocate.

"If you don't have feelings for me, if you don't think you could fall in love with me, given the chance, then walk away now. I'll let you go. I won't bother you about this again. But if you're only walking away because you're scared, because you have the feelings, but you're afraid to act on them, I know how that feels. Because I love you, Domi."

Her mouth dropped open, but no noise came out. It felt as if the entire world had come to a halt. There was no noise, no movement, everyone in the restaurant staring at him while he made a complete and utter fool of himself—and it didn't matter.

None of it mattered except Domi.

"I've been in love with you for weeks, but I couldn't admit it, not even to myself. I tried so hard not to be like my dad, but I became exactly like him. I can't fix what I've already done, but I know he would have never done *this*. He would have never made himself this vulnerable." She was still standing there, staring at him without reacting. Fuck. Maybe he needed to let her go. "So, it's okay if you don't love me back… I just… I just needed to try." He dropped his hands, feeling increasingly foolish.

The whole room waited with bated breath. They'd stopped watching him and were now watching Domi, waiting to see what she said. If she'd walk away from him now.

Maybe he should get off the table.

"Be like the girl from *Transformers*! Get in the car!" a woman shouted from the other side of the room.

Domi's head whipped around, her nose wrinkling in confusion. "What?"

The dark-haired man sitting next to the woman who had called out had put his hand over her mouth, and Mitch had a jolt of surprise. That was Master Justin and Jessica. The third part of their triad was sitting across from them. Master Chris caught Mitch's eye and gave him a thumbs-up, then jerked his finger back at Domi.

Oh, right.

Because he was as big a nerd as his dad, he knew exactly what Jessica was talking about, and fuck, it made sense.

Looking back at Domi, he held out his hand in front of him, beckoning, hoping she could come take it.

"In the *Transformers* movie, one of the main characters hesitates to get into the Transformer when it's a car. The guy asks her, won't she always wonder what it would have been like if she'd gotten into the car. I know I'll always wonder, Domi." She took a step closer to him. "You're right. There are no guarantees, but there are missed chances." Another step. Then another. "I love you, Domi. I don't want to miss my chance." She was almost to him, eyes shining with tears.

Her hand reached out, and Mitch crouched down so her fingers could touch his.

"I think... I love you too, Mitch."

The entire room exploded in applause. Mitch grinned, grabbing her hand and pulling her onto the table with him. She squeaked in surprise but went willingly, then laughed against his lips as he kissed her with all the relief, love, and joy threatening to explode his heart. Kissing him back, she wrapped her arms around his neck, clinging to him, and he could feel the wetness from the tears on her cheeks, could—

"Mother fucker!" He jerked away from the kiss, jumping in place, one small spot on his ass burning from a fiery sting that felt exactly like...

Mistress Olivia glared up at him, tapping her crop threateningly against her hand.

"Get. Off. My. Table. Now."

Whoops.

Cheekily, Mitch saluted her, pretending his ass didn't have a spot that felt as if it had been stung by a bee, and jumped down before helping Domi down. Olivia watched them with narrowed eyes, looking as though she wanted to hit him with the crop again.

"No standing on tables in my restaurant." She pointed the crop at him threateningly and dropped it after he and Domi nodded their agreement. Behind Olivia, her boyfriend Luke—and one of the actual owners of the restaurant—was at the bar cracking up. She gave Mitch a terse smile. "Good job on making the right decision, though."

Resting her crop against her shoulder like it was a bat, Olivia sauntered away, causing quite a few whispers throughout the rest of the restaurant. No one said anything directly to her. Past her and Luke, at the end of the bar, Mitch could see the door to the kitchen was wide open, and people were watching from in there as well. He hoped they'd enjoyed the show.

As Olivia moved away, Rae and Avery came rushing out of the hallway next to the booth where he and Domi were sitting, and Mitch blinked in surprise. Had they been there the whole time?

"Holy shit, that was amazing!" Rae slammed into him, wrapping her arms around him in a massive hug. Mitch did his best to hug her back, although he refused to let go of Domi's hand, so it was a one-armed effort. "I was cheering for you the whole time." She suddenly pulled back, glaring up at him. "But don't you ever hurt Domi again."

"I'll do my best not to."

"Do better than that."

Chuckling, Mitch squeezed Domi's fingers as Rae pulled away from him, looking between her and Avery. He should have known Domi wouldn't show up undefended. Avery grinned at him. She might not be as exuberant as Rae, but she clearly approved.

"Do you two want to join us?" There was plenty of room in the curved booth for all four of them.

"Yes, please, I'm starving," Rae said, already moving to sit before Domi could protest.

"Hey! This is my date!"

Chuckling, Mitch dropped a kiss to the top of Domi's head.

"I'll take you on a real date," he promised. "Soon."

"Will you wear the suit?" she asked.

"Absolutely."

"Fine." She said, sighing and letting him scoot her into the booth.

Domi

Was she making the right decision?

She had no idea.

But sitting next to Mitch, tucked under his arm, with her friends, felt a hell of a lot better than walking toward the door had.

There were no guarantees, but he was right... that didn't mean something wasn't worth trying.

And she was in love with him.

That was no small thing. Maybe it was stupid, but seeing him willing to make a fool out of himself—not in the usual Mitch-way, goofing off to try to make people laugh—literally putting himself out there where everyone could hear him and watch him be rejected... It had made her realize how cowardly she was being. How few risks she was willing to take, even when she'd thought she was giving him a real chance.

They still had some work to do, but she was determined to try in a way she hadn't before. It seemed he was as well, so she needed to meet him halfway.

The server came by with napkins, and Mitch helped her clean up the mess he'd made when he'd jumped on the table. They all ordered some more drinks—as well as asked for menus for Rae and Avery, not that Avery needed one. The server clearly recognized her and hurried away even faster than she'd been moving.

Domi was looking over the menu, enjoying being snuggled next to Mitch for the first time in days, when a handsome man in a chef coat stormed up to the table and glared at Avery—dark hair, blue eyes, and seriously hot, even though he looked ticked off. He planted his hands on his hips, and Domi totally got a yummy Dom vibe from him. She could understand why Avery was attracted, even if he wasn't in the lifestyle.

"Why didn't you tell me you were eating here this morning?" It wasn't a question but a demand for information directed straight at Avery, who looked taken aback.

"I didn't know I needed to tell you all my meal plans," she responded dryly.

Nick scowled.

"Only when you're going to eat here." He reached out, snatching the menus from their hands. Domi was so surprised, she let him without a fight. Even Mitch surrendered quickly. "I'll send food out." Without even saying goodbye, he stormed off again.

They all looked at Avery, who covered her face with her hands and groaned.

"There is seriously something wrong with me that I found that hot," she said.

"No, no, it was hot," Domi reassured her. Mock growling, Mitch snuggled her closer and nipped her ear, sending a flash of heat through her. She turned her head toward him, patting his thigh reassuringly. "Don't worry, you're hotter."

"Damn right." Mitch nodded decisively, making all of them laugh.

Was there a part of her still worried? Of course, but... maybe it was all going to be okay.

CHAPTER TWENTY-FIVE

Domi

Holding the phone in place with her shoulder, she finished her explanation to Marcus.

"So, you want him to come to dinner on Wednesday?" he asked, sounding a little dubious. She supposed it did sound a bit weird when she left out all the kinky sex stuff.

"Yes. Or a Wednesday when he can. Sometimes, he has to work evening shifts." Why did that still feel so hard to say? Maybe because Marcus' approval meant something. Yeah, her parents' approval had meant something, but her *mami* wasn't very picky at this point, and they were far away. She had to deal with Marcus every week and finally realized part of the reason she'd wanted to keep Mitch and Ana separate had been because she'd been scared to have this conversation with Marcus.

Scared if he didn't approve of the guy she was dating, it would upset the balance of their co-parenting or worse, even cause custody issues. Even though she hadn't had any reason to think Marcus would be a hardass about her dating or introducing a guy she was serious about to Ana, she'd been scared of the possibility.

It was a sobering revelation how fear had ruled so much of her life without her realizing it.

Asking Mitch to a Wednesday dinner so Marcus and Julia could officially meet him was her first step in integrating him into part of her life, although she hadn't told him what she was doing. She figured she'd wait to see how Marcus felt, then talk to Mitch about it. He'd been great about not pressuring her to let him meet Ana right away, though that may have more to do with him having to go into work right after brunch and barely getting to see each other after that, so she didn't want to get his hopes up.

This way, she'd be able to tell him either he was invited, or she had at least initiated the process of getting Marcus and Julia comfortable with the idea.

"And you're serious about this guy?" Marcus still sounded a little dubious, and Domi couldn't blame him. She'd never brought a guy around before and hadn't mentioned Mitch to him before Ana's birthday, though he'd heard plenty about Murse Mitch from Ana. "How long have you two actually being seeing each other?"

She bristled at the question, but she got it, so she tamped down her automatic defensiveness and thought back. Well, if she counted the time they were fuck buddies, which was when they'd been building the relationship...

"Holy shit. Months." She sounded shocked, even to herself. How had that happened? The time had sped by faster than she'd realized.

"Months?" Amusement crept into Marcus' voice. "Did you just realize that?"

"Well, we've only been official for about two months." This time she didn't bother to hide her defensiveness. "We were seeing each other, mostly exclusively for about six months before that. I guess I never really added it up. I've known him for longer than that. We were friends before we started... seeing each other." She wasn't really sure she should call what they'd been doing as bondage buddies as 'dating.'

Though it had been... they'd rarely gotten together for just a quick fuck. They'd always talked, joked, and enjoyed spending time with each other, even when they were casual.

Damn.

They'd been building a relationship, and she hadn't even noticed until now.

"Well, then we'd be happy to meet him. Officially."

"Really?" Relief flooded through her.

"Should I be insulted you're so surprised?" Marcus chuckled. "You've been seeing the guy for months, Domi. You obviously have strong feelings for him. While last Wednesday might not have been the best first impression, any guy who can convince you to give him a second chance... well, I kinda assume he's in for the long haul. Plus, Ana will be thrilled."

There was that. Domi felt almost saggy with relief as she sat back on the couch. After saying goodbye to Marcus, she laid there for a long moment, feeling like she'd run a marathon.

She was still nervous as hell, thinking about including Mitch in her family time, but it was the right step. The *next* step if she wanted a serious relationship with him, and she did. Why was change so scary, even when it was a good change?

Maybe because it was so out of her control.

A submissive with control issues. Though, she guessed it made sense. She'd hardly be the only submissive who enjoyed giving up control in the bedroom because she felt like she had to be in control everywhere else.

The front door slammed open, taking her by surprise. Domi jumped up with a small cry. Spinning around, she stared at Rae, who stared back at her. Despite her dark skin, she somehow managed to look pale, and her dark eyes were wide and almost frightened. Domi had never seen her look like that.

"Someone bought my book."

"What?"

"I looked at my sales dashboard, and someone *bought* my book."

They stared at each other for another long moment as what Rae said sank in.

"Oh my God!" Squealing, Domi raced around the couch, throwing herself at Rae. Once they were hugging, Rae finally responded, starting to bounce up and down with Domi in happy excitement. "Someone bought your book!"

"Someone bought my book!"

"Someone bought your book!"

"Someone bought my book!"

"I told you so!"

"Woman…"

MITCH

Waking up next to Domi was the best kind of morning.

He'd come over late the night before after his shift. Domi had invited him over to help her and Rae celebrate Rae's first book sale. He didn't tell them he'd been the one to buy it as a gift for his mom. What? She liked romances. He wasn't sure if she read romances with two men usually but doubted she'd object. Plus, it would give his dad something to worry about if his mom told him what she was reading.

And if she liked it, she'd tell her friends. She was in a book group with a bunch of other women her age, and Mitch had overheard them talking before. They were a bunch of filthy perverts, despite their white and grey hair and normally prim demeanors. Mitch wasn't sure how dirty Rae's book was, but going by the cover, he guessed it would be at least a little dirty.

Head resting on the pillow next to Domi, he studied her features. She was snoring, very softly, and her curls were a rumpled mess. Soft. Vulnerable. He doubted she'd appreciate hearing either word used to describe her. Content to watch her sleep, he felt warmer, happier than ever.

Last night, she'd invited him to dinner with her family. While he couldn't go tonight, he'd be able to next week. Scary in its own way but exciting. They were really doing this.

Her phone went off. Unlike him, Domi didn't have extra ringtones, but she used the ones provided by her service to assign to different people. Mitch recognized Marcus' tone immediately, and so did Domi. Before Mitch could move, she was lurching toward her nightstand, hand outstretched, and he wasn't sure she was actually awake yet.

"Hello?" Voice thick with sleep, there was still a fair amount of panic, and Mitch felt his own worry surge, feeding off of hers. Apparently, she hadn't been expecting a call.

With her phone pressed against her ear, the high-pitched voice—a woman's, so it must be Julia—was muffled, so Mitch could only make out a few words here and there, probably because he was so used to hearing some of them, Ana... throwing up... doing... sick...

He was already moving when Domi put down the phone, stumbling to her feet, half asleep and half-panicked.

"Julia says they're all sick and throwing up... thinks it's the flu or something... I gotta go, I'm sorry."

Mitch snorted and shook his head. He already had his pants on and was picking his shirt up off the floor.

"Get dressed, Domi. I'm going with you."

"But... you don't have to do that." She seemed confused. Mitch wished it was because she was asleep, but he had a feeling she'd be the same way if she was fully awake. It was a reflex to be so self-reliant, thinking she had to do it on her own. They'd work on that.

"Domi." He exerted a little authority in his tone, enough she halted her movements and stared at him wide-eyed. "Get dressed. I'm going with you. They're sick, right? I'm a nurse. And your boyfriend. I'm going with you."

"Oh." She gave herself a little shake and started moving again. There was a little frown on her face as if she was trying to figure out why he wanted to go with her. Exasperating woman. "Okay."

Domi

Bringing Mitch had been the right thing to do, even though it felt weird. In her head, she'd been thinking she shouldn't bring him over until after the official meeting, but she hadn't been able to come up with a good reason to argue.

I don't want you to feel like you have to take care of me or my family.

I don't want to be a burden.

She had no idea where these worries were coming from. Single mom guilt? Too long being on her own without leaning on someone else? Hell, she would have told Rae to stay home, not wanting to risk infecting her. That's what she *had* texted Rae when she'd remembered to send her an update. She'd brought up that same point when she and Mitch were already in the car, and he'd reminded her he probably had a better immune system than she did and told her maybe she should be the one to stay home. After that, she hadn't pointed out any more reasons for him to stay away.

"He's a good guy," Julia murmured. Sitting next to Domi on the couch, one hand on her belly, which was more clearly rounded in her fitted shirt than it had been in the dress she'd been wearing last week, she winced as the sounds of Marcus throwing up again came from the bathroom.

Thankfully, Julia seemed the least affected, though that might partly be because she was already on anti-nausea medication for her morning sickness. She was running a fever, though, and was weaker than usual, so Marcus hadn't let her help him in the bathroom. Then Ana had woken up and started throwing up, and Julia had called in reinforcements.

Now Ana was lying with her slightly sweaty head on Domi's lap while Mitch helped Marcus in the bathroom. Even tucked under a thick blanket, she was shivering.

"He is," Domi agreed, stroking her daughter's hair. From Ana's even breathing, she'd managed to fall back asleep, which was probably the best thing for her. Domi had already called the pediatrician this morning and been reassured the most likely cause was a stomach bug that seemed to be doing the rounds.

"I owe you an apology." Julia's words were quiet but sincere.

"You don't." Domi reached out to hold Julia's hand. "I can't imagine how difficult it was for you when I showed up with Ana, but you welcomed her, loved her, and never treated her as anything other than your daughter. That was all I ever wanted."

"I could have been nicer... should have been." Julia let her head roll, so she could look at Domi. "It wasn't your fault, either. I was just so jealous... and worried. If you'd wanted to take Marcus from me, you could have. I knew he always felt guilty about not 'doing the right thing' and—"

"Hey, hey," Domi cut her off, shaking her head. "Absolutely not. I love Marcus as a friend, but honestly, he's more like a brother to me now than anything. We would have been miserable together. He was always meant to be with you."

"Thank you. I'd like it if we could be friends, too. I'm sorry I wasn't ready before. I think it took me a while to really believe you wouldn't eventually want to make your family whole."

"Well, if I'd known all I had to do was make you feel better was to bring a man around, I would have started dating ages ago," Domi said, teasing a little. Julia laughed. It was a weak laugh because she was clearly exhausted, but it was still a laugh. "Seriously, I feel lucky Ana has such a wonderful stepmother. I think we have a great co-parenting relationship, and I'd love it if we made it even better."

"And is Mitch going to be part of the family, eventually, do you think?" Julia's fingers remained in Domi's, keeping a loose but emotionally significant grip. It felt odd to be holding hands with the other woman but good—a sign of a better future together as a family.

"You know..." Domi winced as she heard Marcus throw up again and the low murmur of Mitch's reassurances. It seemed Marcus had gotten the worst of the bug. "I really think he might be."

CHAPTER TWENTY-SIX

MITCH

Helping Marcus back into the living room where Domi, Julia, and Ana were sitting on the couch, Mitch got him into one of the big armchairs. Honestly, he was more worried about Marcus than the rest of them at this point. The man needed to keep something down, or he was going to get dehydrated.

"How's everyone doing?" he asked.

"Much better now that you and Domi are here," Julia said, giving him a grateful smile. Mitch smiled back, hiding his surprise when he realized she and Domi were holding hands. "Thank you so much for coming. Marcus wouldn't let me help him." She gave her husband a mock stern look, but there was plenty of concern.

"You're pregnant. I can take care of myself." Clearly, Marcus' feelings on the matter were pretty set.

"The pediatrician said it should only last about twenty-four hours," Domi said apologetically. "There's a bug going around."

That was good news.

"Alright, I'm going to go call out of work, then I'll get something fixed for lunch. Do you have any broth?" Mitch asked, heading to the kitchen, so he could wash his hands before handling his phone.

"Oh, you don't have to do that," Julia protested.

"No, no, I got it," Domi told her, and a moment later, he could hear her coming up behind him.

Reaching the kitchen, Mitch went straight for the sink, ignoring his girlfriend's approach. He already knew she was going to try to convince him he didn't need to be there, and he'd already decided she was wrong. If nothing else, neither she nor Julia was going to be able to support Marcus if he got any weaker. Marcus wasn't a huge guy, but he was big, and Julia shouldn't be lifting anything, and Domi was... very petite. Though he knew better than to tell her, she couldn't do something.

"You don't need to call out of work—" she started to say.

"I know I don't *need* to, but I'm going to." Turning on the water, he rinsed his hands before reaching for the soap and giving her a stern look. "Unless you're going to kick me out."

"Of course, I'm not! But you need to work and shouldn't have to go to this much trouble—"

Rather than listening to her continued protests, Mitch rinsed off his hands and reached out to snag her around the waist, pulling her in for a kiss and effectively shutting her up. Domi made an aggravated noise against his lips, but after a long moment, she relented, softening against him. Under other circumstances, his cock might have perked up, but his body knew this wasn't the time.

When he finally released her, he raised one eyebrow.

"I'm here to stay, Domi." He meant it in so many ways. This was her family, and she'd invited him to meet them. Was this how any of them would have chosen to get to know each other? Probably not, but he sure as hell wasn't going to walk away when he could not only be useful but was somewhat necessary.

Domi stared up at him for a long moment.

"I love you."

"I love you, too." A stupid grin lifted his lips. "Now get your cute ass back to your daughter while I make lunch."

"No, Julia's got her. I'll help you with lunch," Domi contradicted. "I know my way around this kitchen, and you don't."

"Works for me." He stole another kiss, then relinquished his spot at the sink so she could wash her hands.

"Why are you smiling like that?" she asked curiously as she turned on the water.

"What? Can't a guy just enjoy spending time with his girlfriend and her vomiting family?"

"Yeah, the vomiting part is what makes the enjoyment a little weird," she teased.

"Probably. But compared to the ER..." He shrugged. "Plus, you're here, and there's nowhere else I'd rather be." The craziest part was it was true. Giving her another wink, he pulled his phone out of his pocket, so he could call work.

DOMI

She and Mitch had ended up sleeping over at Marcus' that night. Rae stopped by with dinner, *asopao de andules* and *asopao de pollo,* from their favorite Puerto Rican place, though she refused to actually come into the 'plague house.' That was probably for the best. Domi was already a little worried about her and Mitch getting sick after this.

Stopping by her house to pick up some clothes and her laptop so she could work, she went back to Mitch's with him after only a tiny bit of coaxing. After all, she didn't want to get Rae sick, and Ana was staying at Marcus and Julia's for a few more days. The bug had lasted about twenty-four hours, though they'd gotten through the worst of it in the first twelve. None of them were feeling back to one hundred percent, but Marcus had insisted they go home and get some rest. Domi had eventually caved.

She was exhausted but happy.

"Now that I've met your family, want to meet mine?" he asked, clearing his throat as they got out of the car. They'd driven in silence, both of them too tired to make conversation. "I mean, officially. My mom's going to be mad my dad met you first."

"Oh, is that the only reason you're going to introduce us?" she teased, pulling her overnight bag over her shoulder. Mitch grinned at her.

"Distract my mom from the fact that my dad met you first by bringing you home with me for Passover? That's not an insignificant reason."

"Passover?" she asked curiously, wracking her brain. It took a moment to pinpoint the memory. "I didn't realize you were Jewish." Not that it mattered. It didn't change a thing about him, though her mom might be disappointed she hadn't found a nice Catholic boy. Though probably not since she'd already 'met' Mitch and liked him just fine.

"My mom is, but my dad's Catholic." Mitch came up alongside her, and their fingers entwined as they walked toward the house together. So half-Catholic. Her mom would like that. "None of us are really what I'd call 'practicing,' but we do the holidays. Passover is one of the bigger ones."

"I'd love to go," Domi said. A little flutter of nerves was already tingling in her stomach, but she would get over them. "Will I need to bring anything? Do anything special?"

"Just be yourself and tolerate my mom's burning desire for grand-children." Mitch paused for a moment when they reached the door before putting his key in the lock. "Oooh, do you think we could bring Ana?"

Domi burst out laughing.

"I'm not kidding," he said, opening the door, blue eyes sparkling merrily. "We can use her to distract my mom from *both* of us."

"I'll see what Marcus and Julia have to say about it," she said, grinning. She doubted they'd say no, especially after the past day. Times of crisis could make people into a unit faster than regular times, which had definitely been proven true.

Having Mitch at Marcus and Julia's to help and support her... he'd made everything easier by his mere presence. Also, she didn't think Marcus would have let her help him shower, and he had started to really stink by the evening.

Flopping on Mitch's bed, Domi let out a long sigh. It really was a comfortable bed, even if it wasn't hers. Turning her head, she looked at him standing in the door, watching her with an amused expression.

"Thank you... for everything," she said. He'd called out for two days of work, switching shifts with other nurses so he could stay with her to take care of her family. "I really appreciate it."

"Oh, yeah?" A slightly wicked grin curved his lips, sending tingles sweeping through her body. She'd have thought she was too tired, but apparently, she was wrong. "Think you're up to showing me how much you appreciate it?" The question was made with plenty of seductive heat but no real force behind it, making it clear he didn't want her to say yes out of obligation, only if she was really up to it.

The tingles spread through her lower body. Didn't matter how tired she was, how could she *not* be hot for the man she loved, when he had dropped everything to take care of her daughter and her co-parents?

"I think I could do that," she purred, stretching up and arching her back. She might be wearing yoga pants and a t-shirt, and her hair might be a mess, but Mitch's eyes lit up with arousal, sweeping over her body as if she was in sexy clubwear.

Grinning, he walked toward her, stripping off his shirt and giving Domi a long moment to appreciate the view before he reached the bed and jumped onto it. The sudden movement made her shriek, instinctively pulling her arms and legs in to protect herself, leaving her slightly curled while Mitch knelt over her, the same wicked smile curling his lips.

Taking her hands, he wreathed his fingers through hers, his body angling between her legs and settling there so he could lean down to kiss her. Pressing her hands down on either side of her head, he claimed her lips, kissing her deeply. She opened for him, wrapping her legs around his waist, feeling the thick bulge of his erection rubbing against her.

Her body was already heating up in response to his kiss and his touch, her nipples hardening in anticipation, pussy creaming with desire.

Pushing her hands upward, stretching out her arms, one of Mitch's big hands wrapped around her wrist while the other slid down her arm. He kept kissing her and kissing her and kissing her while his hand curved across her flesh, finding her breast. Domi moaned against his lips, arching beneath him, then whimpering when he squeezed the whole soft mound in a tight grip. Her nipple throbbed, wanting more focused attention as his fingers flexed and kneaded, making her pant as the heat swirled through her.

A moment later, Mitch's lips and weight left her so he could pull at her clothing. There were only a few small curses from each of them as they were delayed by the necessity of undressing.

Putting her back into position—hands above her head, thighs spread and knees pointing to the ceiling with the flats of her feet on the bed—Mitch leaned over and gave her stomach a kiss, right below her belly button.

"Don't move, Domi Darling," he said sternly, using enough of his Dom voice to make her all squirmy.

"Yes, Master Mitch," she murmured, wiggling to make her breasts shake. His blue eyes glinted with appreciation as he bent over the side of the bed.

MITCH

While he kept most of his toys in his equipment bag so he could grab and go whenever he was headed to one of the clubs, since he'd started dating Domi, he'd begun keeping some in one of the drawers built into the base of his bed. Nothing fancy, a few basic necessities— nipple and clit clamps connected by a chain, lube, a vibrator, a butt plug, two floggers, and a ball gag. He was only going to use about half of it tonight.

Picking up the plug, he took it out of its box and dripped lube onto it, holding it up to make sure Domi could watch the process. She smiled up at him, undaunted by the size of the plug, which wasn't the largest he had but sure as hell wasn't the smallest either.

"Lift up," Mitch murmured, tapping her thigh. Domi's hips lifted enough for him to put the tip at the rosebud entrance to her ass. "Take a deep breath, Domi Darling."

He kept his eyes on her face, watching every flicker of her expression as he pushed the plug into her ass—a slow but inexorable push rather than working it back and forth, forcing her opening wider and wider as each millimeter slid into her.

"Fuck!" she gasped, her hips moving upward in an attempt to get away from the plug. Mitch pressed his hand down on her lower stomach, forcing her back down onto it.

"Stay in position, Domi, or I'll have to punish you." Funishment, really, but making the threat turned both of them on even more. She whimpered, squirming, straining, and panting for breath as the plug's widest section reached her entrance. Mitch's cock throbbed, watching her take the discomfort, the sharp ache. Her pussy was plump and slick above the straining hole he was filling, swollen with her arousal.

When the plug finally slid home, her sphincter snapping closed around the narrowed portion between the plug and the base, she sighed with relief and settled back down.

"Good girl." Mitch twisted the plug and pumped it slightly, pulling it to stretch her hole before shoving it back in deep. Domi moaned, her hips moving up again but not because she was trying to escape.

The tweezer clamps he had weren't harsh. Their grip could be adjusted by the little bands wrapped around them. Attached to each other by a horizontal chain that went between the nipple clamps and one long chain from the center of the horizontal chain to the clit clamp, they were perfect for tonight.

Ignoring the urgent need pulsing from his cock, Mitch leaned over to play with and torment Domi's breasts a little. The soft flesh gave under his fingers, and he enjoyed the little whines in the back of her throat as he suckled on one nipple, plucking the other with his fingers. She squirmed beneath him but stayed in position, though he could see her hands twisting together above her head—especially when he bit down on her nipple, making her cry out at the short, sharp flash of pain.

Moving back, he picked up the clamps. His cock bobbed over her pussy as he secured them to her nipples, pushing the band up toward the rubber tips and squeezing the hard buds as much as the tweezer clamps would allow, the chain hanging between her breasts and down her stomach. Domi moaned when he trapped the tiny bud of her clit in its grasp.

"Fuck, you're beautiful," he said, sliding his hands under her ass to lift her so he could slide his cock into her slick heat. They both groaned as he filled her, the plug making her extra tight around his dick, her muscles squeezing and quivering around him as he slid home.

Domi

Pulsing and throbbing, keeping her hands in position without any kind of restraint might be the hardest thing she'd ever done. Her nipples and clit throbbed in the clamps. Rather than being overly painful, the tight constriction made them feel more sensitive, and when Mitch's groin pressed against her clamped clit, she spasmed from the sensation.

"Fuck yes." He pulled out a little, then shoved back in, setting off a similar reaction as Domi sucked in a quick breath. He felt huge inside her, nestled alongside the plug in her ass, with his body rubbing against the extra sensitive bud of her clit, where it peeked out from the clamp.

Releasing her ass, Mitch bent over her to kiss her again, his hands moving up her sides to press down on her arms and help her keep them in position. The wiry hair on his chest rasped over the tips of her nipples, the position pressing the clamp on her clit more strongly. Domi cried out as he began to thrust with long, slow strokes, setting her aflame.

His body slapped against her swollen, clamped clit, sending wave after wave of shock and ecstasy through her, making her writhe beneath him as each thrust brought her closer to orgasm. She screamed against his lips as she tipped over the edge, the rushing pleasure turning to pounding ecstasy. He pulled away from the kiss—not to slow down, but to fuck her even harder.

The chain between the clamps bounced, pulling at her nipples and her oversensitive clit as they swelled against their confinement, sending the sensations into overdrive. The abuse made her scream again, even as another orgasm swamped her senses, dissolving from inexpressible pleasure to exquisite agony as Mitch moved harder, faster.

She fought against his grip, unable to stop herself, tears sliding down her cheeks at the intense torment at the hands of her sadistic lover. It was excruciating bliss, going on and on and on until she finally felt Mitch slam fully inside her and pulse.

Warmth surrounded her, his body half-collapsed on top of her as he filled her, his cock throbbing against her own shuddering walls until it softened.

Panting, Domi let him take care of the toys, whimpering softly as each one was removed. Mitch soothed her with kisses and caresses, his lips gently laving the hurt from her nipples and clit.

Finally, they were curled up around each other, Domi's head pressed against his chest, arms and legs intertwined. She listened to his heartbeat, steady against her ear, felt the warmth of his skin against hers. Being here in his arms felt safe. It felt like home.

"I love you," she murmured. She liked hearing herself say it.

Mitch's arm tightened around her, hugging her closely.

"I love you too, Domi Darling."

Twenty-four hours later, as Mr. My-Immune-System-is-Better-Than-Yours worshiped the porcelain god, while Domi wiped his forehead with a damp cloth before offering him the glass of water she'd brought him, she raised her eyebrows.

"Still love me?" If he was mad her family had gotten him sick, it was his own damn fault for insisting on being there... but some little part of her was still worried.

She shouldn't have been.

Blue eyes opened, and one winked wearily.

"More than ever, Domi Darling." He put a hand over his chest. "This is just the price I must pay for my love."

She burst out laughing. She really did love him.

From bondage buddies to serious relationship—she would have never thought it possible, but here she was… and she wouldn't change a thing.

EPILOGUE

AVERY

It felt really weird to be wearing a corset again. Going to a club again. Especially because the club was also work.

She wished she'd asked Domi and Rae if they could go to Stronghold instead of Marquis, but it was too late now.

Besides, there were good reasons they'd chosen Marquis. Once they were at their table, no one would be watching them, and she wouldn't have to worry about someone asking if she wanted to scene. All she would be doing was watching. She was really interested in seeing if kink still turned her on, but she also wanted to fit in with her new friends.

Domi and Rae had been the first ones to reach out to her since she moved here. They were sweet, fun, and hearing them talk about the kink club had reminded her of how much she'd enjoyed kink… enjoyed being submissive. Their interest wasn't the *only* reason for her renewed interest, but she was self-aware enough to know it was part of it. Besides, they also wanted to celebrate. Rae had recently self-published a book and had sold twenty copies in the first month, and Domi's boyfriend was taking her home to meet his parents for an upcoming holiday.

She hadn't told them, but she was quietly celebrating being friends with them.

Making new friends was hard for her. The other sous chef, Lloyd, worked days and had made it clear he wasn't there to make friends with *anyone*. He just wanted to do his job, collect his paycheck, and go hang out with his 'real' friends. She couldn't be *too* friendly with the line cooks because, as the sous chef, she was technically their manager. That hadn't stopped her from getting too friendly with the executive chef, but… that was different.

Besides, she and Nick weren't friends.

They weren't even really dating.

They were coworkers who had had a few clandestine and totally hot kisses that set her on fire and left her aching all over. At first, she'd thought maybe something would come of it, but he never asked her out on a date. Though he had kissed her again last week after she'd told him off for yelling at a delivery guy. It hadn't been the delivery guy's fault Nick had rushed when he'd put in the order.

Maybe it was a good thing she was trying out Marquis before things went anywhere with Nick. It had been a long time since she'd dated anyone seriously–the restaurant schedule wasn't exactly conducive to relationships—and she did miss kink. Was it a necessity to her life? She didn't know.

She was hoping she'd find out tonight.

She was also really, really, really hoping none of her coworkers saw her.

Thankfully, Domi and Rae didn't mind hurrying in the back entrance to the club with her.

"Coast is clear," Domi said after peeking her head through the door. She opened it wider, gesturing with her hand. "Go, go, go!"

The gleeful way she and Rae were having fun sneaking Avery in made it fun for her. She laughed as she hurried up the stairs behind Rae, with Domi bringing up the rear to the BDSM club. The sounds of the restaurant faded as they went up, and every step made her feel a little lighter with relief.

The servers who worked the second floor wouldn't say anything about her presence there, and the ones who worked in the main restaurant weren't allowed up to the second floor. The moment she stepped foot into Marquis' lobby, she let out the breath she'd been holding on a long sigh.

Safe!

"Hello, ladies." Standing behind the front desk, Freddy grinned when he saw her there with Rae and Domi. "Avery, I'm so excited you're joining us on the second floor."

Avery smiled back. She liked Freddy. He ran the front desk at Marquis, though he wasn't always there himself since he had a full-time job during the day. Not that he talked about that job, just that the club was his escape from all that.

"Thank you," she said.

"Alright, let's see it," he said, gesturing to her jacket. Even though it was warm out, she'd worn a light jacket that went down to midthigh to cover her outfit, just in case anyone saw her on her way in.

Feeling both nervous and a little excited, Avery unzipped the jacket and shrugged it off.

"Doesn't she look amazing?" Rae enthused beside her, clapping her hands. Avery couldn't help but laugh. Of course, Rae and Domi thought she looked good. They'd basically dressed her up like a doll for the night, combining some of the few pieces she had left from her previous time as a submissive with offerings from their wardrobes.

Clapping his hands gleefully, Freddy gave her an approving once over.

"Hell, yeah, she does! Do you—"

The door to the manager's office opened behind him, and the last person she wanted to see in the entire world stepped out. Their eyes met, Avery's widening with horror, Nick's with shock.

"*Avery?*"

Shit! Run! Her brain screamed, but it was too late. It had been fight, flight, or freeze, and her stupid ass froze.

Beside her, she could sense Rae and Domi freezing as well. Even Freddy went still, despite not knowing about her and Nick's flirtation, clearly realizing something was very amiss. Though he probably thought it was nothing more than not wanting her boss to see her like this.

"What are you doing up here?" Nick asked, staring at her like he couldn't really grasp what he was seeing.

"What are *you* doing up here?" she asked in a high, squeaky voice that made her cringe. Seriously, what the hell was he doing up here? He should be down in the kitchen, running the kitchen. Dinner had already started in the dining room. She'd been worried one of the servers or busboys would see her, not *Nick*. It shouldn't have been possible.

NICK

In her chef coat and pants or wearing a tank top or t-shirt once she took off her coat, long brown hair in a ponytail or bun, sweaty from the kitchen, Avery always still managed to turn him on. She had a serious girl-next-door vibe going on that had always been his 'type.' She was sassy, confident, and not afraid to go toe-to-toe with him, even when he was at his most bad-tempered. All things great in a sous chef, but add in their chemistry, and it took things to a totally different level.

Now she was standing in the middle of the lobby of a sex club, dressed like she belonged there.

The tank tops she wore under her chef coat had revealed she was curvy, but the corset pushed her breasts up into a deep cleavage that wasn't possible with mere fabric. It also pulled in her waist to improbable proportions that made him want to rip the damn thing off her, so she could breathe again.

Uh-huh. Sure. That's *why you want to rip it off her.*

The black leather skirt hugged her legs tightly and was so short, he was pretty sure if she bent over, it would roll straight up to her waist. His dick pulsing at the idea, Nick shifted his stance uncomfortably, hoping his erection wasn't obvious. Fortunately, his drawstring pants were pretty loose in the crotch. Three cheers for chef pants. Not the first time he'd been grateful for that since he started working with Avery.

"I had to ask Olivia a question," he answered. He was about to ask what the hell she was doing there, except he already knew. From the way she was dressed, it was pretty obvious. "Do you... do you do *this*?"

He gestured at the door to Marquis' exhibition room. Nick hadn't been in it while there was a show going on, but he knew what happened up here. Tried not to think about it too much, partly because he didn't want to think about what his brother got up to with Olivia up here and partly because the whole thing disturbed him on a deeper level.

Nick and Luke had been raised to respect women. Not that the women up here seemed to feel they were disrespected—he didn't think Olivia would ever tolerate any woman here being disrespected —but he still had trouble wrapping his head around it. Wasn't sure *he* could do it.

Liar. You like the idea. You're afraid you like it too *much.*

Looking at Avery, dressed like *that*, it was hard to argue the point. She straightened her shoulders, throwing them back, and took a deep breath, which pushed her pillowy breasts up even more. Nick gritted his teeth against a groan. Fuck, did she have any idea what she was doing to him?

"I used to," she said almost primly. Her hands twitched as if she was having trouble not covering up. The two women with her—Rae and Domi, if he remembered their names correctly—moved closer to her on either side, offering their silent support. It grated on his nerves they thought she needed it.

He wasn't going to chew her out. What she did with her private time was her business, but... but...

Fuck.

"I used to do 'this.' Be submissive. Kinky. I came here tonight to watch the show and get an idea if it's something I still want." Avery's eyes darted to Freddy, then back to Nick, her expression turning uncertain. As if she didn't know whether he would be okay with her outing their...

What did they have going on between them? An attraction? A flirtation?

Something.

Nothing.

He should let her go in. Let her have her night, and he'd go downstairs and work his shift. They could hash it out later. Give them both time to think, then talk about what they wanted from each other, where to go from here now that he knew more about what she was into. Let things play out.

Yeah, that didn't sound like him at all.

Spinning around on his heel, he turned back to his brother's girlfriend and Dominatrix. Olivia sat behind her desk, watching him with utter amusement on her face.

"Nick?" Avery asked, sounding as though she was coming closer. He ignored her.

He was about to prove Olivia right about something, and that chafed, but right now, it felt like the lesser evil.

"Okay Olivia, you're finally getting your way. I want to sign up for the Dominant 101 course."

Olivia smiled, and behind him, he heard Avery gasp.

THANK YOU SO MUCH FOR READING BONDAGE BUDDIES! I HOPE YOU ENJOYED the first Masters of Marquis book. Avery and Nick are next up in Master Chef - make sure to Click Here to preorder so you don't miss out.

Also, curious about Mitch's parents? Gavin and Leah have their own story coming in May 2021 - Click Here to pre-order Dungeon Master, the first in my kinky later-in-life romance series.

My newsletter is chock-full of exclusive teasers, fun stories, and everything you need to know about upcoming releases - Click Here to join us and pick up several free books from me as well!

ABOUT THE AUTHOR

Golden Angel is a *USA Today* best-selling author, Amazon Top 50 bestselling author, and self-described bibliophile with a "kinky" bent who loves to write stories for the characters in her head. If she didn't get them out, she's pretty sure she'd go just a little crazy.

She is happily married, old enough to know better but still too young to care, and a big fan of happily-ever-afters, strong heroes and heroines, and sizzling chemistry.

She believes the world is a better place when there's a little magic in it.

www.goldenangelromance.com

BB bookbub.com/authors/golden-angel
g goodreads.com/goldeniangel
f facebook.com/GoldenAngelAuthor
instagram.com/goldeniangel

OTHER TITLES BY GOLDEN ANGEL

CONTEMPORARY BDSM ROMANCE

Venus Rising Series (MFM Romance)

The Venus School

Venus Aspiring

Venus Desiring

Venus Transcendent

Venus Wedding

Venus Rising Box Set

Stronghold Doms Series

The Sassy Submissive

Taming the Tease

Mastering Lexie

Pieces of Stronghold

Breaking the Chain

Bound to the Past

Stripping the Sub

Tempting the Domme

Hardcore Vanilla

Steamy Stocking Stuffers

Entering Stronghold Box Set

Nights at Stronghold Box Set

Stronghold: Closing Time Box Set

Masters of Marquis Series

Bondage Buddies

Master Chef (Coming Fall 2021)

Dungeons & Doms Series

Dungeon Master

Dungeon Daddy (Coming Fall 2021)

Dungeon Showdown (Coming 2022)

Poker Loser Trilogy

Forced Bet

Back in the Game

Winning Hand

Poker Loser Trilogy Bundle (3 books in 1!)

HISTORICAL SPANKING ROMANCE

Domestic Discipline Quartet

Birching His Bride

Dealing With Discipline

Punishing His Ward

Claiming His Wife

The Domestic Discipline Quartet Box Set

Bridal Discipline Series

Philip's Rules

Gabrielle's Discipline

Lydia's Penance

Benedict's Commands

Arabella's Taming

Pride and Punishment Box Set

Commands and Consequences Box Set

Deception and Discipline

A Season for Treason

A Season for Scandal

Bridgewater Brides

Their Harlot Bride

Standalone

Marriage Training

SCI-FI ROMANCE

Tsenturion Masters Series with Lee Savino

Alien Captive

Alien Tribute

SHIFTER ROMANCE

Big Bad Bunnies Series

Chasing His Bunny

Chasing His Squirrel

Chasing His Puma

Chasing His Polar Bear

Chasing His Honey Badger

Chasing Her Lion

Night of the Wild Stags

Chasing Tail Box Set

Chasing Tail... Again Box Set

Made in the USA
Middletown, DE
25 September 2021

49067983R00136